# A HUNDRED MILES TO WATER

## MIKE KEARBY

·
ReadWest,
an imprint of Goldminds Publishing, LLC,
Springfield, Missouri 65804


First Edition 2010

Second Printing January 2011


ISBN 978-0-9788422-4-6

Library of Congress Control Number: 2010912159




*Dustjacket Design: Jake Kearby*

*A Hundred Miles to Water* is a fictional work. Certain real locations
and public figures are mentioned, but all other characters and events
portrayed are products of the author's imagination or used fictitiously.

Printed in the United States of America
at Morgan Printing in Austin, Texas

*Many thanks to:*
*Mindy Reed, Weldon Edwards,*
*Fred Tarpley, and Danielle Hartman*

# PART ONE

June 20, 2011

# Feud

(n). a mutual quarrel or enmity

June 20, 2011

Charlie "July" Walker
Born July 4, 1839
Died September 21, 1928

"Little Black Bull Come Down the Mountain"

The following
is from the Journal of Charlie "July" Walker.

## JOURNAL ENTRY

*I rode up the trail several times. I had occasion to know some good men, and some hard cases. I never shirked from a job that needed to be done; and I always helped a friend when called to do so. I reckon that's what kept the fret from my life. It was the code; above all else a man had to be true to his fellow cowboys. It was Mr. Charlie's eldest son who taught me that, and that's why we all called him Pure, because he always backed the ≡R brand, right or wrong and no matter the consequence.*

# Pure

(adj). free from moral fault or guilt

## JOURNAL ENTRY

After Mr. Charlie died in '77, Pure took over the ranch and that's when things began to change. Along the southern scrub, what old-timers called the brasada, the rustlers had banded into large outfits and the Gunn boys were the worst of the bunch. Some folks tell that Mr. Gunn went crazy after losing his oldest son, Ethan, at Antietam in '62. And because none of Mr. Charlie's sons fought during the war, terrible stories soon spread through McMullen County that the Restons were nothing but "No-good Yankee" sympathizers. Now it wasn't any secret who started these untruths, but Mr. Charlie just ignored them and for years that's all there was to it. But after Mr. Charlie passed, old man Gunn took a peculiar delight in stealing ≡R open range cattle and re-branding them as his own, most times right on Reston land. It was like he was testing Pure. And when Mr. Gunn took off down that trail, well that's when Pure turned the ≡R into a gun outfit. And I still remember the day that the dust-up with the Gunn clan moved past the name calling. It was a wet April day during the spring round-up. That morning Pure sent Buckshot Wallace and Billy Green to *search for thirty head that went missing after a lightning storm the night before. And you know what? Things never did get back right after that.*

# Blood Feud

(n). a feud between clans or families

# ONE

*April 1878*
*McMullen County, Texas*

⟫⟫⬥⟪⟪

**B**uckshot Wallace curled his toes inside a pair of rain-dampened boots. "Two things I never could learn to tolerate," the old-time cowhand lamented and then stuck the tip of each boot directly into the hot ash of the morning campfire. "Punkin rollers and cold toes."

Pure Reston, ranch boss for the ≡R outfit, watched in curious fascination at the smoke coming off Wallace's boots and nodded his agreement. The early morning air, fresh and unspoiled by the harsh sun that would later lift over the range, was as addicting as laudanum or opium to a brush-popper. Pure and Wallace always rose early to get as much of that intoxicating air as possible, unwilling to share its soothing effect with the rest of their bunch.

"You better watch it or you're going to get ash on those prized spurs of yours," Pure remarked and concealed a grin, well aware of the story that always followed.

Wallace leaned forward on his toes and looked down, admiring the polished silver spurs. "Did I ever tell you of how I came to own these spurs?" he asked, but didn't wait for Pure's reply. "Well, I bought 'em in San Antonio from an old vaquero, called Alavez," Wallace bragged.

Pure stood in silent reflection and enjoyed the old cowhand's moment.

Wallace gazed off into the sky and smiled at the memory. "Hammered them himself, he did."

Pure inhaled through his nostrils and filled his lungs with the morning air.

The moon, bright and full, still hung high above the horizon, not ready to dissolve under the coming morn. A seasoned veteran of the cow range, Wallace allowed his gaze to linger on the illuminated orb for a few more

16

seconds before lowering his chin. Stretched from east to west along the camp, a chorus of snores harmonized with cricket and morning dove. Wallace smiled and nodded at his fellow cowpunchers. "If they only knew what they were missing this time of day," he sighed. "This is what makes all of the bruises, and bumps, and scrapes worthwhile."

Pure agreed with a slow exhale and then suddenly all business, nodded to the south. "I want you to take the kid and ride down the scrub this morning. We need to find those steers that cut out last night."

Wallace ignored the request and fidgeted from one foot to another in the warm ash.

Pure waited for Wallace's response. The ☰R owner was a small framed, unimposing figure whose eyes carried the droop of riding herd in the Texas sun for fifteen odd years. He had taken rein of the Reston cattle operation a year earlier and was considered a hard but fair boss by both his brothers and the ranch cowboys. He was a man who said little, more inclined to let his gun speak for him. He holstered his Colt low. The six-shooter's handle, even with his wrist, ensured unhampered quickness. Along the trail, and by those not kin, he was simply known as Mr. Reston.

Wallace lifted his chin and scratched at a morning's worth of whiskers.

Pure studied the ☰ R cowhand's serene stateliness with silent admiration. Wallace was a cowboy through and through. He could ride the brush for days on a single biscuit and a swallow or two of water.

Wallace dropped his hands to his hips and rolled his shoulders back without an utterance.

Undismayed at Wallace's silence, Pure rubbed his left shoulder and repeated his request, "I want you to take the kid and ride down the scrub and find those steers that cut out last night."

Wallace scooted his boots out of the fire and snorted under his breath. "I heard you."

Pure's eyes wandered over the ☰R rannie. Wallace had worked for the Reston outfit since Pure was a ten-year-old kid. Wallace was a top hand and a family friend. And Pure knew that snort all to well. He suppressed a grin and asked, "What's stirred up your war bag so early?"

Wallace exhaled an exaggerated breath, paused, lifted one boot and dusted the gray ash from its toe. "It's the kid, that's what."

The grunts and groans of a waking camp began to stir the air. Several fits of swearing flashed like lightning as cowhands hopped about desperately, determined to push dampish socks into wet boots. Pure glanced over at Billy Green. The youngest member of the Reston outfit was just climbing out of his hot roll. The kid yawned sleepily and patted the ground in search of his boots. Pure removed his wide-brimmed hat and dragged a hand through his thinning hair. "What about the kid?"

"Might delicate concerning his courage."

"He's thin-skinned, that's a fact."

"Doesn't like to listen neither."

"He's only fourteen."

Wallace dipped his chin. "Youth can be a deadly disadvantage in our line of work."

"How were you at that age?"

"Open-eared and that's a well-known truth."

"He's a good kid," Pure said.

"I reckon the bone orchard is filled with good kids."

"Likely so, but I'll bet none of those kids had an old moss back like you for a teacher."

Wallace tossed a hard look at Pure. "You're wasting your loop," he said. His voice boomed with sarcasm.

A chuckle rippled deep in the ranch boss's chest. "Hard to catch a horned jackrabbit if you don't throw your rope."

Wallace glanced right to hide a wide grin.

Pure stared straight ahead and waited for Wallace to look back.

When the ≡R rannie swung his head around, his expression was as sober as a judge. He locked eyes with Pure and asked, "What if them head ain't running free this morn?"

Pure returned Wallace's glare. A thin frown tightened the corners of his mouth. "You expecting to find trouble out there?"

"Has nothing to do with expecting or finding."

Pure's mouth tightened.

"There's plenty enough of it running the scrub these days."

"That figures to be about right."

"I 'spect we'll run headlong into it."

Pure lifted his chin and stared east, mulling over Wallace's words. A slight glimpse of orange lit up the horizon. "I've got a schedule to meet."

"That's a fact."

"With all the work to be done here, I can't afford to send more than two men out looking for strays."

"Figures."

"You know that," Pure said.

"Don't need more than two," Wallace mumbled. "Just don't need the kid."

Pure dug his toe in the wet earth, deep in thought, and then ran a hand over his lower back. "Take one of the dogs with you," he muttered then almost as an afterthought added, "and the kid."

Wallace nodded with an abrupt snort and started for his gear.

"That's all I can give you."

"I heard." Wallace responded and then lifted a horsehair halter from atop his saddle. Halter in hand, he shuffled toward his cow pony. "I'll have 'em back by night," he muttered in the lifting darkness.

"The dog or the cattle?" Pure joked, trying to lighten the mood.

"Depends on which sulks and fights the most."

Pure smiled and grabbed a tin cup from the hanger. As he reached for the coffee pot bubbling in the fire, he offered, "We'll have hot grub waiting for you."

Wallace snorted once more and slid the halter over a piebald mare. He mumbled, "Hot grub my backside . . . be nice if once before I die, I could get the ramrod of this greasy sack to bring in some canned peaches for a man to eat."

Pure smiled at Wallace's grumbling, then as an afterthought remarked, "Watch yourself out there."

Another snort.

Then from the blackness, Wallace boomed, "Get alive, kid, you and me are going on a cow hunt this morning!"

# Two

*April 1878*
*The Brasada, Texas*

———⊰•◊•⊱———

**B**uckshot Wallace leaned off his saddle and studied the muddied set of tracks and trampled grass leading into a dry ravine several miles above Cita Creek. A look of concern darkened his expression.

"What is it?" the kid asked.

Wallace snorted and ignored the question and the kid. At least six horse prints now mixed with the cattle tracks.

*Appears them beeves picked up some company.*

Wallace shifted in the saddle and surveyed the landscape. He knew this place well.

Cañón Cerrado.

A hundred yards down the ravine, the gorge swept left and followed a dry riverbed into a natural box. Hardly a canyon by appearance, the south and southwest sides of the ravine were covered in a dense thicket of prickly pear, black chaparral, and Spanish dagger as high as a horse's head. A rolling hill of mesquite bordered the southeast side. Wallace, considering the landscape, made a face and pushed his boots against his toe-fenders. He knew wild beeves would seek the brasada for cover, but the more calm Reston beeves might work their way into Cañón Cerrado where the sandy floor would be free of thorny vegetation and out of the wind. Wallace had driven many a stray into this natural corral for branding. It was an oasis to a brush cowboy. "Soft-work" was how C.A. Reston described working in Cañón Cerrado. The canyon also made an ideal area for any working rustlers to re-brand ≡R beeves. Wallace took a long look down the narrow entrance and tugged at his right earlobe.

"What is it, Buckshot?"

Wallace snorted but wouldn't look over at Billy Green. "Kid," he said. "You see that mesquite hill back to our southeast?"

"Yeah, I see it," the kid answered with a long drawl. "Why?"

Something about the smug way that the kid answered caused an uneasy tightness in Wallace's stomach. His expression soured. He glanced from the canyon entrance to the trail behind them.

"Well what is it?" the kid asked. His voice dripped false concern.

"Back outta here and swing your pony around to the top of that hill."

"Why?"

"'Cause I told you so," Wallace grumbled.

The kid tossed a quick glance toward the hill. "What's going on up there?"

Wallace inhaled and counted to three, resisting the temptation to slap the youngster out of his saddle. He rolled his neck from side to side. Years of riding the scrub yielded the audible pop of bone against bone. He glanced over at the greener with little regard and said, "When you get to the top, find yourself a nice hiding spot." Wallace paused and pointed at the carbine slung off the kid's saddle horn. "Then you pull that Winchester and keep your sight steady on my back."

The kid glanced down at the rifle in its leather scabbard, then his face lit up. "Trouble coming?"

"Maybe."

The kid took a deep look into Wallace's eyes. "Somebody fixin' to wake the wrong passenger?"

"Not if you do what I say. Now get going. I'll give you a five-minute start, and then I'm going to ride into the canyon with the dog."

The kid reined his horse left and clicked his tongue. "Don't you worry," he said and straightened in the saddle. "Me and this Winchester will make sure no harm comes your way."

Wallace watched the kid ride off and then snorted, "I surely hope you do just that, kid, I surely do, or you just might end up getting the both of us killed."

Wallace pushed both toe-fenders outward and glanced down at his spurs to pass the time. Five minutes later, he lowered the stirrups, eased his pony down the trail, and pulled rein with a soft, "Whoa." He turned an ear into the ravine, listening for any sound, the clop of a hoof or the bawl of a beeve. The piebald, an old trail hand, instinctively understood what the seasoned cowman wanted and stood unmoving and quiet. Within seconds, from down the ravine, the sound of milling beeves caught Wallace's attention. He lifted his head, paused, and then lowered his ear back toward the faint, yet distinct sound.

*"Hold him, Street!"*

Wallace winced at the voice.

*"Hurry up, Nate!"*

Normally hard to stir, Wallace chewed on his bottom lip, wondering. A small part of him wished that the voices he heard inside the canyon were nothing more than the sound of wind against brush, but he knew better.

*"Drag that next one to, Foss!"*

Wallace made a face. He had had the feeling when he tossed off his hot roll this morning. Cowpunching for twenty-five years provided a man with an intuitive understanding of each day and the difficulties that always seemed to follow. A cold shiver rattled his shoulders. It was as if someone had walked over his grave. He dragged a dry tongue over a chapped lower lip and for a few seconds thought about canned peaches. The natural fragrance of sugar filled his nose. His mouth watered at the taste of the thick sugary syrup. A half-smile tugged at one side of his mouth.

*"Let's go boys!"*

Wallace scowled.

"Damned Gunns!"

Wallace straightened in the saddle, his wool-gathering interrupted by the sound of his own voice, strong, angry, and cursing. He recognized the voices in the canyon, knew all of their names, and understood his predicament. "Damned Gunns!" he swore again and then with some reluctance clicked his horse forward, well aware of what he had to do. Knowing Nate Gunn's reputation with a pistol and his own quick draw limitations, the grizzled cowhand unholstered his pistol.

*You best confront the lot of them with a full hand.*

And then as an afterthought, he glanced about and whispered through his teeth, "I hope all six of them are in there."

Exposing a full grimace, Wallace clicked his tongue twice and turned his spurs into the sorrel. Ten yards down the ravine he shot a glance back at the dome-top hill and a second after that, he turned the dog loose.

## JOURNAL ENTRY

*In those days, it was common knowledge throughout McMullen County that the Gunns were rustlers. It was an occupation that just seemed to come natural to them. Old man Gunn, whose given name was Echol Brocious, went by E.B., and every one of those Gunn boys did anything E.B. asked of them. I often thought it was a shame that those boys didn't take to a respectful living as they could rope beeves and turn brands quicker than any outfit in the county. We found out later that E.B. had an arrangement with a group of border bandits. E.B. would push his stolen beeves to the Nueces and exchange them for the bandits' stolen Mexican beeves. Both sides would then go back to their own localities and sell what appeared to be legitimate brands . . . and as we later came to understand nobody knew that better than Pure.*

# THREE

*April 1878*
*Cañón Cerrado, Texas*

⇒·◇·⇐

Street Gunn secured a half-hitch around his oversized saddle horn with expert finesse. The far end of the leather reata was looped tightly around the broad horns of a ≡R steer. With his rope set, Street lifted the reins and walked his horse rearward, tightening the reata's loop with each backward step. Meanwhile, his brother, Clark, kept a ketch rope taut around the back legs of the steer.

Nate Gunn, the second child and oldest son, braced his left shin against the steer's back bone and pressed his right knee into the steer's midsection. His hands were wrapped with thick pieces of hide. Skilled at his trade, Nate rolled a cherry-red cinch ring over the steer's existing brand. At the cinch ring's placement, a yellowish blue cloud billowed from the steer's hindquarters. The branding smell was sweet to the accomplished rustler but served only to make the thousand-pound steer all horns and rattles. Within fifteen seconds, Nate had deftly transformed the ≡R brand into the EB brand. His task complete, Nate hollered, "Drag that next one to, Foss!"

The oldest of the Gunn boys then turned back, dropped the cinch ring into the fire, and grabbed its white-hot replacement. Hearing Nate's call to Foss, Street flipped loose his reata and made ready to rope the next beeve as brother, Clark dragged the newly branded EB steer away from the work area.

Out on the perimeter, Foss planted his feet deep into his stirrups and eyed a lanky mossback on the outside of the small herd. His horse responded to a slight neck rein and moved sidewise and then forward to encourage the steer from his surroundings. When the steer was separated from the bunch, Foss leaned over his horse's right side and with a quick flip of his wrist pitched a loop at the steer's back legs. The steer started forward, and the loop settled perfectly on both of the beast's hind legs. With steel-spring precision, Foss tugged the rope tight and quickly wrapped a half-hitch around his saddle biscuit. Five seconds later, the struggling, bawling steer was dragged toward Nate, Street, and the branding fire. Street jumped his horse forward and roped the incoming steer's horns. In the meantime, Clark freed the re-branded steer and turned his horse into the remaining cattle when the bark of a running dog sounded from the neck of the canyon.

Nate Gunn turned his head in the dog's direction and pushed his eyebrows together. "What the—?" he barked. Annoyed he immediately dropped the hot cinch at his feet. "Dog!" he yelled to alert the others and then, with a frightening calmness, pulled his .45 and fired. The slug hit the fast-approaching animal square, killing it immediately.

Street looked beyond the downed dog and watched a piebald cow pony race in at a hard gallop. *Restons!* He glanced up at the horse's rider and frowned. It was well known that Reston cowboys were the only bunch in the county who, to a man, rode piebald horses, with their unique black and white spotting pattern. Street sucked in a quick breath. The ≡R cowboy raced by the dog without even glancing down. Unruffled, Street finished wrapping his half-hitch and then filled his hand with a pearl-handled Colt. "Lookey, lookey," he sniped. "Here's an old friend come to help."

Nate immediately recognized the old circle rider from the ≡R spread. Figuring four to one odds favored his position; he holstered his pistol and tilted his hat back, welcoming.

Wallace pulled rein ten yards in front of the branding fire kicking up clods of dampened soil.

"Howdy, Buckshot," Nate offered with a pleasant grin.

"Howdy, Nate," Wallace replied calmly and took a quick glance left, then right, at the well organized brigands. "What have you boys got going on here this morning?"

Nate tossed a quick look at Street and winked. "Just branding up some strays for the old man."

Wallace pushed his hat back and scowled. "Mighty industrious for such a steamy morning."

Nate cleared his throat and glanced at the sun. "Yeah, well, we all kinda figured it would only get steamier as the day moved ahead."

Wallace nodded. "Probably so," he replied.

Nate nodded back and mumbled, "Yeah, probably so."

"Where'd you find 'em?" Wallace asked.

"Huh?"

"The strays . . . where'd you find 'em?"

Nate ignored the question and glanced beyond Wallace to the dead dog. "That your dog?"

Wallace took a casual glance behind him. "Yep," he said without concern. "Sorry I shot him like that, but he could have stirred up our branding."

"No worries, there seems to be as many dogs as beeves running wild out in these parts."

Nate crossed his arms across his chest and sighed, "Ride far?"

Wallace shifted slightly in the saddle and lied, "No, we've got the whole outfit working a mile or so away."

"Hmmmph," Nate answered, acknowledging the lie, then asked, "Is that right, what Brother Street said? You come to help us?"

"Help you boys work beeves already branded with the ≡R?" Wallace glowered. His tone suddenly turned serious. "That sounds too much like double duty for me."

Nate tilted his head and following Wallace's lead quickly sobered his own expression. "I guess it depends which side of the brand you're riding for," he said sullenly.

Wallace noted Nate's sudden facial change and felt the rustler's play would come soon. His eyes left the eldest Gunn and darted speedily around the canyon floor, counting the brothers.

*One.*

*Two.*

*Three.*

*Four.*

*Uh-oh.*

*There's two missing.*

Wallace's face paled. His scowl deepened. He leaned forward in the saddle.

*Where are the other two?*

The unaccounted-for Gunn brothers could be a real concern.

Foss loosened his rope and flipped it free of the steer's legs. "Anything wrong, Buckshot?" he said and eased his pistol from its holster. "You sure looked spooked."

Wallace tossed a fast glance at Foss and then turned his attention back at Nate. The ≡R cowboy's left hand rested on the saddle horn, his Colt was visible across his left forearm. "Where's your other brothers?" he casually asked.

Nate shrugged and moved carefully toward Wallace's horse. "You mean Ben and Charlie?"

Wallace nodded.

Nate raised his brow and grinned. "Heck, Buckshot, who can tell with those boys? They might be back home drunk on the porch, or if you know Charlie, just as likely still losing at the card tables."

"That sounds about right," Wallace agreed.

Nate tipped the back of his hat forward to shade his eyes. "I can't ever depend on him."

"Uh-huh," Wallace said. He kept a steady gaze on the oldest Gunn brother.

The rustler avoided Wallace's eyes and rested a hand on the ≡R cowboy's saddle cantle. He motioned for the cowpuncher's Colt while whispering, "You're outgunned here, Buckshot. You might want to hand over that Peacemaker."

Wallace took a deep calculated breath.

A sneer crossed Nate's mouth.

Wallace forced a tight smile and in a barely audible voice said, "Nate, just so there's no misunderstanding here, there's a ≡R cowboy sitting back yonder on that round-top hill looking straight down the barrel of a Winchester at you right now."

Nate's mouth fell open. His eyes darted toward the hill. "That cowboy set to hole me?" he gushed in fake surprise.

Wallace exhaled through his nose and stared into Nate's smiling eyes. And then it struck him, and then, he knew exactly where brothers Ben and

Charlie were. His eyes darted toward the round-top hill.

Nate followed Wallace's eyes and suppressed a grin. "Everything okay, Buckshot?"

Wallace quickly composed himself and rolled his eyes toward the rustler. "Couldn't be better, Nate," he said, bluntly.

"Well you looked like you was about to overheat there for a minute."

At that moment the soft slush of hooves galloping in sand sounded down the canyon neck.

Wallace turned his shoulders and looked back.

Three riders approached. A trussed-up Billy Green rode in the middle spot.

Wallace snorted as the riders got within fifty feet.

"Howdy, Buckshot," greeted Ben Gunn.

Nate laughed.

Foss, Clark, and Street joined in.

Wallace twisted his mouth and arched his back, nettled at the predicament he now found himself and the kid caught in.

"Or," Nate tilted his head slightly and added, "Brothers Ben and Charlie might be watching our backs from that same round-top hill, Buckshot."

———◆———

Wallace and Green, bound with ropes, and placed back-to-back near the branding fire, sat in stunned silence. Street Gunn stood over the two while his brothers worked in the background.

Wallace ignored the youngest Gunn and stared ahead, expressionless.

Billy Green's normal bravado was long gone. His back trembled every few seconds, causing his legs and shoulders to jerk uncontrollably.

"Take it easy, kid," Buckshot whispered.

Suddenly, two gunshots erupted behind the captive ≡R cowboys.

Two dying bawls followed immediately.

"What are they doing?" the kid asked and twisted against the rope binding him. His shivering became more pronounced and impossible to repress.

Wallace took a deep breath, uncertain of how to answer the kid. After a shallow exhale, he said, "Just shut-up, kid and take whatever comes along like a man."

Street glanced down at the terrified Billy Green and barked, "That's good advice, kid. Take whatever comes to you like a man." The younger Gunn brother then looked sideways at Wallace. "He's kind of a high-strung colt, ain't he?"

Wallace bit his tongue, spurning a reply, and pressed his back stiff against the kid's. "Take it easy," he grunted softly. "Keep it inside you."

Behind the bound pair, Nate Gunn holstered his Colt and took a long draw at the two shot ≡R steers. Ben Gunn stood to the right of Nate and dragged the blade of a castrating knife under a dirty fingernail, bored. Next to Ben, Foss lazily scratched the back of his neck while brother Clark yawned at Charlie and shrugged.

All waited for Nate to decide. Something. Anything.

After a moment's time, the eldest Gunn looked back at the two trussed-up ≡R cowhands and rubbed a day's worth of beard. He hesitated for a breath, then muttered to the others, "Awright boys, get them hides peeled."

Street whooped at Nate's pronouncement. "Hwooo!" he laughed. "This is going to be something, Buckshot."

Wallace stared up at the youngest Gunn with black eyes.

Street's smile faded slightly. "Oh come on, Buckshot," he lamented. "You'd be doing the same to me where our fortunes turned."

"Shut-up, Street," Nate hollered at his brother and walked tensely over to the roped cowboys.

"Awwwh," Street moaned, "I was just ribbing these boys a 'might."

Nate motioned for his brother to move away and glanced down at Wallace. "No hard feelings, Buckshot?"

Wallace exhaled sharply and lifted his gaze toward Nate. "No . . . no hard feelings. What Street said was true, were it reversed, I'd do the same to you."

Nate smiled and nodded.

"What's going to happen, Buckshot?" Billy Green asked in choked breaths, panicked.

"Calm down, kid," Wallace answered coolly.

"What are they gonna do to us?"

"Quit asking so many questions."

Billy Green trembled uncontrollably. "They're gonna kill us, aren't they?"

"You're riling everybody up, kid," Wallace warned.

"I ain't ready to die, Buckshot."

Nate shook his head in disgust. "Hell, kid, who is?"

"But why you gotta kill us? Keep them strays for all I care," the kid cried. He pushed hard against Wallace's back. "Right, Buckshot?"

Wallace stared straight ahead, emotionless. "Shut-up, kid."

Tears began to drip down the kid's face. "Tell 'em, Buckshot . . . tell 'em to keep the strays."

Wallace remained silent.

The kid began to rock back and forth, pleading, "Tell 'em, Buckshot. Tell 'em!"

Nate ignored the kid's whining and lifted his chin at Wallace. "Can I get you anything?"

Wallace thought hard, shook his head no, and then resignedly added, "Nate, I'd be mighty beholden if you'd take my spurs."

"Tell 'em, Buckshot," the kid continued to spout.

Nate pulled his Colt and poked the butt of the pistol against the back of Billy Green's head. "Shut-up, kid or I'll shoot you right where you sit!" he shouted.

The kid snapped his mouth shut, but couldn't stop his whimpering or crying.

Nate shook his head and glanced down at Wallace's silver spurs, suspicious. "Why would you want to go and give me those spurs of yours?"

Wallace rolled the toe of each boot to the side and admired the handcrafted silver. "They're something ain't they?"

Nate directed his gaze on the spurs. "You're serious?"

"As a Nueces steer," Wallace spouted, never looking away from his prized possessions.

Nate's eyes brightened at the offer. "You'd really do that? Go slick-heeled and all?"

Wallace kept his focus down his outstretched legs and motioned with his chin at the spur's rowels. "I bought 'em in San Antonio from an old vaquero, called Alavez," he said and then added proudly, "hammered them himself, he did."

Nate's face lit-up. "I'd be much obliged to have them."

Wallace strained to look back at the remaining Gunn brothers. "This Alavez was a real craftsman."

Nate nodded, tight-lipped and squeezed Wallace's shoulder once before turning to join his brothers.

Wallace watched the rustler walk away, and then after a moment, called out, "There is one other thing, Nate."

Nate turned back, silent, and lifted his brow, waiting.

Wallace licked his lower lip and asked, "You fellas' wouldn't by chance have any canned peaches with you?"

## JOURNAL ENTRY

*Mr. Charlie had a saying that we all repeated, it would have been hard not to . . . for he recalled it at least twenty times during a work day. If any cowpuncher ever complained about his lot on the trail . . . whether it be riding a wind-broke pony, or wearing a kerosene poultice . . . well that cowboy always got the same sympathetic lecture. The old man would push both hands into his back pockets, rock on the heel of his boots, stick his chin into the complainer's face, and in a booming, gravelled voice, whoop, "Blazes, Rawhide, it ain't the hundred-mile to water problem! Toughen up, and be a cowboy!" And what the old man meant by that was driving two thousand thirsty longhorn beeves a hundred miles over dry land to water . . . now that's a problem. Not getting enough sleep or riding in a thunderstorm were and would always be small irritations to Mr. Charlie. And on the morning that we rode into Cañón Cerrado, we knew right away that we were all fixing to git off into a hundred-mile to water problem.*

# FOUR

———⟫◆⟪———

The four ☰R cowboys sat on their piebald ponies in stiffed-back silence and stared down the cut of a low dome hill in the southern scrub. Peacemakers hung from each man's waist. The Colts were all black, rubber-handled, and neatly tied mid-thigh. The men's expressions were serious revealing hard-bitten character. Not dally welters, but honest-to-God real rawhides, wholly intent on the job at hand and all of a fixed purpose.

From the shade of a mesquite tree, Pure Reston squinted at the canyon floor, uneasy. Buckshot and the kid didn't make it in to camp the night before and Pure knew that only meant trouble. A light scent of hide drifted between his upper lip and nose. He flared his nostrils at the faint odor and shook his head, indignant. He had caught the smell first. He always did. His pa, C.A., Charlie Albert Reston, had once bragged to a neighbor that Pure could smell the singe of cow hide, no matter the instrument used, from a mile away.

And then from below, a thin gray plume, barely visible through the mesquite caught Pure's eye. A branding fire simmered its last embers. The fire, small but adequate, was almost entirely spent, and across one corner a rolled-up piece of cowhide rested. Pure inhaled painfully and worked a piece of Snapping and Stretching gum from back in his mouth to his front teeth while his eyes swung over the canyon floor. The rolled-up cowhide was the cause of the rising smoke. Pure didn't allow his eyes to stray from the fire. He chewed the gum resignedly; his lips drawn tight; his mouth closed. He chewed slowly at first, judging the scene below and then faster in angry realization of what the fire indicated.

The three remaining men, brothers, Isa and Paint Reston, and ranch foreman, July Walker, recognized the sign. Pure was thinking. And more often

34

than not, when he chewed his gum in such a fashion, unpeaceful things were soon to follow. The three cowboys instinctively slid the Peacemakers from their holsters and hunched over, then checked their loads in a deliberate, patient manner.

A moment later, Pure stopped chewing, looked up from his cogitating, and muttered, "Let's go around."

<hr>

Inside the dry ravine, dozens of tracks, moving in two directions marked the area. Pure stopped chewing and stared at the mid-day sun. For days after a rain storm in this country, the air was slathered with a wet heat that exhausted even the strongest of men. Pure pushed back his hat and wiped his forehead before sniffing the air once more. "They came this way that's a certainty," he muttered and nodded at July Walker.

July, the son of free slaves, had worked for C.A. Reston since he was a young man. C.A. had taken an instant liking to the hard-working cowhand and always treated him like one of his sons. It was C.A. who nicknamed him July after he showed up at headquarters looking for work during the rise of the brightest summer star. July stood six-foot-four inches tall. He was a mountain of blackness, a bull of a man, and a pistoleer of great skill. July stepped out of his stirrup and bent down to read the track. After a few minutes of study, he straightened and pointed at several spots in the sand. "Mixed," he sighed and glanced up at Pure. "Eight horses and thirty head of beef."

Pure lifted his chin slightly to indicate his agreement and stared down the narrow draw. Fifty yards ahead, the long cut meandered left. He began to roll the gum around his mouth again. His eyes darkened. The rolled-up cowhide flashed in his head. "They went down there," he said.

The youngest and tallest of the Reston brothers, Isa, pursed his lips and squinted down the draw. "The thirty head or Buckshot and Billy?"

"Both."

The middle Reston, James, better known as Paint for the generous spat of freckles running across his nose and cheeks, nudged his pony forward until he sat even with his older brother and pointed down the ravine toward

35

Cañón Cerrado. "Well, are we riding in?"

Pure pinched his lower lip between his forefinger and thumb. "Suppose we better," he said and with a slight lift of the rein started his horse down the gorge.

Paint clicked his tongue and jogged his pony forward, staying even with Pure. His Peacemaker filled his right hand.

Pure glanced over at the gun and said, "You won't be needing the Colt."

Paint frowned. "How can you be sure?"

Pure dropped his eyes back on his horse's neck and lifted the rein chest-high. "Because what's done is done."

Paint shrugged, holstered the pistol, and then swung his attention back at Isa and July. "Put 'em away, boys," he called out. "Pure says, what's done is done."

## JOURNAL ENTRY

Pure's pa, Charlie Albert Reston, or C.A. as the boys called him, had brought his family to this country in '60. Soon after, the Millers and the Gunns arrived. All had come from Clay County, Kentucky, for one reason and one reason only, the abundance of feral Longhorns. There was good money to be made with beeves after the Big War, but it took a man with a lot of hard-bark to do so, as wildness and gunplay always rode alongside that good money on the range. Miss Sally Anne, C.A.'s wife died in '63 and before his death in '77, C.A. had built the Reston brand into one of the largest cattle operations in the area. C.A. raised his three boys and me on the ≡R, and he worked all of us like any other hand on the ranch. And that's why, even though a continual cycle of that Clay County misfortune and violence dogged us the rest of our natural lives, I rode into Cañón Cerrado that morning with the boys, for all three were as close to me as any brother I would ever have in this life.

# FIVE

*April 1878*
*Cañón Cerrado, Texas*

———⟫·◇·⟪———

Inside Cañón Cerrado, Isa Reston turned away from the branding fire carnage and placed both palms on his knees, his upper body wracked with convulsive dry-heaves.

Paint and July stood in stunned, morbid silence.

A building rage boiled Pure's face. "*La muerte de vaca*," he muttered through clenched teeth.

"Hell-fire," Isa muttered.

Pure made a gesture with his head toward the fire. "The Spanish call it the death of the skins," he said solemnly.

Paint pulled the rolled hide from the fire. Wrapped inside was the kid's body. He exhaled in disgust and glanced over at Pure. "They wrapped them in ≡R branded hides."

The men had been enfolded inside the green hides while still alive. A heavy binding of leather strapping imprisoned both victims within the animal skin. Over a day's time as the hides gradually shrunk under the sun's heat, the life was slowly squeezed from each man. It was a painful, agonizing death.

July removed his hat and lowered his head. "Smothered alive," he said and shook his head slowly. "That ain't a proper way for any cowpuncher to go out."

Pale, Isa moaned and turned back to the ghastly scene. "They suffocated them with rustled ≡R cattle?" he panted.

Pure remained unflinching, his face ashen and lined. "Let's get them out of those hides," he muttered, softly. "And get them buried proper-like."

"Here?" Isa asked. "Bury them in the canyon?"

Pure nodded at his younger brother. "Can't think of a better spot for Buckshot," he said and glanced skyward. "He'll have a wide open view of the sky every morn."

"He would like that, Isa," July murmured, tight jawed.

Isa's eyes darted across the sky. "Yeah," he uttered. "Maybe he would."

Paint ignored the conversation and pulled a six-inch blade from a leather sheath on the back of his belt. Kneeling, he cut the rope binding Billy Green's body and asked weakly, "Are we a hundred miles to water, Pure?"

Pure stood silent. His Adam's apple bobbed uncontrollably. A sad, bitter expression hung on his face. His gaze was fixed on Buckshot's body. He pushed his lips tight against one another and pushed his hat down over his eyes. He was blank, spent, and ireful.

Paint looked over to his older brother and awaited a response to his question.

After a moment, Pure leaned over and cut the ropes binding his friend, then slowly unrolled the ≡R rannie's body. He studied the old cowpuncher's features with a doleful exhale.

"I said, are we a hundred miles to water, Pure?" Paint asked again, impatient.

Pure ignored his brother and continued to study his friend's body. Lowering his head in respect, his eyes drifted to the dead cowboy's boots. He studied Wallace's boots carefully. Then a befuddled frown quickly darkened his expression. He unleashed a barely audible moan followed rapidly by a string of swearing.

"What is it?" July asked.

Pure pushed his lips closed. He moved closer to Wallace's feet. His fists clenched tightly as he stared at the old cowpuncher's boots.

"Damn it, Pure, are we a hundred miles to water?" Paint shuddered, his tone, a notch higher now.

Pure inhaled mournfully and knelt beside Wallace's body.

*I bought 'em in San Antonio from an old vaquero, called Alavez.*

He imagined Buckshot's last thoughts and formed in his mind the ghastly picture of his friend, lonely, scared, but defiant as the last breath was squeezed from his chest.

*Damned Gunns!*

Pure clenched his teeth, saddened that as boss, he had no one to share his pain with. *Toughen up*, he cautioned himself, aware that his brothers and July were waiting and watching. He reached down and crossed Wallace's arms across his chest. "Thanks, old friend," he whispered. "I got the message. Sleep well."

July crowded close to Pure and cast his eyes over the ranch boss's shoulder.

Pure lifted one of Wallace's boots by the heel. His hand trembled slightly. He clenched his jaw and glanced back at July. "See?"

"What?" July asked, puzzled. "What is it?"

Pure turned the boot toe-down. A vicious snarl deformed his mouth. "Look closer!" he said. His voice was more forceful and laced with growing impatience.

July, vexed, pushed his eyebrows together and squinted at the dead-man's boots.

Pure shook his head in a growing rage. "Hell, July! Gunn is what it means," he snapped and gently lowered Wallace's boot to the ground.

July wiped his mouth and swallowed hard. "How can you know that for certain, Pure?"

Frustrated that his ranch foreman didn't comprehend, Pure poked a finger at Wallace's boot heel and uttered, "He's slick-heeled, July."

The black cowboy's eyes widened in understanding. Pure's words hit him like a kick in the belly. "Buckshot would never be found without his spurs," he muttered.

"Are we a hundred miles to water, Pure?" Paint screamed out.

Pure turned his head and bore a hard gaze straight through his brother, far out to the west. After a moment, he reached down, grabbed a fistful of sand, and muttered, "The Gunns have drawn from the Reston well one time too many."

July offered Pure an outstretched hand. "Rankles a man mightily enough this thievery," he said, "But the killing . . . how can you be sure it's Gunns that did it?"

Pure pitched the sand toward the open end of the canyon. He grasped July's extended hand and pulled himself to his feet. "Who else would have need for such provocation?" A dangerous tone sounded in his voice. "It's them for sure, and there will be a payment extracted, this time, July," he vowed.

"Hell-fire, Pure!" Paint bellowed. "Are we a hundred miles to water?"

Pure jerked in anger and locked stares with his middle brother, offering only a cold, violent look in reply. His eyes dulled like the earth. "I'll bet my life that one of the Gunns is wearing Buckshot's spurs," he hissed and then nodded back at Wallace's lifeless form. "Don't y'all see that?"

July's face relaxed in understanding. "Even a Gunn wouldn't stoop so low as to take a dead cowboy's spurs."

Pure bit down on his lower lip and uttered, "Finally."

July exhaled. "Unless they were given willingly."

Pure nodded and muttered, "Buckshot gave those spurs to his killer."

"But why?" July asked. "He so loved those spurs."

"So we'd know who it was done him in."

July clenched his jaw. The muscle visibly protruded below his cheekbone. "Whoever is wearing those spurs is his killer," he muttered.

Paint lowered his head at Pure's revelation and in a meek whisper of a voice, gasped, "A hundred miles to water, Pure?"

Pure dug his fingers into his palms until his knuckles whitened and nodded at his middle brother. "Yeah, Paint," he uttered through clenched teeth, "I reckon we're a hundred miles to water."

# Six

*April 1878*
*Cañón Cerrado, Texas*

———◆———

Pure grabbed a handful of his piebald's mane and swung up into his saddle, his gaze, steely and cold, never left the two fresh graves mounded at the back of Cañón Cerrado.

Off his right side stood July, Paint, and a sullen Isa.

"You sure this is way you want to do this?" Paint asked.

Pure remained silent.

"Alone and all?"

Pure glanced down at his brother and shook his head.

"Because we're more than up to the task ahead."

Pure rolled the Snapping and Stretching gum to his front teeth and thought about his brother's words. He started to answer but was interrupted as Isa stepped forward and said in a cracking voice, "I'm coming along whether you like it or not."

Pure studied his youngest brother. A tormented expression of pain and anger hung on Isa's face. Pure's expression weakened. He had always allowed Isa a little more slack than Paint or July. He understood Isa's anger, or thought he did anyway. Growing up without a mother was tough in this country, and Pure had determined early on in Isa's life to be both mother and big brother to him. "Not this time, Isa," he drawled.

Isa turned and motioned at the two graves. "I just buried two friends, big brother."

"I'm aware."

"Two cowboys who rode for us."

"Don't push it."

"What about your damned code?"

"Don't lecture me, Isa."

"The code you're always preaching to us?"

"Not today, I said."

"Two cowboys . . . two ≡R cowboys!"

Pure looked away.

"Look at me!" Isa shouted. "Damn you and your code!"

Pure remained unmoved. He stared down the canyon.

"Two of our own, Pure!"

Pure inhaled a long breath and looked down at his brother. "You're too emotional right now."

"Buckshot and the kid, killed by Gunns," Isa growled.

"Emotional can get a man killed."

"The hell with you, Pure!"

"Emotional can get the rest of us killed too."

"Two of ours, Pure!"

Pure looked away. "You've said that."

Isa's expression turned to scorn. He twisted his lips tightly. "And you know what? I can't make myself cry or pray for either of them."

Pure blinked once and lifted the rein. A swallow of grief hung in his throat. He turned the piebald's head west.

Isa grabbed the horse's cabresto and stopped his older brother from leaving. "All I can think of is making those responsible pay for Wallace and the boy's murders."

Paint shoved both hands into his pockets. His eyes flicked toward Pure.

Isa stepped in close. "You understand what I'm saying, Pure?"

The muscles in Pure's jaw corded tighter than a half-hitch knot. "I understand," he pronounced, solemnly. Then in a deliberate, cold voice answered, "But this ain't your fight, yet . . . and don't get any notions that it is."

Isa glared bitterly at his older brother's cold demeanour. "It's blood that's been dishonored!"

"Hold your tongue," Pure warned carefully.

"It is my fight!"

A flush of heat rose up Pure's neck. His face glowed red. Isa and Paint were not hardened from the same forge as he was. Paint was brash and hotheaded, and Isa was young and impulsive. He was determined to keep the pair out of the Gunn fight for as long as he could. "It's not your fight until I say so," he snapped. "This thing falls to me as the oldest son."

Isa showed his teeth, seething. He stared into Pure's determined, contemptuous eyes, and with visible disdain dropped his hand from the cabresto.

Finished with Isa, Pure directed his attention to July and Paint and pointed east, "Seven cowhands are waiting for you boys at headquarters. A lot of livelihoods depend on you getting them beeves to the Kansas railhead on time."

July stiffly chewed on his lip and nodded his understanding.

Pure carried his gaze over to his middle brother. "Paint?"

Paint inhaled and held his breath for several seconds then nodded with a great exhalation.

A noticeable tension descended over the canyon floor.

July inhaled a deep breath and then grinned large, lessening the unspoken hostility. "How do you aim to find them, Pure?" he asked.

Pure recognized July's gambit and returned a thin smile. "The finding will be straightforward; this bunch has no choice in their trail."

July looked west. "To the river," he muttered.

Pure nodded. "The land is always the dealer in this card game," he said. "They'll head first for Cita Creek and then down to the Nueces."

July tightened his lips against one another and mumbled, "A beeve herd moves from water hole to water hole."

Pure laughed softly, "That's what C.A. always told us boys."

Paint shuffled his feet and joined in the conversation. "You figure the Gunn boys to be meeting up with a much larger herd?"

Pure hesitated briefly and then frowned. "I hope so. If not, then they killed Buckshot and the kid for only thirty head of Reston beeves."

July wrinkled his forehead at the thought and then stared at Pure, expressionless. His mouth hung slack at the possibility. "Damn them all," he cursed under his breath.

Pure nodded and exhaled in disgust. "Seems a man's life ought to be worth more than thirty beeves."

The canyon became silent and still.

Pure breathed hoarsely and stared down. A sheet of blackness slowly swallowed the ground in front of him. He lifted his chin and stared at the April sky. A bank of clouds blowing in from Kansas shadowed the sun.

*Rain's coming again.*

Pure gathered his rein and gentled his horse forward. His hand brushed lightly against his pistol handle. "Caring for your friends is a man's greatest responsibility, one I refuse to suffer lightly. I sent them boys out, and I'm the one accountable for righting the slate. I aim to find the man wearing Buckshot's spurs and bring back our stolen beeves."

His brothers stood speechless, well aware that an unstoppable storm of vengeance was brewing and blowing west toward the Mexican border.

As he reached the neck of the canyon, Pure flipped the rein across his horse's neck and gathered the cow pony into a lope. "I'll meet all of you at Fort Griffin in six weeks," he shouted out, thankful that his back hid the tears welling in his eyes. "And if I've missed you there, I'll catch up to you at Doan's Crossing on the Red."

The three glanced at one another with fearful worry.

"What's done is done," Isa uttered mockingly and looked out toward the canyon neck with an insolent glare. "This is the very last time I'll take an order from him."

July gathered up the reins to Buckshot's and the kid's horses and tied them on a string behind his piebald. He knew nothing or no one could stop the events that were now in motion. He stepped into his stirrup and plopped down on the worn saddle.

Paint and Isa followed suit.

July cast his eyes on the two and smiled in recollection. "You know Buckshot taught your brother how to rope," he lectured respectfully. "Taught him how to be a brush hand and more important, taught him how to be a man."

Isa glared at July and mumbled, "No matter and it doesn't give him the right to act like C.A. all the time."

**45**

"It gives him every right, Isa!" July shot back. His voice betrayed a growing impatience with the younger Reston. "Buckshot was just like a daddy to Pure."

Shocked at July's outburst, Isa leaned back and glared at the ranch foreman.

Paint took a second to mull over July's words and soon after grasped the tip of his hat brim and nodded his thanks.

Then they sat, all three, unmoving, stifling the desire to talk, each holding his own thoughts.

After awhile, July broke the somber apprehension. "Well, no matter," he boomed optimistically, "I'll bet the both of you that Pure get's every last one of those Gunn boys."

Isa clicked his tongue and turned a light spur into his pony. He muttered sarcastically, "Yeah."

"You'll see," July said, encouraged. "He'll end this thing once and for all."

Lagging behind the others, Paint raised his brow and gigged his pony toward the canyon neck. "I hope so too, July," he mumbled, prophetically. "Because if he doesn't, then there is going be more than just a little bit of hell to pay over this for a long time afterward."

## JOURNAL ENTRY

*There was an old saying back in those days that went: Texas is all right for men and dogs but hell on women and horses. But I'm going to tell you right now that back then Texas was hell on everyone. It seemed as if every living creature or plant in that country had horns, thorns, or fangs. How any of us cowpunchers survived all of those things plus the rustlers and border bandits had to be some kind of miracle. By '73 any buckaroo with an inclination toward thievery could drive re-branded cattle to the Nueces and sell them to Mexican thieves for four dollars cash. Texas did little to stop the lawlessness, and the Mexicans, still stewed over the loss of their land west of the Nueces, considered the rustling justified. The Mexican bandits called the stolen beeves, Nanita's cattle or "grandma's" cattle. They felt the land and everything west of the Nueces still belonged to them and that included the cattle. And looking back, the one thing I always regretted in my life was letting Pure ride into that defiant outlawry all by himself that April morn.*

# SEVEN

———⊰⬧⊱———

S ixty miles south of Cañón Cerrado, on the edge of midnight, the rain started to fall. The deluge was in its own antagonistic way, incessantly harsh and memorable in severity. In a very short period of time the monsoon had turned the brasada into a viscous ocean of muck.

Tucked away in a small stand of mesquite a hundred yards northeast of the Gunn herd, Pure sat hunched on his piebald and chewed the Snapping and Stretching gum between his front teeth. Hapless, his oilskin of little use, the ≡R ranch boss shivered under the chilling rain and between lightning strikes kept a keen eye on the goings-on in the Gunn brothers' selected bedding ground. He had settled in the mesquite hours earlier, during daylight, and now patiently surveyed the drive layout and noting the watch changes. Even in his discomfort, Pure still inhaled a reassuring breath.

*You boys might have slipped up a 'might.*

The Gunns, although expert rustlers, were inexperienced drovers, and the night's extreme weather proved that fact. While the bedding ground was far enough from the Nueces, a half mile west, and the main camp, a mile to the east, the landscape itself was littered with scrub and sage thicket that would make a stampede impossible to control.

Pure peered out from his wide-brimmed and looked skyward. A barrel of water drenched his face and high up, a streak of chain lightning raced across the sky. C.A.'s caution about thunderstorms and cattle drifted back to him as he wiped a handful of water from his mouth and chin.

*Ride for hell and beyond when the lightning turns blue and jumps for mother Earth.*

Looking back at the herd, his eyes widened in amazement as will-o'-the-wisp, phosphorous balls of electricity, jumped from horn to ear to horn, before dancing on all thousand or so cows at once. A loud crack illuminated the sky directly above his head and caused him to jerk forward abruptly spitting out his gum in the process. Swearing at his loss of balance and gum, he quickly righted himself and threw his gaze out at the herd. The cattle, their long horns reflecting each flash, milled about fretful and uneasy under the storm. Pure winced as another crack exploded above him. He prayed the herd would remain calm a while longer and allow him to finish what he had come here to do.

Fifty yards outside the herd, two night-herders in slickers circled the beeves in opposite directions. Even from his distance, Pure heard the riders as they mumbled a soft, garbled, nonsensical melody in an attempt to soothe the circling beasts. From experience, Pure realized that the confused beeves were just a little north of spooking.

*Hold them cows, boys.*

Both men had dropped their pistols to the ground earlier. Pure knew it was dangerous to keep a chunk of metal strapped to your waist during a storm of such veracity. He wrapped his hand around the handle of his six-shooter and started to lift the gun from its holster, then paused, thinking. Against his better instincts he pushed the gun back into its holster and decided he would risk a lightning strike this night.

*Just hold 'em now, cowboys.*

The night-herders, unmistakeably miserable, kept a steady line of glances rolling toward the main camp, desperate for replacements and ready for the warmth of their hotrolls. Pure grinned at their discomfort.

*God help you boys if these beeves start to run, because without any open ground to turn 'em, there'll be no stopping a stampede.*

Without glancing down, his eyes fixated on the dark shadow of the herd; Pure slipped an Elgin stem-winder from his pocket and waited for the next lightning strike. Seconds later, the sky crackled and lit up in yellow brilliance. Pure dropped his eyes and peered at the watch face.

*Five minutes 'til midnight.*

He gentled the Elgin back into his pocket as the yellow-lit sky faded to blue and then darkness. Out in the herd, one of the night-herders turned his horse east and unable to gallop, ploughed through the mud for the main camp.

The sky illuminated once more.

Pure's grin sharpened.

*That's it, cowboy; go wake up the next shift.*

He lifted his mouth skyward and took a gulp of rain.

An electrical flash swam sideways across the sky.

A thousand beeves wailed with a chorus of bawls.

The stench of sulphur hung in his nose.

*There'll never be a better time.*

Then with an easy flick of his spur, he directed his piebald cautiously toward the bedding ground and the lone night-herder. Ankle-deep mud would assure that the next watch would take at least fifteen minutes to reach the bedding ground. Certain of his aggrieved decision, he reached in under his oilskin, slipped the Peacemaker from its holster, and rested the gun across his covered lap. Right or wrong, Buckshot Wallace's silver spurs no longer occupied a place in his mind.

# EIGHT

*May 1878*
*The Bedding Ground, Texas*

———◦◇◦———

Pure walked his piebald onto the bedding ground unnoticed. At each thunderous crack, he pulled rein and held the seasoned cow pony in place, waiting, and lurking in deadly silence. Once the sulphurous flash dissipated, he would start the horse forward while never taking his focus off the remaining night-herder.

When he approached within fifteen feet of the solitary watchman, he slid the Colt from under his oilskin. A flash of lightning moved closer to earth and discharged a thunderous crack that caused the night-herder to roll his shoulders forward in the saddle.

"Blazes!" the rider swore, unsettled, and then sank back in the saddle.

Pure remained calm, squinting as a steady deluge of water rolled off his hat brim.

The night-rider shivered once and then seemingly spooked, glanced around as another bolt illuminated above the bedding ground.

Pure twisted his lips against one another. He recognized the face. His expression softened, but only momentarily. This was the one Gunn brother he had hoped he would not have to face tonight, but even so, he would not be deterred from carrying on, the code demanded such.

Startled by the figure saddled behind him, the watchman jumped and then cursed loudly, "Hell! It's about time! I'm all done playing cow nurse for tonight."

"Hullo, Street," Pure hissed through closed teeth. His voice was level and ice cold.

A hellish bright orange bolt rolled overhead lighting up the landscape.

Street compressed his neck into his shoulders and glanced askance at the figure in front of him and then the piebald horse. His eyes tightened. *Restons!* He was familiar with the pony and the oldest Reston brother. His right hand instinctively dropped toward his holster, but only air filled his palm. A regretful frown gathered at his mouth.

Pure inched the piebald forward. "You tossed it on the ground, remember?"

"What the?"

"Funny thing," Pure smirked. "A man throws his gun down in a lightning storm to be safe and then still ends up dead."

"What the hell do you th . . . think you're doing out here, Pure?" Street stuttered.

"I promised to tally up the books for an old friend."

"What kind of nonsense are you ranting about on a night like this?"

"I'm the tally man for tonight's herd."

"What?"

Pure's right hand moved slightly. "Call it professional pride," he uttered. "Every roundup needs a tally."

The click of a Colt, a click so unmistakeable, hammered back, and sounded in the rain.

Street's eyes widened. He sucked a gulp of air through a half-closed mouth. "Whoa, whoa now, Reston!" he said in a rush of panic.

Pure levelled the gun at the youngest Gunn's chest and lifted his eyebrows. He waited for the rustler to acknowledge that he knew why Pure was here. "Say it!" he ordered.

"Say what?"

"Say it!"

Street eased both reins toward his chest. His horse took a step back. "You're loco, Pure."

"*La muerte de vaca?*"

Thunder boomed and lightning flashed simultaneously.

Street rolled his head to the right, confused. "Now what in the hell does that mean?"

Rain danced off the Colt's barrel. "The death of skins, Street," he said, steady. His voice smouldered with contempt.

"Never heard of that expression before."

"Com'on you remember, Street."

Street glanced into the distance. "Night crew will be riding in here any minute."

"Not likely."

"You prepared to take that chance, Reston?"

"How come it is that bad eggs like you always talk in circles?"

Street sucked in a breath and brushed his hand against the empty holster. "It's not there, remember?"

Street leaned forward in his saddle. "You still got time to ride out of here, Reston."

"With my tail between my legs, Street?"

"Better than dying in the rain a long way from home."

"You said it, boy."

Street pushed back hard. "Damn you."

"You and your brothers have been throwing the big loop on Reston land for too long now."

"There ain't no proof of that, and you know it!"

"I figure I've got all the proof I need."

"So, now what?"

"*La muerte de vaca?*"

"I told you before that I don't know what that means."

"Oh, you know, Street."

"The rain must have got you all loco, Reston."

"It's how you and your sorry lot of brothers killed two of my men."

Street's jaw quivered. "That's cr . . . crazy," he stammered.

"Two Reston cowpunchers."

"You're sniffing in the wrong bush, Reston."

"Two of my own . . . family, Street."

"Why wo . . . would we want to kill Buckshot?"

Pure tightened his grip on the Colt, more incensed now, no longer caring which of the Gunn brothers it was. He leaned forward and whispered angrily through clenched teeth, "Who said anything about Buckshot, Street?"

Street's shoulders dropped. "You did?" he responded nervously. "Just before." His attention never wavered from the Colt.

Pure started to answer the lie but held-back as the near-deafening rain suddenly stopped.

Street blinked twice and then glanced up, nervous.

An electric chill rolled through the air.

Pure's eyes swung toward the bedding ground.

The herd had stopped milling. Every cow's neck was stretched northwest. A strange silence descended through the blackness.

Street swallowed and looked out at the herd. "That's mighty unusual," he said, unsteady.

Pure knew the signs. He felt the hair on his arms stand up.

*It's fixing to hit right on top of us.*

He lurched off the piebald as if shot and squatted beside his horse, holding both reins tightly.

Street glanced at the riderless piebald. A puzzled looked froze his expression. Then sensing an opportunity, he flipped the rein and turned his horse toward the leading edge of the herd. Rolling his spurs against his horse's side, he screamed, "Git up!"

A deep prolonged growl reverberated from west to east. The sky boiled fire, and a sharp crack exploded overhead.

Pure's head shot up. A low rumble shook the ground beneath him. "They're running!" he screamed, and swung back up in the saddle, desperate to put distance between him and the crazed herd.

A series of lightning strikes ignited and bore violently into the bedding ground. The jagged blue bolts gnawed repeatedly in the middle of the herd. A rolling mass of bawls and bellows followed and soon the stench of melted hide burned the air.

Out in front of the stampede, a string of curse words echoed in the darkness quickly followed by a gut-wrenching scream.

Pure tossed a glance to where he last saw Street. The rustler's horse was stopped dead in its tracks, swinging its head from left to right, flailing and whinnying in terrifying shrieks.

Pure gritted his teeth unable to look away.

The animal was hopelessly bogged down in the muck.

"Get behind your horse!" Pure screamed above the roar. He knew the rush of cattle prone to split around men and horses would never see Street or his horse in the darkness.

Street's horse gave one last wail and then collapsed on its side under a horrific crack of bone.

Pure raised both hands to his mouth and leaned as far forward over the saddle as he could. "Get behind him, Street!" he shouted through cupped hands.

The exhausted horse lay sideways in front of the leading edge of the stampede.

Pure cursed the boy's youthful ignorance and spurred the piebald away for the mesquites and safety.

Darkness descended once more.

Thirty seconds later, clear of the rush, Pure reined his piebald to a stop and glanced back. Both he and the horse huffed for breath.

A solitary flash illuminated overhead.

Pure exhaled a labored breath and surveyed the carnage. Hundreds of dead cattle littered the bedding ground in a neat circle. The remaining beeves rolled in wild headlong rush for the Nueces. Street Gunn and his pony were nowhere to be seen. Pure dragged a wet palm across his mouth and cursed aloud, "You damned fool!"

The sky faded from orange to charcoal to black.

Then softer with regret, "You damned fool."

Pure waited in the darkness, knowing he should turn and ride away but for unfathomable reasons sat paralyzed, cold, and empty. Lightning flashed on the eastern side of the bedding ground. He looked up, stock-still.

*Storm's moving away.*

Overhead, the departing storm flashed a departing grumble. The electrical charge flicked weakly across the sky.

*Get going. There's nothing more you can do for him or here tonight.*

Pure lifted the rein and turned his piebald back northeast but unable to contain his curiosity as to the boy's fate, he took one final look back. Another lightning flash sparked in the east. Beneath the cracking bolt, hurried movement caught his eyes. Two riders rode into the bedding ground slaughter, gesturing wildly.

*Are they pointing at me or the die-up?*

Pure flipped the rein and turned the horse around. He stared at the two riders as the light faded to black.

*Did they see me?*

Anxious, he took a quick glance skyward and prayed the lightning wouldn't flash again.

*Did they see me?*

But he knew the answer to his question before it even left his mouth. If he could see them, then they sure enough could see him.

*Calm down. They could never make-out who you were at this distance.*

A sputter of lightning flashed overhead.

He glanced down at his pony and started to rein the animal to the northeast but paused. His eyes remained fixed on an oval ink spot on the horse's neck. His mind raced. He gritted his teeth and kneaded his brow with his thumb and index finger. A sense of dread shivered down his spine and gooseflesh rolled up his arms.

*If they saw me, that means they saw the piebald too.*

His head drooped toward his chest. He gripped the saddle horn with both hands and leaned all his weight against leather wrapped pommel. A sense of inevitable bad luck shook his thoughts, and inside he cursed himself.

*Everyone in South Texas knows that to a man only the Reston outfit rides piebald ponies.*

# Nine

*May 1878*
*The Gunn Bedding Ground, Texas*

⟫◆⟪

In the shadowy first light of morning, Echol Brocious Gunn stared down at the mash of horse, man, and mud mixed together and flattened into an oval depression. E.B., as he liked to be called, was a squat, iron-fisted, cruel man and no stranger to thievery or violence. His eyes, one blue, the other gray, discomposing to even the most hardened rowdy, melted black at the horrific sight.

The brothers Gunn watched patiently as their father stroked a full-faced beard that hung past two buttons on his undershirt. The boys knew better then to speak. E.B. was reckoning, working himself up, and getting angrier with each glance at the flattened corpse of Street. They all knew that a fire was boiling inside their father's belly, and when he did speak, it would be of a desperate order filled with rage.

"Didn't leave much of him."

Nate looked on. "Damned, Restons," he said under his breath.

"Yeah," E.B. said.

"Calls for an answer from us," Nate said.

E.B. ignored Nate. His attention was preoccupied with the gore at his feet.

The other brothers shuffled glances elsewhere and didn't answer.

E.B. coolly pointed at the mush. "Is that Street's ribs or the horse's?"

Clark and Foss turned their heads back and cleared their throats.

E.B. glanced at the pair, shook his head, and then looked toward the river. "Gawdallmighty, them beeves is probably spread from here to Mexico."

Nate nodded but held his tongue.

E.B. looked back at his oldest, tightened his mouth, and then glanced back at the muddy depression. "Nothing more to be done for Street," he said matter-of-factly. "You boys saddle up and start rounding up those stampeded beeves. The Mex will be here tonight to trade."

Ben furrowed his brow and before considering, asked, "We just gonna leave him like that?"

Nate winced.

E.B. turned on his heel and gave a quick tug at his beard. His eyes melted into one another. "Damned you, Ben," he cursed wildly, "you got cow chips in those ears of yours."

Ben pushed his lips together and lowered his eyes.

E.B. took three quick strides toward the now submissive boy and with a powerful swing slapped him flush across the jaw.

Ben stumbled slightly. His hat toppled from his head. He winced but didn't raise a hand to his face.

"I told you, boy, to mount up and start looking for beeves!" Spit flew from E.B.'s mouth. His voice was frighteningly deliberate, and ice-cold. He spun toward the others. "Well? What are y'all waiting for?"

The boys scrambled for their ponies.

Ben reached down and retrieved his hat. He walked quick-like for his pony, never looking back at his father.

E.B. watched Ben saunter off. His glare on the boy never softened. When Ben stepped into the stirrup, he yelled, "Boy!"

Ben pushed a reluctant glance toward his violent father.

"After you get all them beeves back to camp, you can throw some rocks or something over your brother."

———◇———

Later toward dark, several miles west of the bedding ground on the far side of the Nueces, Nate tallied the rounded-up cows.

E.B. sat on a dun next to his oldest and breathed noisily through his nose, impatient for the count.

Nate poked at a line of charcoaled Xs marked on his horse's neck. Each

X represented twenty head of beeves. "We're missing thirty head," he said without looking at his father.

E.B. pushed down his beard and looked grimly north. "How many head did you say you boys cut out of the ≡R herd?"

Nate turned his head slowly toward E.B. The old man's lips were already mouthing the answer. Nate held back a grin. *Sharp as ever*, he thought and then answered, "Thirty."

E.B.'s face shook in a frightful tremor. "Them thieving, Restons," he mumbled.

"What you want to do about this," Nate asked.

"Ought to hang every last one of them no-good Yankee liars."

Nate's mouth contorted, stifling a good laugh. *Hang the Restons for stealing their own cattle back from us, that's E.B. through and through.*

E.B. dragged the back of his hand across his mouth and squinted at the rustled herd, pondering. After a moment, he whipped his eyes back at Nate. "I'm going to trade with the Mex. Clark stays with me."

"Okay, E.B."

"You take the rest and follow them Restons to the railheads. You boys should catch them easy afore they leave the Nation."

Nate wiped his hand over the charcoal Xs and allowed, "I'll handle it, E.B."

E.B. rolled his neck at Nate, his eyes bore into his youngest son. "You git them thirty head back."

Nate lifted his gaze and studied his father's eyes. Even with E.B.'s drooped eyelids, he knew what the old man was thinking . . . knew all too well what the old man wanted. "Yes, sir."

"And thirty more to even the tally."

"I'll see to it."

"And Nate."

Nate peered at E.B., suspiciously.

E.B. looked down at Nate's boots. His eyes danced in delight at the sight of the shiny prods.

Nate pursed his lips and waited.

"Them new spurs?"

Nate glanced down at Buckshot Wallace's handcrafted beauties. "Yep."

"Where'd you get 'em?"

"Back in the canyon."

"From one of the Reston cowboys?"

"Yep."

E.B. rolled his hands around one another in child-like delight. "Which one?"

"Wallace."

E.B.'s grin broadened. "Buckshot?"

"Yeah. Gave them up willingly."

"Naw."

Nate nodded. "Swear."

"Buckshot Wallace?"

"Swear."

E.B. eyed the spurs greedily and motioned for them with his index finger. "Give 'em here."

Nate shook his head, amazed, and lifted his right boot from the stirrup. He undid the spur buckle and handed the prod to his father.

A wide smile brightened E.B.'s face as he studied the craftsmanship of the spur. He looked back at Nate and motioned for the other impatiently.

Nate obliged with an accompanying frown.

E.B. held both spurs head-high and nodded, pleased. "Thanks, boy," he said. "Now git about the business we spoke of before."

Nate didn't move.

E.B. stared right into his oldest son's soul.

Nate inhaled, waiting.

Minutes passed. Silent minutes.

Nate coughed into his hand.

"Well, whataya got to say, Nate? Don't be shy now, boy."

"What about Street?"

"What of him?"

Nate mulled over his next words, and questioned if he should even ask them.

E.B. straightened. His face began to redden.

*Wonder if he's going to try and hit me too*, Nate wondered.

"Go ahead boy, spit out what you're chewing on. I ain't got all day for socializing."

"Don't you want to even the score for his killing?"

"Is that so important to you, Nate? Is that your real question?"

"He was my brother."

E.B.'s eyes contracted and sank deep into their sockets. "Not full, he wasn't," he snarled, turned, and spit on the ground. His expression showed a brewing storm. "He weren't from me, anyways."

"Well, to me he was, and I aim to settle things with the Reston clan for his murder."

E.B. leaned over his saddle and muttered, "You do what you gotta do, boy, but make damn sure you secure those sixty head of Reston beeves first."

"How come you never liked him, E.B.?"

E.B. trailed his tongue along his upper lip. "I liked him as well as any stray a man takes onto his property."

Nate started to reply and then thinking better, lifted his rein to leave.

E.B. grabbed his oldest son's forearm.

Nate glanced down at his forearm with a frown.

A flash of evil sparked in each of E.B.'s eyes. "You want justice for Street?" he said with a quick nod, "then do it."

Nate's eyes narrowed into small points. "I plan to."

"You're old enough to act on your own."

"Don't need you to tell me of that fact."

An evil smile crossed E.B.'s mouth. He squeezed Nate's arm harder. "But if you're gonna do it, do it like the Good Book says, an eye for an eye, boy. You take their youngest in return."

Nate slid his arm out of E.B.'s grip and nodded. And that was it. The old man had conceded. There would be no holds barred with the Restons going forward. He nodded his acknowledgement of E.B.'s orders all the while wondering when the old man had ever read the Bible.

E.B. smiled, wicked and villainous, then quickly frowned. "And Nate," he said, showing his teeth, his voice edgy. "If any of my real sons git themselves killed during your bandying about, it'll be you I'll hold the blame to."

Nate choked back a shiver and held his composure with steady eyes. For all the old man was, Nate knew that he wasn't ever a liar.

## JOURNAL ENTRY

*Around the last week of June, I believe it was, Pure caught up with the drive herd at Doan's Crossing on the Red River. And true to his word, he drove in with him twenty-eight re-branded ≡R beeves as well as two head carrying the EB brand. Being that those two were to make up for the two beeves the Gunns killed in Cañón Cerrado. We were all excited to see him back safe, but Pure acted funny that day, closed, sad-like, and to himself. He refused to answer any questions about finding the Gunn boys, or the whereabouts of Buckshot's spurs, and there wasn't an hour that went by that he didn't squirm in his saddle and watch the drag. It wasn't until a few days later when we reached Brushy Creek in Indian Territory that he told Paint, Isa, and me about the lightning storm on the Nueces and the demise of Street Gunn. And then I understood why Pure fidgeted in his saddle so much because soon I found myself checking the drag too. All the way through the Nation, I checked it. For I knew once E.B. settled Street into Mother Earth and traded our stolen beeves, he would send the rest of his boys after any cowpuncher riding for the ≡R brand. What I didn't know, not until much later, was why*

*Street's death caused Pure so much anguish . . . and the real cause of this running argument between Gunns and Restons.*

# TEN

*July 1878*
*The Western Trail, Indian Territory*

———⟫◆⟪———

The line of ☰R cattle stretched for a mile or more down Otter Creek in the northwest corner of Indian Territory. Soaking spring rains had left the grass full of protein and the watering holes filled. The drive was operating without a hitch which made Pure uneasy and nervous. He rode from point to drag repeatedly preaching, "Keep your eyes peeled and don't be getting too comfortable."

The ☰R cowhands, confused by Pure's out of character barking, simply lowered their heads and concentrated on their drive duties.

"I don't want any problems reining us in today."

July, riding on the wind side point, noticed Pure's anxiousness and stopped the trail boss as he rounded the curve closest to the Reston ranch foreman. "What's crawling up your spine today?" he asked, dry throated.

"Just don't like getting overconfident."

"We're covering ten miles a day."

"Like I said."

July squinted, thinking. "And right on schedule to arrive in Dodge City with one of the first herds."

"And I aim to make sure that doesn't change," Pure said, more agitated now.

July ran his tongue over his lips. "Ok, boss," he conceded.

Pure cut a rough glare at his foreman and then eased his pony in beside the cowboy.

July lifted his brow, waiting for Pure to speak.

Pure worked the Snapping and Stretching gum forward from the back of his jaw. "I almost wish something would happen," he rasped and then kneaded the gum rapidly between his two front teeth.

"You just can't stand good fortune," July joked.

Pure's thoughts drifted back to the lightning storm and Street's demise. "Well it's just that this prosperity you speak of always seems to come with a heavy price."

"In all the years that I've known you, I've never seen you afraid of a gamble."

"This ain't a card game, July."

"True enough. I reckon it's just life and that's always been a bet whose odds favor the house."

The tension in Pure's face eased some. "I ain't got the time to listen to philosophizing," he said.

"Would you relax if I sent a scout up ahead?"

Pure twisted his mouth in thought and chomped hard on his gum. After several moments of contemplating, he glanced over at July. "Yeah, I would," he said and without a thought added, "Send Isa."

"Okay. Anything in particular you want explored?"

Pure looked at the vast emptiness on the western horizon. "Yeah, tell him to scout the next few crossings carefully."

"He's gonna want to know why?"

"'Cause I said so," Pure huffed.

"Like I said, he's gonna want to know why."

Pure exhaled, annoyed. "You tell him that with the rivers and creeks running full and with two other Texas outfits in close proximity, I need to know that the waters are safe for our beeves to swim."

July hid a grin. "I'm sure he'll appreciate that answer," he said.

The tendons in Pure's neck rose visibly. "And you also tell him that if the water is suspect, then he is to find us another crossing spot."

July nodded.

Pure stared ahead with feigned agitation. "Any other cowboy working for me that I need to do any explaining to?" he asked.

July kept his gaze up the trail and refused to look in Pure's direction.

Pure bore a hard glare on July. "You're sure?"

"I'm sure."

"Then get back to it."

July nodded and turned his pony's head, but before riding off, offered, "You know he ain't gonna to be too happy about being singled out for this job."

Pure raised one eyebrow at July. He stared at his foreman for two seconds and then said, "He'll get over it."

"I know he will, but he's gonna feel like you're punishing him."

"He's just one more cowboy on this drive, July."

"I know, but—,"

"That's how C.A. treated every one of us boys."

July tightened his lips and thinking, nodded his head.

Pure ran his tongue over his lower lip, unconcerned. "He's like a young colt testing his bucking legs right now."

July grinned. "More like a young man rebelling against a father figure," he said and then clucked his tongue loudly, loping his piebald toward the right swing position where Isa was riding.

Pure watched July ride off and muttered, "He's no different than you and I were at that age."

⟫◆⟪

Isa stormed across a stretch of flattened prairie, silent and gloomy, still angry over his dust-up with Pure in Cañón Cerrado. He mulled over July's orders.

*Isa, Pure wants you to ride out ahead and check the water crossings.*

The youngest Reston seethed, cussed and muttered to himself as he drove his pony up the trail toward Brushy Creek.

*Yeah, Mr. big-shot trail boss, in case you didn't know, prospecting is your job, not mine.*

Five minutes later, he crossed the creek still upbraiding Pure mentally. His pony, a thick-legged, easy-gaited horse called Crow-hop by the Reston cowpunchers, became restless during the swim to the other bank. The cow pony got his name for his penchant to bucking when he sensed trouble about.

Crow-hop had been Isa's mount since his first day as a cowpuncher. The youngest Reston could read the horse's temperament and signals expertly, but today, as he tossed Pure's comments from the past several weeks back and forth in his head, he missed all of the horse's visible signs of irritability.

*This ain't your fight, Isa.*

Crow-hop came out of the creek irritable. His nose sniffed high into the air. A low whinny rumbled from the pony's throat.

*And it won't be your fight until I say so.*

Angry, Isa kept a blank gaze downward and all of his focus inward, oblivious to his surroundings. He paid no heed to Crow-hop's rapid head movements or disquieting snorts.

*Caring for your friends is a man's greatest responsibility. Hah!*

Half a mile out of the creek, the land was open and often used as a bedding ground by the ≡R outfit on the yearly drives. Crow-hop faltered at the open ground, and then stopped altogether, refusing to move any farther ahead.

*Well, to hell with you big brother. I'm just as smart as you.*

Isa was suddenly aware of Crow-hop's balking and taking it as stubbornness, he rolled his spurs along the pony's side and shook the reins. The pony resisted with a shake of his head and remained firmly in place, unmoving.

*Maybe I'll go off with my own. One third of the cattle profits from this drive are mine.*

Abandoning his idle-indulgence, Isa quickly directed his attention to Crow-hop's insistence on not moving forward, He lifted his gaze to the horse's neck and muttered, "What's gotten into you, Crow-hop?"

The cow pony snorted twice, then turned his head left, and smelled Isa's boot.

"Hey," Isa mumbled, annoyed and jerked Crow-hop's head around.

Crow-hop backed up, irritated.

Isa glanced at the horse's flank and raked his spurs a little deeper in the animal's side. "You get up, here."

A rousing round of clapping sounded in front of him. Isa pushed his eyebrows together and tossed a self-conscious glance ahead.

Charlie Gunn swung a wide-brimmed sombrero off his head. "Ride 'em buckaroo."

Isa squinted and looked left to right. Riled, Crow-hop danced on his back legs and swung his head up and down.

"Hee-yaw, cowpuncher!" Foss Gunn pulled his reins chest-high and imitated riding an outlaw pony.

A feeling of tightness compressed Isa's chest. He cursed his stupidity. Ben Gunn sat directly in front of him, gun drawn.

Isa swallowed and pulled hard on the left rein. "Whoa," he said forcefully. Crow-hop settled immediately.

From his right side he heard, "Look at how he handles that cow pony, boys," the voice laughed.

Isa's face paled. He twisted toward the voice and then shrugged abjectly at the figure. "Howdy, Nate," he said, sullen, suddenly wishing Pure, and Paint, and July were riding beside him.

"Howdy," Nate replied and then gestured at Isa's holster. "I'll be needing that pistol of yours, Isa."

"How's that?"

Nate pointed at Isa's holster. "Your gun. Hand it over."

Isa gathered himself. "It's dangerous for a man to be without his gun on the trail, Nate."

Nate glanced around at his brothers and then looked back at Isa with a hard grin. "We'll keep ours then as protection."

"So you want to protect me?"

"Why not? We are neighbors after all."

Isa twisted in the saddle and looked down the trail. "You know, I think I'm going to keep my Colt, Nate," he said and spun back toward the Gunns.

Nate fell silent.

Isa studied the oldest Gunn brother's face intently.

After a minute, Nate said, "That's too bad."

Isa felt the blood drain from his face. A single drop of perspiration beaded on the tip of his nose.

Nate pushed his hat above his forehead. "Yeah, that's too bad."

The pained images of Buckshot and the kid flashed in Isa's head. *La muerte de vaca.*

Nate frowned. "I just saw something in that expression of yours that troubles me, Isa."

Isa stared blankly past Nate.

"We ain't gonna have any trouble here, are we?" Nate asked.

Isa broke away from his thoughts and fixed an uneasy stare on the oldest Gunn brother.

Nate's face dropped slightly. "Are we?" he asked louder and more forcefully.

*La muerte de vaca.*

Nate tilted his head and tightened his mouth, waiting.

"No," Isa smiled with a blank stare. His right hand lurched toward the Peacemaker. "No trouble at all."

# ELEVEN

*July 1878*
*The Western Trail, Indian Territory*

———◆———

An hour before dark, Nate, Charlie, and Ben sat saddled on the far side of Brushy Creek. Nate held the rein to the riderless and saddle-free Crow-hop in one hand.

A mile to the south out on the open prairie, the rising outline of a drive herd appeared.

Nestled on the ground between Charlie and Ben, Foss stoked a fire of dry cow chips and dead mesquite. A piece of cowhide was strapped to his right hand wrapped with several strips of rawhide.

Nate tossed his gaze a little west of the first herd. A second outfit came into view. He looked down at Foss, lifted his chin, and held out Crow-hop's rein. "That's plenty hot. Get going."

Foss picked up a hot cinch ring from the fire with his covered hand and stepped up in the stirrup. Once settled, he took Crow-hop's rein and nudged his pony toward the first herd.

"Make sure you put enough heat on that ≡R pony so that he runs through their herd like a bay steer," Nate added as a reminder.

Foss never looked back as he hoisted the cinch ring head-high. "Oh, he'll run and play hell, big brother, that I guarantee."

Nate nodded, tight-lipped, and looked back at Ben and Charlie, then off to the second approaching outfit. "Off you go, boys. Make sure you get a good circle on that outfit's beeves and drift them into the Reston herd."

The two brothers nodded, turned their ponies, and scrambled west.

———◆———

July, riding the left point, saw it first. He leaned forward in the saddle and squinted. A hundred yards ahead, a piebald pony ran head long for the herd.

"Holy Lord," he muttered and whistled through two fingers to catch Pure's attention.

Pure tossed a quick glance at his foreman who was motioning frantically ahead of them. Pure moved his gaze toward the creek and saw what unmistakeably was Isa's pony bounding for the lead beeves.

"He's going to split 'em!" July screamed.

Pure focused on a rising dust cloud behind Crow-hop. Four deep furrows appeared on his forehead.

*What's he dragging?*

The answer fell off his lips.

*Isa!*

July raced to intercept Crow-hop's charge.

Jolted from his disbelief, Pure screamed, "No!" and raked his spurs across his piebald's side.

July waved his hat high above his head, shouting, frantic to turn Crow-hop. The wild motion spooked the leading phalanx of cows, and the herd began to pick up speed.

Midway down the herd, riding swing, Paint watched July sprint away from the point position. "What the?" he said and lifted himself out of the saddle. The cows to his right began to run. Paint shook the rein and jumped his pony ahead.

Crow-hop turned his head at July's approach. Undismayed, the ≡R foreman leaned right and deftly snatched the leading rein that dragged beside the spooked piebald. "Whoa," he shouted out and then glanced behind the horse. A long, length of rope, tied at the base of Crow-hop's tail, held a thoroughly mangled Isa.

Seconds later, Pure reached his younger brother's horse. He rolled off his pony at a dead sprint simultaneously pulling a skinning knife from his belt with his right hand.

July tightened his grip on Crow-hop and tossed a quick glance back at the building stampede. "They're on us," he shouted.

Pure ran his left hand down the rope tied to Isa and with a downward slash of the knife severed the lariat in half, his concentration fixed fully on his brother's badly mauled body.

Thirty-yards back, the leading edge of the herd began splitting left and right in front of July. The black cowboy watched, stunned, as the remaining ≡R drovers tried futilely to gain control of the explosive rush. A faint wave of despair swept over his expression followed by a cold anger. "Damned Gunns," he swore under his breath.

Behind, an anguished moan drifted above the stampede's chug. July glanced back at Pure. The ranch boss knelt beside Isa and clutched his brother's shirtless body tight against his chest.

"Damned Gunns!" July's tortured scream pierced the air.

Paint rode up in a fury and swung out of his saddle behind Pure. "What have they done?" he cried out. "What have they done, Pure?"

Pure's rocking slowed at the sound of Paint's voice.

"Why?" Paint screamed.

Pure refused to look at his middle brother. His face was void of expression. He was spent, blank, and uncommunicative.

Paint collapsed across Pure's back, sobbing. "What have they done? What have they done?"

Pure stopped his back and forth motion and gently placed Isa on the ground. He rose and turning, grabbed Paint under both arms and squeezed his brother uttering softly, "They've killed him, Paint." Then in a guttural whisper, "They shot him six times."

A low moan grumbled in Paint's throat.

Pure bore a steely gaze at July. "Shot him down like an animal," he said in a dry rough voice. "Just like an animal."

"No," Paint screamed toward the sky.

"Just like an animal," Pure cried.

"Damn them all!" Paint shrieked. "Damn them all."

Pure rubbed the back of Paint's head and slowly turned his mouth close to his brother's ear. "Don't you worry none, Paint," he whispered. "For now, I aim to kill everyone of them."

A half mile to the west, two appendages, which extended from a dark object lying on the prairie floor, moved in a wavy, rising, and falling pattern.

Out of view from the second trail outfit, Ben Gunn sported a large grin as the outfit's cattle refused to approach the flailing black lump and instead drifted at a quick pace east away from the obscure spook.

The nearest point man of the crew yelled across the drifting cattle, "Let 'em go, boys! Just try to keep a little rein on those lead steers!"

Ben held his Colt head-high and fired off one shot.

The herd jumped at the explosion, and the massive ball of hide began to pick up speed.

A fit of cursing erupted from the point riders.

Charlie stifled a belly laugh, coughed, choked. He gazed at Isa's shirt, which was tied securely through his saddle's gullet. The youngest Reston's shirt sleeves flapped wildly in the late afternoon breeze.

Ben glanced over at his brother and panted, "Now who was it said that no Reston could ever be good for nothing?"

Charlie, unable to hold back any longer let loose with a howling laugh. "Whew, brother," he bellowed and slapped his chest as the second herd turned into a full stampede under the falling twilight. "Weren't me, that's for sure."

Ben raised his brow and exhaled a deep breath. He watched the second herd running directly into the oncoming Reston stampede. "I'd sure hate to be the cowboys who have to straighten out that mess."

Charlie nodded and turned his pony around. "Might take days or weeks. It'd be a real shame if them Reston boys didn't make the railhead in time."

# TWELVE

———◆———

N ate Gunn sat horseback and looked across a prairie of horns, pleased at the big cut of beeves. E.B. wanted sixty head and Nate was determined to provide those sixty and more. He watched Foss mark his gelding's neck with charcoal Xs, but Nate already knew the count. He had rustled enough cattle to have a fair figure of how many head grazed in front of him.

*One hundred head, most ≡R, but some from the second outfit, the —∞.*

Foss stuffed the charcoal back in his front pocket. "A hunerd," he said, confident.

"Whew," whistled Charlie.

"Pa's gonna be happy to see this haul, Nate," Foss Gunn said with a broad smile.

"Maybe."

Charlie frowned. "Whataya mean, maybe?"

"Just what I said."

"Pa was pretty clear in what he said, Nate," Foss argued.

Charlie chewed on a dirty fingernail. "I sure didn't hear any maybe coming out of his mouth."

"He wants to look out from the porch and see Reston cattle in his front pasture," Foss said. "That much was clear to me."

"Now that's where you're wrong, Foss." Nate's eyes twitched slightly and flashed a cunning wickedness. "Pa ain't ever gonna see 'em."

"But Nate," Ben leaned into the conversation. His mouth turned down at the corners. "Pa will skin each and every one of us if we don't bring these

74

beeves in like he said."

Nate bore an icy stare right through Ben. "You've let him slap you around too much. You're all punchy from it."

Ben turned away. When he glanced back at Nate, he did so with lowered eyes. "Well, he won't like it a bit is all I'm saying."

Nate showed his teeth, and then poked his tongue deep into his lower lip. "You're a might shaky today, Ben."

Ben exhaled and scratched the corner of his eyebrow. "I know how he is, Nate, more than you anyway. Besides, none of us, including you, has ever gone contrary to his wishes."

"Well don't worry your little head so much. Pa ain't going to see the beeves, but he's going to see ample proof that we took the tallow out of them Reston boys' pockets."

Foss chuckled. "What's rolling through that head of yours, Brother Nate?"

"Money, sure and simple."

Out in the herd, Charlie heard the conversation turn to money and edged away from the milling beeves. He sidled his ponies in close to the group.

Nate beamed as Charlie rode up. The oldest Gunn brother loved holding court with his siblings. "The way I figure it, we've got the perfect opportunity to finish off them Reston boys once and for all."

"Do tell," Charlie sang out. Excitement coated his voice. "For I surely hate Restons."

Nate pointed at the rustled herd and said, "It'd be senseless to waste so much time driving these beeves all the way back to South Texas."

Charlie glanced over at Ben. "That's sure enough so."

Nate leaned back in the saddle and said in a devilish voice, "We're going to split up."

The remaining brothers chattered at the pronouncement.

"Charlie, you and Ben are taking this herd to the town below Fort Griffin."

Ben raised an eyebrow. "Fort Griffin?"

"There's a man there, goes by Cap Millett."

Ben shot a warning glance at Nate. "I don't know, big brother," he said and nodded at Charlie.

Nate ignored Ben. "He lives north of the fort."

Charlie made a face. "You're sending us into a soldiering town with stolen beeves?"

Nate chuckled. "As wild a town as you'll ever see, Charlie."

Charlie settled all his attention on Nate.

"Don't worry, the Millett ranch is a good ways from the fort."

A broad smile stretched across Charlie's face. "Your plan is beginning to make sense, Nate," he spouted.

"Wait-a-minute, Nate, how can you be so sure this Millett fella will even see us?" Foss asked.

Nate smiled. "He's a man goes after our own heart. He'll take the beeves or find buyers for you."

Charlie shrugged. "So, who is this Millett fella?"

Nate snarled at Charlie's questioning tone. "He's a rancher who dabbles in thievery, especially against plow-chasers. E.B.'s traded with him before . . . back in '76, as I recall."

"What's he get out of the deal?"

Nate rolled his shoulders from side to side, exasperated. "Hell, Charlie, those beeves there didn't cost us a thing 'cepting a couple hours work. Give Millett whatever cut he wants. We'll still come out ahead."

Charlie nodded. A flicker of a smile gleamed from each eye. "And after we're finished with this Millett fella, you say the soldiering town is only a few miles south?"

Ben made a face. "Don't even think about it, Charlie," he said.

Nate noticed the spark in Charlie's expression. "Charlie, you stay away from the card tables while you're working for me."

Charlie peered at his brother with mock astonishment. "Me?"

"I mean it," Nate said harshly, and then looked over at Ben. "You watch him."

Ben raised his brow and nodded with little enthusiasm.

"Foss and I'll meet back up with you there in a week or so."

"And me and you?" asked Foss. "Are we just going to sit around here in Indian Territory for a week?"

Nate eased his horse close to Foss and grinned. "Nope, you and me are headed north."

Foss returned Nate's grin. "North is a big place, brother."

Nate slapped Foss across the back. "Well, sure it is, Foss, so we'll be stopping off in Dodge City."

Foss twisted his head, confused.

Charlie looked at Foss and mouthed, *Dodge City?*

Nate flashed a flinty look at the pair. "I reckon if we want to finish this thing with Pure Reston that's where we need to go, because he still needs to get the rest of his herd to the railhead."

Charlie nodded and then wrinkled his brow with some uncertainty.

Nate stared at his brother and clicked his tongue against his teeth. "What is it, Charlie?"

Charlie made a face and asked, "How come you and Pa hate the Restons so much?"

A soft murmur arose from the other three.

Nate studied them all briefly and then parted his lips in a scornful grin. "Has to do with Street," he whispered, and then added playful, but serious, "And whenever any of you boys' dispositions gets rank enough, then you just go ahead and tell old E.B. you want to hear all about it."

# JOURNAL ENTRY

The morning after, Pure dug Isa's grave all by himself, and he wouldn't allow me or Paint to help with it. When he finished digging, he scooped up Isa and placed him in the ground. He didn't even say words over him, just covered him up, and then Pure just plopped down on Isa's grave. He sat there most of the morning without speaking a word to anybody. A little later, Paint gathered up the boys and rode out to try and round up the herd. I stayed back with Pure and waited. And after a long time, Pure stood up, dusted off the back of his britches, and said, "Let's go for a ride." We rode across Brushy Creek, and a little ways after crossing we came across a small burned out fire and six spent shells. Pure bounced those shells around in his palm for some time, thinking mighty hard over them. Then he pocketed those shells and as serious as I ever saw, looked me straight in the eye and said, "You know C.A. was Street's daddy." Well, I must have looked like a mule kicked me right in my stomach because Pure walked over, put his hand on my shoulder, and added, "Happened after momma died and Mr. Gunn was away during the war." Course, I didn't know what to say to that, so I just stood there balking like a Missouri mule. Pure said C.A. told him the story before he died. And then Pure said that with the killing ahead, he wanted the truth of the matter known just in case he didn't make it through the difficulty. But after today, he didn't ever want to talk about it again. Ever. And he didn't. But that revelation carried its toll and on that very day Pure changed. His face lost its color and turned hard and chiselled like limestone. I never saw him smile again in my whole life, and when he did set his gaze on you, it would chill your backbone. When we rode back to camp that day, Pure told Paint and the boys to spend the next two days rounding up the beeves as best they could and then drive what they could muster on to Dodge City. "Don't worry about finding them all" he told Paint. "For the Gunns are of such vengeance that they will retrieve the thirty beeves I took back plus some." When Paint asked Pure what he was going to do. Pure just glanced south and said he and I were headed for Fort Griffin, that he and I had an appointment there in the town below the fort. Locals called it The Flat, and it was a place filled with gamblers, lowlifes, and owl hoots of all persuasions. Pure said it was just the place the Gunn boys would drive the stolen cattle to sell. And it was there that I became involved in one the most talked about shoot-outs in Texas.

# THIRTEEN

*August 1878*
*Cap Millett's Ranch, Texas*

Charlie Gunn squeezed his eyes shut and pounded two trail-hardened fists on a cedar-planked table that occupied a prominent spot on the front porch of the Millett house. The card table bounced once on uneven legs, and its contents—playing cards, gold coins, and cigarette fixings scattered to the edges. The other card players at the table—Cap Millett, Frank Coe, and Virgil Lattimore, all leaned away at Charlie's outburst. The three pushed their backs hard against their chairs as if an eight-pound cannonball had landed square in the middle of them.

Charlie glanced at the startled trio with an upturned lip. "What are you gawking at?" he muttered and then slammed his fists on the table once more, cursing every card in the playing deck.

Cap Millett smiled respectfully at Charlie's blow-up but kept a cautious eye on the steady Ben Gunn, who leaned against the porch railing, shaking his head from side to side. Millett tugged at his earlobe and waited patiently for Charlie's tantrum to subside. The earlobe tug was a signal every Millett hand understood: keep your hand close to your pistol. Several of the Millett cowpunchers moved closer to the porch and the Gunn brothers.

Frank Coe, a hired gun fighter of some distinction, sat directly across from Charlie. He stared at the coins scattered across the table and counted his winnings aloud. "Ten, twenty, thirty, and . . . five. Thirty-five dollars."

Charlie fumed at the gun hand.

Coe took notice of Charlie's increased frustration. "Let me see," he said and jingled the coins in his right hand. "I better count this again . . . just to be sure."

Cap Millett sat tight-lipped and tense.

Coe looked up at Charlie and placed his winnings on the table.

Charlie's face turned beet red.

"Ten, twenty, thirty, and . . . five. Thirty-five dollars. Yep, it's all here." Charlie muttered under his breath.

Coe glanced over at the south Texas rustler. "That didn't bother you none, did it, Charlie?"

"What?" Charlie growled. "What bothered me?"

"Me counting my winnings right in front of you?"

Charlie leaned back, surprised by Coe's arrogance, and shook his head angrily.

"'Cause by my accounting, it appears you've played like hell again, Charlie," he laughed and reaching over, picked up his winnings once more.

Charlie's face reddened with rage. Put into a fury at the gunfighter's chortle, he swung his left hand across the table and grabbed Coe by the left wrist. "Shut your fly-trap, cowboy," he swore. His eyes flashed dark anger.

Coe tightened his smile and glanced down at his wrist, composed. After a long pause, he rolled his eyes up at Charlie and pushed a full set of bushy eyebrows together. "What'd you say?" he chuckled, daring, and threatening.

Charlie snarled at Coe's suppressed laugh and, even more angered, reached to yank his Colt, but before he could blink, he found himself staring into the shooting end of Frank Coe's Peacemaker.

"Some folks in these parts call me fast?" Coe said.

Charlie inhaled and gritted his teeth. His eyes widened in amazement at the man's quickness.

Ben reeled back, astonished and shocked at the gun hand's draw speed.

"I can't really tell. Do you think I'm fast, Charlie?"

The veins in Charlie's temples bulged. He glared at Coe without making a sound.

Coe glanced over at Ben. "How about you, Brother Gunn?"

Ben looked at Charlie, then to Cap Millett, and finally back to Coe. He nodded slightly.

Coe smiled and cocked the gun's hammer with his thumb. His eyes contracted into tiny beads of black. He leaned across the table, pushed the pistol into Charlie's cheek, and smiled. "Go ahead and pull that leg iron, Charlie. It'll be the last thing you ever do in this world."

All of the Millett cowboys, Ben, and Cap tensed, unsure of Coe's intended play.

Charlie stared bravely into Coe's eyes, but his half-opened mouth told another story.

After several uneasy seconds, Cap reached over the table and patted Charlie's wrist, but kept his full gaze on Ben. "Don't do anything foolish, Charlie," he said with a fair measure of respect and then added, "Why don't you let go of Frank's wrist before something unfortunate happens?"

Charlie inhaled and quickly scanned the porch. Eight Millett cowboys surrounded the table. He looked at Coe roughly and then released his grip on the gun hand's wrist.

Coe pulled his hand back and slowly removed his Colt from Charlie's face. "You're in a sure enough horn-tossin' mood, huh, Charlie?" he said and shook his head slowly.

Charlie rubbed his flushed cheek, but kept his hard glare on Coe.

Coe, enjoying the stage and Charlie's embarrassment, pushed his tongue against his bottom lip and continued to taunt the rustler openly by thrusting the barrel of the Colt toward Charlie, "You must be some kind of hard egg, a real buckaroo?"

Millett squared his eyes at Coe and shook his head in disapproval.

"Come on, Charlie," Ben stated and started forward only to find his progress cut off by two Millett cowhands.

Millet smiled and lifted his hand from Charlie's wrist. He glanced over at Ben and said, "Now boys, you both might be angry about losing all your cattle money, but this game has been on the up and up the whole way."

Charlie relaxed slightly and placed both hands on the table, still eyeing Coe and the Colt. "That so, Cap," he muttered.

"That's so," Millett said forcefully.

"Then how come I played two straight days with your boys and never won a pot?"

Millett ignored the question and glanced over at Coe. The ranch owner gave his hired gun a slight nod of his chin.

Cole swung his eyes to the pistol and then with a click of his tongue holstered the gun.

Millett eased his gaze back to Charlie. "Hell, son, I don't know," he said with feigned ignorance. "Maybe you just ain't a card-hand."

Ben moved past the two Millett cowboys and up to the table. He sunk both hands into the clasp of his gun belt and studied Millett carefully from head to toe. "Well, E.B. won't take too kindly to your hospitality, Cap, I'll promise that."

Millett eyed Ben menacingly and inhaled deeply. "Don't you try and threaten me you petticoat cowboy," he exhaled through clenched teeth. "I've killed sorts who were three times the man you are or will ever be!"

Ben twisted his lips together and started for his Colt.

In a flash, eight Millett guns cleared leather and fell on Ben.

Millett pushed his lips tight against one another and held up a hand. Regaining his composure, he signalled for his hands to holster their guns and then smiled broadly at both Gunn brothers. "I know E.B., son, and it ain't me he's going to be angry at."

Charlie slapped the table once more at Millett's pronouncement. "Damn," he muttered and turned his head away from the table.

Millett leaned back in his chair and dug into a vest pocket. "Since I know your pa and how he gets, I'm going to give you boys enough coin to get you back home," he said and laid six five-dollar coins in front of Charlie.

Charlie exhaled roughly, stared at the coins, and then picked each up.

Millett smiled. "Good," he said, and then called toward one his cowboys, "Get these boys their horses. I believe they are ready to leave our hospitality."

Minutes later, a red-faced Charlie took his reins from one of Millett's gunmen and stepped up in the stirrup. A painful awareness of his inadequate play before Coe still riled his thinking. Before riding away, he looked down at the gun hand and uttered, "How far to the soldiering town?"

The Millett gun hand kept a straight face and pointed south. "Ten miles or so," he said. "You looking to rid yourself of Cap's free coin?"

"Watch your mouth," Charlie growled and turned his pony's head toward The Flat. "I'm lookin' to find a place where a man can git a decent drink and an honest card game."

# FOURTEEN

*August 1878*
*The Flat, Texas*

———◆———

P ure and July dusted their pants and stared through the doorway into the front room of the Cattle Exchange. The saloon was a favorite haunt of many trail dusters in the grimy town below Fort Griffin known locally as The Flat. Amidst the carrying-on of the saloon's brisk trade, Pure spied Ben and Charlie Gunn. Both men sat at a card game with their backs to the door.

Pure nudged July and pointed at the two brothers.

July's gaze followed the outstretched arm and then came back to Pure. "You had those boys pegged dead to rights," he whispered and then pushed his hands against his gun belt, settling the band comfortably on his hips.

Pure watched Charlie throw a handful of cards on the table and then swear loudly. "Be damned, Coe! These cards are cooked through and through!"

The buzz of the Exchange stopped, but only momentarily, at the outburst.

The man dealing across from Charlie turned crimson at the call. "I thought you might have learned something out at the ranch, Gunn," he answered obligingly. "But it appears not."

Charlie jumped to his feet but respectful of Coe's draw, kept his hand away from his Colt. "What'd you say?" he shouted and placed both hands palm down on the table.

The corners of Frank Coe's mouth curled up. "I said that I'm glad the boys told me you were headed this way, Charlie. I thought I'd come over and get Cap's thirty-dollars back."

Pure kept a tight eye on the dealer and inhaled deeply. "That's not your average card preacher, July. Keep a good eye on his gun."

July nodded and eased behind Pure and into the saloon. He worked his way along the rough planked wall to a position that gave him a front view of Charlie and Ben and the back of the card dealer.

Pure waited for July to get into place and then strode to the bar.

The bartender ignored Pure's approach. His attention fixed on the disruption at the card table to his left.

"Some place, huh?" Pure shouted over the roar. His voice carried a raw edge to it. He removed his hat and ran a hand through slicked back hair. "Appears to be some cold-blooded sons of Texas in here."

The bartender tossed a quick glance at the slight-framed cowboy in front of him and then turned his concentration back to the card table. "What can I get you?" he asked dismissingly.

Pure twisted his body slightly and stared at Charlie Gunn's back. "Those boys certainly have gotten cross-grained with one another."

The bartender never glanced back but asked once more, "What'll it be, cowboy?"

"Beer," Pure obliged and pushed his gum forward in his mouth.

Charlie Gunn eyed Frank Coe and lifted both hands from the table. "You're a long ways from the ranch, Coe and you don't have Cap Millett or his boys to protect you now."

Pure watched the build-up to gunplay. The code demanded that he and no one else settle things with the Gunns. Determined to interject himself into the fracas, he drifted a few paces from the bar and whooped loudly, "Well, look at this everybody!"

The patrons closest to Pure turned at the hoot of excitement.

Pure swivelled at the on-lookers and spoke to the man nearest him in a thunderous voice. "I never figured the day would come that I would see one of the Gunn brothers take a man's play head-on!"

The saloon quieted at Pure's statement.

"No sir, I never did."

A growing murmur circled the saloon floor. Some of the regulars, recognizing the vilification headed for the doorway; others, eager for action, remained but moved out of the lane between the card player and the slender cowboy.

Ben jerked his head in the insult's direction, seething. He fixed a hard stare on Pure, inhaled deeply, and after a second of recognition, loosened a slow smile. "Well lookey, Brother Charlie," he said, "it's our neighbor from back home."

The remaining Exchange patrons stepped back several more steps upon hearing Ben's jovial tone and resumed their own boisterous exuberance. Still, each kept a watchful eye on the card players and the lone cowboy.

Charlie lifted his shoulders and shrugged at Coe before turning back toward the bar and Pure. "Howdy, Pure," he said and rested his right hand on his pistol butt. "You alone," he squealed and then looked around the Exchange. "Or is the little black bull still slobbering after you, hungry for that Reston teat?"

The movement and noise of the saloon stopped abruptly at Charlie's words. All eyes settled back on Pure. Gunplay was familiar here and the Exchange customers all recognized the warning signs.

Pure's expression glazed over at the affront, but he held his tongue and instead scanned the room hurriedly, searching for Nate and the others.

July leaned forward from the wall and spoke in a low voice, "Little black bull come down the mountain, Charlie." The low, dull, authoritative grumble caused all heads to turn toward the black cowboy.

Charlie spun slowly on his heels at July's voice. The rustler's eyes wandered along the front wall of the Exchange before his gaze settled on the six-foot-four Reston ranch foreman. His gaze dropped to July's gun. He paused for several seconds and then curled his lips away from his teeth. "Hoe, boy, hoe!" he sang and clapped his hands together in rhythm. "Chop that cotton all the day long."

July, his right foot braced against the Exchange wall, stared at Charlie, expressionless.

Charlie, all smiles now, glanced down at Coe. "Get up, Frank," he said dryly and swept an upturned hand toward Pure and then July. "I want you to meet some neighbors of ours, Pure Reston and his colored slave boy."

Coe slipped out of his chair with little effort and took to his feet with a tip of his hat.

"And Pure," Charlie continued with a raised brow and a voice thick with contempt. "This here is Frank Coe. His boss speaks highly of the fine breeding of ≡R cattle."

Pure retrieved his hat from the bar, pulled it securely to his head, and nodded at the Millet gun hand. "Mr. Coe," he said respectfully.

Charlie turned and squared his shoulders at Pure. "I heard about your brother, Pure, and want you to know both Ben and I think it was a terrible tragedy," he said. His tone dripped with insincerity.

Coe smiled at Pure and then turned toward July. The hired gun held his hands chest-high and his palms turned out.

"Howdy, friend," Coe said.

July acknowledged Coe's signal with a quick nod and motioned for the gunman to move several paces to his left.

Coe gave July a slow nod and moved as instructed.

Pure waited until the gun fighter settled away from both Gunns and then gestured at July to watch the gunman.

July's answering nod was quick and barely discernible.

Turning back to Charlie, Pure crinkled his brow and then just as quickly widened his eyes. "I forgot you Gunn boys never learned to read nor write."

"Watch your tongue, cowman," Charlie warned.

Pure smiled softly. "So it's understandable that neither of you would know that the slaves were all freed in '63."

A murmur of laughter filled the Exchange.

A blush of anger rushed across Charlie's face at Pure's taunting.

Ben looked at his brother and then took a step forward. "It's okay, Charlie," he said. "Pure, here, is just trying to rile your temper up some."

Pure turned toward Ben and exhaled loudly through his nose. "Where are Nate and the other two, Ben?"

Ben glanced over at Charlie and scratched the back of his head. "Where are those boys, Charlie?" he asked quizzically.

Charlie shrugged, puckered his lips, and in great exaggeration rubbed his forefinger down the corner of his mouth as if deep in thought. "Let me see if I can remember," he said.

During the lull, Coe lowered his hands slowly. Pure caught the gunman's movement and cleared his throat loudly.

Coe stopped his hands at Pure's warning.

Ben glanced at Charlie and then mumbled, "Oh, you know what?"

Pure tossed a look at July and shifted his eyes toward Coe.

"What's that, brother?"

July removed his leg from the wall and focused his attention on the gunman's back.

"Clark is with E.B. trading cattle," Ben chuckled and then pointed at Pure. "And Nate and Foss are headed north."

Charlie slapped his thigh. "That's right, brother."

Ben looked at Pure smugly. "They were looking to meet up with . . . why . . . you, Reston . . . all the way up the trail in Dodge City."

Pure's face dropped slightly at the mention of Dodge City. His body tensed and a grim foreboding raced through his thoughts. *Paint.*

July saw the change in Pure's expression. "Just like a bunch of cackle hens, Pure," he called out in an attempt to jar Pure's attention back to the mess at hand. "Nate and Foss are obviously too frightful of a town like The Flat."

Charlie's face flushed crimson. He jerked his head around at July. "Nobody asked your opinion, colored-boy!" he shouted and lowered his gun hand toward the Colt handle protruding from his holster.

Pure snapped back to the present, narrowed his eyes, and watched as Charlie, Ben, and Coe moved into fighting stances. "I'm sorry boys," he said, sharply. "Appears July struck a chord with you."

"This isn't going to happen in here!" the bartender growled furiously and swung a double barrel shotgun from below the bar. He levelled the gun on each man in turn and then ordered, "Take it outside! Now!"

Ben tossed an angry glance at the bartender. "Mind your own business, sagebrush, or you'll find yourself done up just like the fella next to you is fixing to be!" he warned.

Pure relaxed and focused on the room.

Ben looked away from the bartender and turned his attention back to Pure. "You didn't strike a chord with us, Reston, we're fine," he said tight-lipped.

Pure exhaled. "You're fine, Ben? You sure of that?"

Ben rolled his fingers against his palm. "Yeah, I'm sure."

"Because you don't look fine."

"Don't press it, Pure."

"You almost look a little peaked, if you ask me."

Ben's finger stretched out full. "I said watch your mouth, Reston."

"You're not poorly, are you?"

"No!" Ben blurted out, and then regaining his composure said, "Me and my brother are just a little tired from working so much lately."

Pure sensed Ben's growing irritation and decided to prod him into a fight. He tossed a quick gaze back at July and said, "You hear that, July?"

"Uh-huh," July muttered never letting his glare leave Coe.

"Now that has got to be big news."

"What's that, Pure?" July asked.

"Two Gunn brothers tired from working."

July chuckled aloud. "Never heard of such a thing."

Charlie's face flushed at the back and forth.

"Imagine a pair of heel squatters like these two doing actual work."

Charlie lashed back. "Watch your tongue, Reston or I'll –"

Ben laughed aloud. "It's nothing but a joke, Charlie," he said, calm and deliberate. "Ain't that so, Pure?"

Pure narrowed his eyes. He ignored Ben and bore a hard, killing look right through Charlie. "Watch my tongue or you'll do what, Charlie?" he asked coldly.

July wrapped palm flesh around his Colt handle.

Charlie twisted his lips together and clenched his fists until his knuckles whitened.

"Easy, Charlie," Ben whispered. "Easy, brother."

"Outside!" the bartender screamed again.

Pure pushed harder. "You'll do what, Charlie, bushwhack me outside somewhere?"

Charlie looked around the Exchange at a mob of now interested faces. "Shut-up, Reston!" he screamed.

"How about I just turn my back to you?"

"I'm warning you, Reston!"

"So you can drill me with six bullets?"

"I mean it!"

"Six on one, that's the way you Gunn brothers fight, ain't it, Charlie?"

Charlie slid his hand toward his holster.

"You can't fight fair, because deep down you're a coward," Pure said in a rising voice.

Charlie dug his heels into the floor. "That's enough of it, Reston," he growled.

"What'd you say, Reston?" Ben screamed. "Did you call us cowards?"

"I said anybody goes by the name Gunn is a low-down, thieving, rustling coward."

Charlie squirmed from foot-to-foot. His face turned into a distorted mask. "I've had enough of you, Mister high and mighty, Pure Reston!" he shouted and yanked his Colt free.

Pure smiled, bent his knees, and in a lowered crouch, yanked his Colt to a firing position.

Enraged at Pure's crouch, Charlie aimed his gun at the ≡R boss and hollered, "Stand where I can take a good shot, you weasly coyote!"

Pure didn't flinch. With calm and deliberate spirit, he leaned forward and extended the pistol toward his target. The Peacemaker was solid in his grip. "You smell like a dead man, Charlie," he uttered with great composure.

A long exasperated silence followed, and then an enraged yell as Charlie squeezed his trigger and re-cocked the hammer in rapid succession.

The Exchange erupted in gunfire. The bartender dropped behind the bar cussing loudly.

Two shots rang out seconds apart from each other after Charlie's initial volley.

Charlie Gunn frowned and slumped ahead on wobbly legs. He pressed his left hand against two bullet holes in his chest. His Colt fired twice into the Exchange floor.

Ben glanced at his brother, issued a blood-curdling scream, and then turned and began firing at Pure.

Pure rose out of his crouch and pivoted toward Ben just as a shot whistled by his waist.

The whole of the Exchange suddenly exploded in a panic of cursing and screaming.

Ben shouted out, "Damned you, Pure!" A flash of lightning lit-up the barrel of his Colt. "I'll kill you for that!"

A stinging sensation whipped across Pure's thigh. His leg went slack and then numb. He winced and hurriedly returned Ben's fire. His first bullet sailed over the Gunn brother's shoulder. The second hit the far wall of the Exchange.

Ben squatted. His left hand waved at the smoke-filled room while he fired once more in Pure's direction.

Pure sent two more errant shots Ben's way.

Stirred to enter the fray, Frank Coe stepped toward Pure and filled his hand with killing steel. "Reston," he uttered calmly and raised the gun to shoulder level.

Seeing Coe's play, July straightened and bellowed out, "Behind you, Coe!"

The gunman hesitated briefly, dipped his shoulders, and then wheeled toward the voice, his gun firing.

July raised his pistol, thumbing the hammer and squeezing the trigger on the way up. The gun bucked once, carrying July's shoulder upward.

Coe dropped in a heap, dead.

The Exchange turned into a stampede of frightened humans, waving hands and shuffling feet.

July rushed over to the downed gunman. A single bullet hole dotted Coe's forehead. His expression was locked forever in a mask of disbelief.

Pure fearlessly limped toward Ben. He held the Colt in his left hand with the gate open. Ejected shell casings fell at his feet as he reloaded with each step.

Ben flashed a crazy smile. "You've done yourself in now, Pure!" he hollered and thumbed back his gun's hammer.

"Maybe."

"You'll pay for Charlie!" Ben cried and pulled the Colt's trigger. The gun clicked blankly.

Pure glared straight through Ben's soul. "You're out of cartridges, Ben," he whispered in a deliberate, unemotional utterance. "I counted them. You should have as well; 'cause now you're as dead a man as your brother."

Ben swore loudly and fumbled to pull cartridges from his belt while watching Pure's approach.

Pure moved within ten feet and snapped the loading gate on his Peacemaker shut.

The sound of the gate snapping into place brought Ben's gaze up. Re-load cartridges fell from his right hand and bounced around his feet. His face trembled in fear.

July raced for Pure's side.

Pure kept his advance, now muttering and repeating, "*La muerte de vaca.*"

Ben's expression turned to frightened incredulity.

Pure's gun moved to shooting height. "This here's for the kid," he mumbled as the Colt erupted in fire and smoke.

Ben grabbed his left shoulder and moaned. Blood seeped through his shirt.

Pure's Colt bucked again. "And this is for Buckshot."

Ben's knees collapsed under him. A dark liquid seeped from his right thigh. "Damn you, Reston!" he cried out, pained.

Pure stood over the down man. His glare was dispassionate and icy. He aimed the gun at a spot directly between Ben's eyes. "Hell's riding for you at a full gallop, Ben."

Ben's leg muscles trembled wildly, causing his spurs to jingle unnaturally. "Don't kill me like this," he cried.

"Pure," July called out in a whisper and shook his head no. Then softer, "Don't do it this way."

Pure glanced over to July and flashed a grimace.

July dragged his tongue across his lips. "He's empty."

Pure paused briefly, blinked twice, and then looked down at the writhing figure of Ben Gunn.

"Don't, Reston," Ben said and cowered behind raised hands.

Pure's mouth curled back in a snarl at the man. *Don't?* He mouthed, confused at the Gunn brother's plea, then pushed the Peacemaker closer to the man's head. "Don't?"

"Please," Ben sobbed.

Pure's hand shook in rage. "Please?"

Ben glanced over his raised hands.

"Did Isa ask for mercy, Ben?"

Ben glanced back at the floor. "I don't know, Pure. I don't know."

"Well, I know, Ben. He didn't. Restons don't beg cowardly-like."

Ben sniffled. "Whataya want me to say? Tell me, and I'll say it."

Pure's face turned cold. "I don't want you to say anything, Ben. I'll do the saying, and what I say is this, this is for my brother, Isa," he hissed, and cocked the Colt's hammer once more.

"Pure," July pleaded. "Think about what you're doing."

Ignoring his friend, Pure groaned, loud, guttural, exasperated that this thing, this killing, could not be stopped now, and then slowly squeezed the Peacemaker's trigger.

Ben fell back in an awkward and inglorious pose.

Unable to look away, Pure watched the rustler's muscles tremble in death. He pushed the Colt back into his holster and curled his top lip in disgust.

July sidled next to Pure.

Pure didn't acknowledge his friend and instead tapped Ben's foot with the toe of his boot. "Hell's come, Ben," he said. "Hell's come and won't be denied."

# FIFTEEN

*August 1878*
*The Flat, Texas*

—————◆—————

July held Pure under both arms and slowly lowered the ≡R boss to the floor of the Exchange. "You okay?" he asked.

Pure nodded and glanced down at his thigh. Ben's bullet had ripped opened a three-inch-wide gash in his upper thigh. "I was lucky," he said. "The bullet gouged me a 'might, but it only creased the outside of my leg."

The sound of excited Exchange customers milling back into the bar caught July's attention. "Well, we need a doctor to look at that wound, and then we need to skedaddle out of here."

Pure lifted his chin at the gawking on-lookers gathering around the dead men. "You reckon anyone of this bunch will vouch for us?"

July looked back and shrugged. "Hard to say," he muttered. He pulled his bandanna from around his neck and circled Pure's leg with the cloth, tying it tight just above the gunshot wound. "Right now, I'm more concerned with stopping this bleeding."

Pure glanced down his leg. "Yeah, well I'm concerned with Paint alone in Dodge City with Nate Gunn on his trail."

July patted Pure's shoulder. "He's not alone. There are seven ≡R hands with him. He'll be just fine," he offered with an optimistic tone. "Besides, if we headed out right now, it would still take a full week of hard riding to get there."

From out of the crowd, the bartender's voice broke the morbid silence. "I told you! I warned you to take this outside!" he bawled and approached Pure and July brandishing the double-barrelled shotgun. "Now you're both going to deal with me."

July studied his bandaging job, then straightened, and with perfect timing jerked the shotgun from the man's hands. July towered over the startled bartender. "You're not going to do anything!" he snarled. "Except find a doctor and get him over here."

The bartender gulped hard and froze in place, staring back at his gun in July's hands.

"Now!" July barked.

The bartender nodded and hurried around July in a rush for the door.

"He sure won't head for the doc's office," Pure said.

"Probably not," July allowed. He leaned down bore a hard gaze straight into Pure's eyes. "How many of these Gunns are you aiming to kill?"

Pure twisted his head sideways and looked up at his ranch foreman, grim-faced. "This isn't your fight, July. It's mine, and I don't expect you understand the why of it or to stay with me."

"That's not what I asked?" July said softly and rested his palm on Pure's shoulder. "And I don't figure to back away now."

Pure nodded. "I know you wouldn't," he said.

July frowned. "Then why'd you even ask?"

"I wanted to give you a way out seeing how this thing with the Gunn's can only trail in one direction."

"So how far are you willing to take this thing?"

Pure extended a hand and lifted his chin at July.

The ranch foreman extended a massive hand toward Pure, locked palms, and gently pulled his boss and brother to his feet. A distant twilight shone in Pure's eyes.

Pure wobbled unsteady for several seconds and then regaining his equilibrium looked into July's waiting face. "Before C.A. moved us to Texas, back when I was six or seven years-old, there was a she panther killing livestock on our land in Kentucky. One fall morning, C.A. scooped me out of bed and told me we were going to hunt that old girl and kill her, no matter how long it took. As we rode up into the hills, he said that once a cat started killing horses and cattle it would never stop."

July listened intently; suddenly aware that Pure's story was more than just a fanciful reminiscence.

"It took us a week to track her back to her den, and while we waited for her return from a night of hunting, we heard the distinct cries of two cubs inside. I told C.A. we couldn't kill her on account of the cubs. But the old man told me firmly that those cubs would inherit her killing instinct for livestock."

July twisted his mouth in anticipation.

"She showed up right at sunrise, and as she started to enter the den, C.A. shot her and broke her spine. To this day, I can still hear that mother's cries. But C.A. seemed immune to her wailing. He just stood and told me to get the horses. That we were going home. And despite my begging, he refused to waste another bullet on her. Don't ever have sympathy for a killer, son, he lectured me, it's best to get them out of civil society in any manner possible."

"What about the cubs?" I cried.

"They'll die soon enough," he answered, "especially, without her to support them."

July wiped his forehead and blinked rapidly.

Pure's face tightened. "We're going to ride to Dodge City and make sure Paint has fared well. And then we're riding back to McMullen County."

July clamped his jaw firmly. His teeth ground against one another.

"I'm going to remove that panther, E.B. Gunn, from civil society just like C.A. taught me."

July exhaled in a loud whoosh of breath.

"And then I aim to exterminate all of the cubs," Pure said, knowing that the Gunn offspring had inherited their father's killing ways.

Pure turned and gazed at the men crowding the Exchange doorway, then looked back at July. A stunned look of disbelief shone in his friend's eyes. Pure studied July's expression intently. Speechless, the ranch foreman's face articulated a veiled hint of doubt and a fair amount of shock at Pure's declaration.

"You think the law will allow us to just swoop down on every Gunn in McMullen County?"

Pure's pulse pounded in his neck. He tossed a hard glance over at Ben Gunn's still corpse. "Here's the thing," he rasped. "If there was any sort of workable law in McMullen County, then we wouldn't have had to bury Buckshot, the kid, and my youngest brother. Damn it, July, E.B. Gunn has been pushing for this since C.A. died, and sitting still won't stop that old man from hunting and killing us to a man!"

July glanced down at his feet, rocked from heel to toe, and in a half whisper said, "Then let's do what we have to do."

Pure clenched his jaw and nodded.

"But, Pure," July said in a warning voice. "I won't spend the rest of my life chasing this thing."

Pure's eyes frowned. He shook his head gravely. "Nor I."

"You're sure this is the road you want to ride? You won't be able to change horse mid-stream, you know."

Pure glanced about the floor of the Exchange. He nodded at the bodies of Charlie and Ben Gunn.

"I understand about these two," he said. "But what about when the Gunns kill more of us?"

Pure frowned. "What do you mean?"

"I mean hell's come alright, but it never makes a distinction as to who it comes for."

Pure stared at the floor, thinking.

Pure continued to shuffle his boots, heel-to-toe.

"You've uncorked the bottle now for sure."

Pure exhaled. "I know that."

"So, is this what you want?"

"It's not about what I want, July. It's more about what I have to do."

Grim, July stopped his fidgeting. "So, let's get on the trail," he uttered. "And get this job, this thing, this murderous killing, finished."

⟫◆⟪

An angry Deputy Sheriff Jim Draper walked past the laid out corpses of Charlie and Ben Gunn and Frank Coe on the street outside the Cattle Exchange. "This better be good," he said. "I was sitting with a full house back there."

The Exchange bartender continued to give his animated account of the gun fight as Draper barged into the saloon. Seeing Pure and July, Draper raised a hand to quiet the rapid-talking bartender. "Enough," he said, agitated. He shook his head at the ≡R cowpunchers in disbelief that the pair could have inflicted such damage. "You boys do all of that?" he asked and nodded outside.

"Sheriff," Pure started.

"Deputy," Draper corrected.

Pure nodded and began again, "Deputy, two of those men outside are the Gunn brothers from South Texas."

Draper rubbed his jaw. He glanced back through the open doorway and across the street to where he was playing cards only minutes earlier. "And you obviously had a beef with them."

Pure filled his chest with a deep breath and inhaled through his nose. "They killed two of my ranch hands and stole thirty head of livestock from me."

Draper tilted his hat back. "You got proof of any of that?"

Pure moved closer to the deputy. "They also shot and killed my youngest brother a week ago."

Draper glanced over at July and then seemingly chafed at Pure's accusations, said, "Yeah, well I still need some sort of proof, cowboy."

Pure rolled his gum forward in his mouth and moved nose-to-nose with the deputy. He spoke in a low growl, "They tied him behind his horse and ran the horse through a herd of cattle we were driving to Dodge City."

July nodded his head in agreement.

Draper inhaled and glanced back at the saloon across the street. "I'll need to ask a few questions from witnesses to make sure this thing went how you said and that you boys didn't draw on them first."

The bartender stared at Draper in disbelief. "Jim, you ain't letting this pair go?"

July narrowed his eyes and made a face at the bartender.

Dumfounded, the bartender stepped back slightly. He glanced at July's Colt, then wheeled, and, muttering to himself, walked back to the bar.

"What about a doctor?" July asked the deputy.

"Down the street."

Pure backed away from Draper and said, "Much obliged, Deputy. And don't worry, we'll be heading north as soon as you complete your investigation."

"Yeah," Draper exhaled and turned to leave. "Just make sure you two don't head north until I say so."

"Deputy?" July called out.

Draper looked back with raised eyebrows.

"Who was this Frank Coe fellow?"

Draper's mouth twisted into a half smile. "Frank Coe?"

July glanced at Pure and shrugged.

Draper rubbed his chin. "He was a shootist extraordinaire in these parts."

July mumbled, "Hmmmph."

"Not anymore it appears," Pure said.

Draper dragged his hand across his chin and tilted his head. "Yeah, well . . . that may be, but he had friends here."

Pure pushed his eyebrows together. "Anyone we should know about?"

Draper's voice got softer. "If you boys end up heading north, you'll ride right through his employer's ranch."

Pure turned his head slightly and chewed his gum rapidly between his front teeth. "And who would that be?"

Draper lifted his brow and frowned. "That would be Cap Millett, and I don't think he or his boys will be too happy with you cowpunchers."

"Why's that? The fight was fair," Pure said.

Draper shrugged. "Fair or not, you boys killed Cap Millett's number one gun hand."

# JOURNAL ENTRY

*After the gun fight at the Cattle Exchange, we got Pure's leg doctored and later that afternoon Deputy Draper told us we were free to go. I believe we were mounted and riding out of The Flat before the deputy even finished speaking. The Flat, now she was a lawless burg filled with a vile population. I was glad to leave that August afternoon and to this very day have never rode close to her again. Pure and me spurred our ponies north as worry for Paint's safety and Nate Gunn's reputation pained us both. About an hour or so before sunset we crossed a wide-open prairie filled with grazing beeves carrying all kinds of brands on their hides. Sitting horseback in the middle of that prairie was Cap Millett and seven of his ranch "hands." But right away, I noticed these weren't your average cowpunchers. Each man in Cap's crew wore two-gun holsters, something that in all my life, I never saw a real cowboy do. Now Cap was a pleasant enough fellow, but after the welcome and niceties, he asked straight out if we were the cowpokes who killed Frank Coe. And Pure, being Pure, well he rose up tall in the saddle, looked Cap square in the eye, and said that we were, but that we had only gone to settle a score with Charlie and Ben Gunn. Cap never blinked* and asked Pure what killing offence the Gunn brothers had perpetrated upon him. Pure said they killed three of his hands, including his youngest brother. Cap nodded his head at that and said, "That sounds like the pair." Pure nodded and added that we didn't know Coe and wasn't expecting him to join in the fray, but he did, and his play wasn't as fast as he promised. Now, I'll tell you what, that was a gutsy move by Pure, for all of Cap's gun hands twisted in their saddles at his pronouncement of Coe's draw speed. Then Pure clicked his pony up close to Cap just as pretty as you please and in a whisper of a voice said that he would understand if Cap wanted to avenge Coe's perceived wrong. I remember Cap took a hard swallow at Pure's frankness. Pure went on, adding that he followed the code and understood anyone else who did the same. But if Cap decided on gunplay to right the tally, it wouldn't be just Pure and I who died on the Millett ranch land that day. Well, that paled Cap's expression, and I watched the old ranchman lean in close to Pure and whisper a few words. Pure nodded, whispered back, and then glanced back at me. It was then that Cap gave me a going over with a frightful stare. It was a hard look that I won't ever forget, and at that point I was plenty worried about leaving that prairie upright. But after a second or two, Pure kneed his *piebald and said, "Let's go, July. Cap has graciously allowed us safe passage across his land." It wasn't until we crossed the Red River that Pure told me what he had whispered to Cap. "I told him it was you who shot Frank Coe straight between the eyes with one shot even though Coe had the bulge on you. And that before we even left The Flat, you swore, if a fight started on Millett land, you'd to do the same to the man who hired Coe in the first place." Later, Pure finished the story, telling me, "To let Cap save face in front of his men, I gave him the stolen beeves that Charlie and Ben brought to him." And I remember thinking how smart a play that was by Pure. But Pure always studied his situation and was never ruffled in the heat of things. I had a good laugh thinking back to Cap's glare at me. Pure wouldn't have any of it though. And best I can recall it was the last time I laughed on the ride toward Dodge City and the ordeal that followed.*

# SIXTEEN

*September 1878*
*A Mile South of Dodge City, Kansas*

———◦———

aint watched Shanks McCoy draw near the ≡R bedding ground on a sorrel mare. The bedding ground lay one mile south of Dodge City on a patch of prairie laden with good Kansas browse. McCoy was a northern buyer with whom C.A. had done business since founding the ≡R outfit. The old man's instructions to Pure, bellowed from his deathbed the previous year, rang clear in Paint's head at the buyer's approach.

*You keep the beeves south of town and make Shanks ride out to you to negotiate. And don't let any of your cowboys take even one sip of scamper juice until them beeves reside in Shank's possession. You do what I tell you, Pure, and you boys will all make out well*

Paint smiled and allowed a rolling chuckle to heave in his chest. There would never be a character, above or below, such as Charlie Albert Reston.

McCoy, dressed in a wool suit complete with vest, tie, and pocket watch, looked like a big city banker and not a cattle buyer for the Chicago meat plants. Reining the mare to a slow stop, McCoy lifted a wide-brimmed felt hat and rasped, "Is this the Triple-Line-R outfit?"

Paint took hold of the mare's reins and smiled. "Reckon so," he said.

McCoy eased out of the saddle and shook Paint's hand with great energy. "Howdy, Paint," he boomed and then glanced around puzzled. "Where are your brothers? Where's Pure? And Isa? And that bull of a foreman, July?"

Paint's expression changed suddenly, and in a barely audible voice, he answered, "Isa's dead, Shanks."

McCoy's face hardened in shock and bewilderment. "Dead?"

Paint nodded. His shoulders drooped as if stricken with an unexpected

103

weariness. "Killed in the Nation."

McCoy looked suspicious. "Surely not by Indians."

Paint led the sorrel over to a picket line extending off one side of the grub wagon. "Rustlers," he growled. "Pure and July have headed for Fort Griffin to settle the tally with the bunch."

McCoy nodded and muttered between tight lips, "I'm sorry, Paint. Isa was a good hand."

Paint draped McCoy's reins over the stringer and exhaled loudly. His shoulders rose and fell with the breath. Turning back, he lifted his brow and all-business, asked, "Coffee before we parley?"

McCoy removed his hat and followed Paint toward the cook fire, "Sure," he offered. "I need something to cut the dust."

<hr/>

Later, the seller and buyer leaned against the sideboard of the grub wagon, sanguine and cordial in their negotiation.

"I think you'll find the beeves better or at the very least as good as the bunch you bought last year, Shanks."

The Chicago buyer rolled his shoulder over the grub wagon and peered over the side-rail at the milling beeves stretched out for a mile or more. "I'm sure. But I'm a little concerned Paint; it doesn't appear that you have the numbers that I initially agreed upon with Pure."

Paint backed away from the wagon and walked toward the cook fire. Once there, his back to McCoy, he reached down and grasped the swing handle of a blackened coffee pot. "I won't lie to you, Shanks. We hit a few rough patches on this drive. I'm short by two hundred beeves," he said and turned to face McCoy.

McCoy pivoted away from the beeves and pushed his cup toward Paint and the coffee pot. "All rustled?"

Paint poured a generous amount of the inky liquid into Shanks' outstretched tin. "The day that Isa was killed, the rustlers stampeded a nearby herd into ours. It took two full days just to straighten out the brands."

McCoy pulled the tin of coffee to his lips and took a long swig. The Chicago buyer shook his head in solemn sympathy.

"By the time we finished sorting, I knew I had to leave right then to make Dodge City in time for you to stay on your schedule, so I don't really know if the Gunns got all two hundred or if some of those are still wandering in the Nation."

McCoy rubbed the back of his neck; a sour look settled on his face.

Paint studied the man's expression. "What is it, Shanks? You can still take what beeves we've got can't you?"

"No," McCoy said hastily and then held up his left hand. "It's not the beeves. Don't worry about that, son."

"What then?"

McCoy turned his tin over and dumped the remaining coffee on the ground. He tried to smile, but his lips hung in an awkward tautness.

"What is it, Shanks?"

McCoy tightened his jaw. "Who did you say rustled your beeves?"

"An outfit from back home. An ornery bunch familiar to most of McMullen County as rustlers and thieves."

"But what was their name?"

Paint rolled the name off his tongue with disgust and anger. "The Gunns."

McCoy went silent for a long moment, mumbling under his breath, then said, "Paint, there's a fella in Dodge City, a bad hombre of sorts by my estimation. He's been drinking in the Lone Star and the Alamo with others of whom I would say were of a similar persuasion."

Paint paled, knowing, but still needing to ask the question. "Who are they, Shanks?"

McCoy inhaled and then exhaled slowly. "The mouthy fella goes by Nate," he muttered and then looked straight in Paint's eyes. "Nate Gunn."

Paint tightened his mouth and tapped his forefinger on the bottom of his coffee tin. He looked down and stared hard into the Kansas dirt. "What else, Shanks?"

"He's making it known to everyone in town that a bunch of Texas trail drivers riding under the ≡R brand killed his brother Street down in Texas."

Paint jerked his head up and yelled, "That's a damnable lie, Shanks!"

"I knew your pa well, Paint, and I know you boys just as well. I know what this fella is spouting can't be the truth, but you have to understand that he's making a case for killing any triple ≡R cowpuncher that comes into Dodge."

Paint slammed his coffee cup to the ground and cursed silently.

"I'd keep my business north of the railroad tracks, Paint"

Paint expelled a bitter laugh and pointed toward the herd. "I've got seven hands that have been on a cattle drive most cowboys would shy from. These boys have been on the trail for three months, Shanks, and they are ready to let the wolf loose. Now, how in *the* hell do you propose that I keep them from riding south of the deadline?"

Shanks shook his head grimly. "I don't know, Paint. All I can offer is to settle with you here and plead that when you drive the herd for the stockyards that you keep north of the tracks where the play will be at least somewhat gun free."

Paint removed his hat and scratched the top of his scalp roughly. "Thanks for the information, Shanks. I'll get the boys to run a tally for you and we'll meet at the yardage pens this afternoon so you can run your own count."

McCoy nodded at Paint and extended his tin.

Paint took the cup and motioned at McCoy's horse. "Sorry we shorted you, Shanks. You can take a fair amount off the tally if you're of a mind to do so."

McCoy moved for the string and gathered his reins. "No need, son. Weren't any of it intentional or by your direction."

Paint nodded and watched the Chicago buyer step up into his stirrup.

McCoy turned his horse's head north and looked down at Paint. "Just remember what I said about staying north of the deadline. After hearing of your brother's killing, I sure wouldn't want to see any further misfortune come your way."

Paint gave McCoy's horse a light slap on the flank and said darkly, "Thanks again, Shanks. We'll see you at the stockyards this afternoon."

McCoy locked stares with Paint for a brief moment, then tipped his hat and started the sorrel toward Dodge City.

Paint watched the buyer ride away at a lope and uttered a low vow, "And after that, I'm going to make an end to the rough string known as the Gunn brothers before this feud of theirs kills every last one of us."

## JOURNAL ENTRY

*Now back in those days, Dodge City was cut in half by the Atchison, Topeka & Santa Fe railroad tracks. The tracks, known to all Texas cowboys as the dead line, divided the town north and south. Each side of the railroad tracks had a main thoroughfare called Front Street. North of the dead line, a cowboy was required by law to check his guns at the livery or hotel upon riding in. And over the years, the Dodge City Gang, a group of businessmen led by ex-7th Cavalry scout Dog Kelley, hired some of the most hard-barked, game lawmen to back up that order. Men like Wyatt Earp, Bat Masterson, and Charlie Bassett. A cowboy who crossed any of that bunch quickly found his match. But the Gang also wanted to keep the Texas cowboys happy and spending their hard-earned money so south of the dead line, law was a very different thing. South Front Street was home to poisonous whiskey, slick card hands, dangerous women, and vile debauchery, a place where a small fine and immediate release was the only penalty for a cowboy's law-breaking. I'll never forget my first trip into Dodge. As we rode into town, I swear there were a hundred saloons and dance halls lining the street. Course there really wasn't that many, but to a* green cowhand, it sure seemed so. Best I can recollect there was the Alamo, the Lone Star, the Long Branch, the Variety, and . . . others I can't likely recall now. Back then almost every place offered the Texas boys the rare opportunity to taste ice and the chance to listen to a piano player. Those were some fun times for the cowpuncher who wanted to get out on a high lonesome. But a shave-tail on South Front Street could just as quick-like find himself in deadly confrontations arising from words that north of the dead line would be considered harmless and insignificant. And it always came about from what Mr. Charlie called prattle fluid. That fluid always seemed to bear some responsibility for a cowboy's demise. Pure never had any call for it. He got that from Mr. Charlie. Neither of them ever paid a driver his full wages until they were clear of Dodge and headed back to Texas. Pure didn't mind others partaking, but he always preached to his cowboys to keep it in small regular doses. And after leaving Cap Millett that afternoon, a good week from Dodge, I hoped to hell that Paint had given the boys the same sermon.

# SEVENTEEN

*September 1878*
*Dodge City, Kansas*

———◆———

Paint stood on the west corner of the railroad depot watching as a somber blackness flattened and rolled across the Dodge City landscape. Two hours earlier, Shanks had taken possession of the trail herd and penned them in the stockyard. Flush with cash, Paint had paid his trail hands full wages and then warned them to the dangers of being caught alone south of the tracks. After all of the transactions were complete, he relinquished the shower, shave, and new clothes that the rest of the ≡R outfit so energetically sought and instead walked to the corner of the depot and waited . . . and watched. The gold coin payment for the cattle filled the inside of a trail-worn leather wallet draped across his right shoulder. His gaze, directed toward the Variety Saloon, was unyielding in its purpose, yet a twinge of guilt twisted his conscience into knots. He knew the ≡R cowboys would soon cross the tracks, ready to frolic at their favorite bar, the Variety. And he reckoned Nate Gunn would be watching too and would most likely follow the boys in. He buried both hands deep inside his armpits as a hint of winter rode in on the darkness. He didn't like using his own cowboys in this ploy, but he reasoned he didn't really have any other choice. West, down the tracks, the revelry of cowboys filled the night air. Paint smiled as the familiar hoots and catcalls of the ≡R merrymakers announced their arrival to the merchants south of the dead line. These were boys ready for a night filled with tonsil varnish and painted cats. Paint skulked west, down the tracks toward the jail house careful to never leave the shadows. When he reached the back corner of the city offices and the jail, he stopped and stayed hidden as his outfit hurried toward the Variety.

*Stay well, boys.*

Paint hunched slightly and cupped both hands around his mouth, pondering. He wanted his draw hand warm and flexible for the expected confrontation with Nate Gunn. Imagining his play, he blew long, hot breaths into his palms and then rubbed his hands vigorously. Folks in McMullen County always bragged about Nate's gun speed, but Paint was confident he could match the oldest Gunn brother with his own Colt as long as the fight was straight up. With his hands warmed, Paint whipped his Colt from its holster in a dizzying blur, pointed the gun into the darkness, and whispered, "Drop it." A broad smile crossed his mouth at his draw speed. After several seconds of holding an imaginary Nate Gunn at gunpoint, he pushed the Peacemaker back into the holster, and questioned the darkness. "Who's the fastest now, Nate?"

From behind, the characteristic click of a trigger being cocked jarred the smugness from Paint's expression, and the unmistakeable feel of a gun barrel pressured his back. A hand slithered from the darkness and eased Paint's Colt from its holster.

Another lifted the leather wallet from his shoulder.

A familiar voice laughed and mimicked Paint. "Who's the fastest now, Nate?"

And then . . .

"Why I reckon you are, Paint," laughed Nate Gunn.

# EIGHTEEN

*September 1878*
*On the South Canadian River, Indian Territory*

———◆———

P ure's stomach curled at sight of the ≡R grub wagon. He rolled the Snapping and Stretching gum to the front of his mouth and pushed it deep into his lower lip. He didn't know why, but the sight in front of him was troubling. The trail camp was silent and sedate and filled with expressionless, faceless cowboys. Not the sort of camp a man expected to find after an outfit was free of their beeves and flush with several month's wages. There wasn't any singing or horseplay or free-spiriting to be seen or heard. Pure shook the reins above his piebald's head and urged the horse to a lope. At his approach, the ≡R hands slowly gathered their feet. Not one in the bunch raised a head, choosing instead to acknowledge Pure with upturned eyes peering from beneath new hat brims. The whole camp was filled with grave apprehension. He counted the cowboys instinctively.

*One*

*Two*

*Three*

*Four*

*Five*

*Six . . . seven.*

*Where's Paint?*

The cowboy closest to him, Willy Barry, cleared his throat and lifted his head.

Pure made a grimace at Willy's appearance. The ≡R cowboy was pale and distressed.

"Where's Paint, Willy?"

Silence, pained and disturbed, hung around the cowboy.

Pure crinkled his brow and looked past Willy. He studied each cowboy's down turned face.

A fit of throat-clearing circled the group.

Goose pimples popped under Pure's shirt-sleeves. He took a heavy, knowing breath and contorted his lips against one another. "Where is he?"

Willy, his eyes glazed, his expression wordless, tilted his head toward the grub wagon.

Pure's eyes darted toward the open air wagon. A sense of dread moved like a wave across his chest. He clicked his tongue and moved his piebald alongside the wagon. His eyes peered down. Inside was a length of wrapped canvas. "What is this?" Pure asked, both shocked and apprehensive.

The ≡R cowboys shuffled in place, uncomfortable and unable to make contact with Pure's glaring eyes.

Pure felt his chest tightened. He bit down hard on his lower lip and uttered, "Is this?"

The ≡R cowboys moved away from the wagon, still unwilling to answer or even look at their ranch boss.

Pure slumped in his saddle. The grief crawled over him slow and painful. "How?" he wailed and glanced back at the cowboys.

Pitiable shoulders shrugged.

The only reply was an unknown, sad whisper from one of the men. "We found him in the yardage pens, Pure. We found him the morning after Shanks took possession of the herd. Whoever killed him also took his wallet with all of the herd money inside it."

Pure moaned. An intense sadness trembled through him. His body suddenly felt tired and old. He dropped out of the saddle and waved a hand faintly at the cowboys. "Leave me be," he said in a thin voice and then crawled into the wagon next to his dead brother.

# NINETEEN

——◆——

A t sun rise the next morning, Pure sat atop the driver's seat of the grub wagon. The mule team's reins rested easily in both hands. His piebald was tied with twenty-foot of lead rope to the back of the wagon.

"I'd feel better if you'd let me ride with you."

Pure fingered the reins tighter and tossed a brief, dark frown at July. The Snapping and Stretching gum bounced around in the back corner of his mouth. He shook his head and then looked away, muttering, "You know C.A. always thought that his life . . . our lives . . . all rose and fell on the price of a damned longhorn cow."

July wet his lips and stared down the cattle trail. "Yep."

"That when God created this world, he somehow decided that a feral cow with six-foot of horn would dictate a man's worth."

"It was the way back then, Pure."

Pure tilted his head sideway, thinking, and then uttered. "But what always happens with men, July, is they gotta make their way the way of every other man."

"I reckon there are those that think like that."

"Well, he was wrong, July. I'm saying it right now to you and those seven cowpunchers waiting at the trail."

"Now, Pure."

"No, C.A. was wrong. And because of it, I've been wrong too."

"The grief is tugging at you hard right now, Pure."

"It ain't the grief talking."

"A cowboy shouldn't try and make sense of God or man when kin is taken and deprived him through killing."

Pure shook his head emphatically. "No, it ain't the sorrow poison that's got me spouting. It's Isa buried behind us, and Paint lying cold in this wagon."

"Those boys loved you, Pure. You needn't feel guilty about their dying."

"Maybe both of them would still be alive if I hadn't been so hell-fired set on protecting thirty long-legged, scrawny-assed cows."

"Weren't your fault."

"I told you that day in Cañón Cerrado that Buckshot's life was worth more than thirty beeves."

"Pure . . ."

"I should've listened to my own wisdom."

July tightened his jaw and glanced down at the canvas covered body in the wagon's belly. "You best get on down the trail, Pure. This poison can't be flushed from your system until Paint is resting next to Isa."

Pure nodded and reflected, "It seems lately that there are many things in my life that I wish I could do over."

July grimaced.

"You warned me of this."

July shook his head. "What's done is done, Pure."

"No, I should have listened," he sobbed, and then in a barely audible voice said, "I should have—."

July turned his piebald for the seven ≡R hands waiting down the trail. "Bury your brother."

"They'd be alive if I hadn't been so set on upholding the code."

"You'll come to know in the days ahead that it wouldn't have mattered. Be it mules or chickens, E.B. Gunn has had a branding iron in his belly about your daddy and the Reston clan since they arrived in McMullen County. He carried that hate all the way from Kentucky."

Pure's eyes darkened in realization of July's words.

"And you know as well as me that the thing with Street is what led us down this road."

Pure exhaled and looked up at his ranch foreman. "You think we could end this thing right here, right now?"

"Won't ever happen, Pure."

"I'm talking about just stopping it all together, peaceable-like."

"Not hardly."

Pure winced and looked down at his boots. "Well fact is . . . I've been doing some thinking . . . and I don't think I have the stomach for it anymore," he revealed. His eyes were slack and blank.

A hard, icy glare fell across July's face. "You remember what I told you in the Exchange about switching horses mid-stream?"

Pure rambled on and refused to listen to his foreman. "I don't think my conscience will hold seeing you or any of those cowpunchers killed by my doing."

July narrowed his eyes. "I said I won't spend the rest of my life chasing this thing."

"July, I know now that once vendetta killings start, they blacken a man's heart and cause the violence to spread like the pox."

July rose up in his saddle and stretched all six-foot-four of his massive frame. His shoulders blocked out the sun. "I asked, Pure. I asked if you were sure this is the road you wanted to ride."

"I'm tired of the killing," Pure said. "Sick of the back-and-forth of it."

July scratched the nape of his neck and blinked his eyes several times before answering, "There's a lot of bad things in this world, Pure."

Pure wiped at wetness building in the corners of his eyes and stared back at Paint. A soft moan, deep inside his throat escaped. "Seems so."

"And we've seen our share of it."

Pure nodded grimly. "Participated in our share of it, too."

"True enough, but always on the right side of it."

Pure shook his head and snuffled. "The right side of it, huh?"

"I think so."

"How come it don't feel so?"

"Because of the grieving, Pure. The grieving takes a fair amount of sand out of a man."

"It ain't the grieving that's got me all balled-up, July."

"What then?"

"It's the dabbling in gore that I've done."

"But on the right side of it, Pure. You have to stop thinking any other way."

"I feel like one of them bad eggs right now."

"There's a lot of bad men in this world, Pure."

Pure drew a shallow breath and nodded.

"Men who seem to have it in their own way of thinking that they should decide who deserves what in this world."

Pure twisted his head toward July. His expression was one of a man who had just been punched violently.

"Unbending, unyielding men who only know how to settle things with copper and lead."

Pure clenched his jaw. "Sounds like us."

July let a thin, tight smile break the hardness of his expression. "Nope, that's not us. We're the ones who rid the land of those men before civilization arrives."

Pure eyes contracted. Unthinking, he began to pound the Snapping and Stretching gum between his front teeth.

"So don't be giving any thought to what might happen to me or those boys over there because we're all only working with the hand, God dealt us . . . and not a one of us could change that now . . . no matter how hard we try."

Pure's hands gripped the reins tighter. A faint flush of red crossed his neck. His knuckles whitened.

"And none of us is going to spend the rest of our lives looking over our shoulders for E.B. Gunn or any man like him."

Pure's head rocked back and forth in understanding.

"And remember, Pure, you've killed three of theirs. That mother panther has got a bad itch for killing now and won't stop because you've had enough."

Pure wet his lips and lowered the reins. He took an easy breath before scooting to the far left of the wagon seat. "Tie up your pony and get in," he said, warmly. "I think I might need company on the ride back to Brushy Creek."

July locked eyes with Pure. "Much obliged," he said and swung his far leg over the back of his saddle.

Pure watched July glide gracefully out of the saddle and then led his piebald to the back of the grub wagon. "Holler at those cowpunchers too. I think Isa and Paint would enjoy hearing their friends speak words over them."

July tied up his cow pony and then crossed under the horse's head. He exhaled a great breath as he strode toward Pure. "I think those cowboys would like that, Pure."

"July," Pure called out as a question, "in your way of thinking, its E.B.'s perceived wrong that won't let him end this thing?"

"Yep," July muttered quickly without doubt and then added with some uneasiness, "leastways, not until he's sent you and me straight to hell."

# TWENTY

—————⬥—————

C ap Millett sat on his porch looking squarely into the eyes of Nate Gunn. A tin of coffee cooled on the cedar-planked table a hand's reach away. He knew why Nate and his brother Foss were on his land. For an instant, he thought about simply ordering the six hands lingering around the porch to kill the both of them. After hearing the story of the gunfight at the Exchange, he figured these two were walking dead anyway. He choked back a smile and narrowed his eyes at the thought. *What did a few weeks matter?* Instead, he rose and stretched his back, then asked, "You boys looking for work?"

Foss grinned and rolled his eyes toward Nate. "Work? That's a laugh, Cap."

Nate tightened his jaw. He counted the guns around him and then pursed his lips, calculating.

Cap eyed Nate intently and wondered why the older Gunn hadn't spoken. "You're carrying an odd look on your face, Nate."

Nate remained silent but slowly eased his mount away from Foss.

Millett understood the movement. He intertwined his hands and tapped his thumbs against one another all the while staring into Nate's eyes. "We ain't fixing to have trouble are we, Nate?" he asked calmly.

"Depends."

Millett shrugged. "Seems a waste for E.B. to lose so many sons in one outing."

"Hey!" Foss snapped at Millett.

Nate issued a dismissing wave of his hand to Foss and then smiled. He tilted his hat back and glanced around at Millett's cowboys. A conflicted look troubled his face. "You know E.B., Cap. I figure it might be better to fight here then go home and tell him that two of his sons were killed after selling a hundred beeves to you."

Millett turned red-cheeked. After a long pause, the outlaw rancher pulled a willow chair from under the table and placed his right boot on the seat. His composure regained, he ran a hand along the top seam of the boot sweeping off a fine powder of dust. "What are you trying to say, Nate?" he asked with a smile.

Nate leaned forward in the saddle and brushed his pony's mane. Without looking up, he said with considerable irritation, "I'm just wondering how come the deputy sheriff in The Flat told me straight out that the undertaker didn't find a single coin on either Charlie's or Ben's bodies?"

Millett quit smiling. "Well you ought to know the answer to that, Nate."

Nate slowly raised his eyes and snorted, "Well, why don't you go ahead and tell me anyway, Cap?"

Millett lowered his boot from the chair with a testy exhale. His smile returned. He poked both hands into the front band of his trousers and drawled, "Hell, Nate, anyone who spent five minutes worth of time with Charlie recognized that brother of yours was a bad gambler."

Foss looked over at his brother and winced.

Nate clenched his left hand into a tight fist. After a moment, he nodded to himself, and stepped down from his horse. "Was his failing, that's a fact."

Millett didn't retreat from his goading. "I'd think E.B. is going to want to ask his oldest, why he sent Charlie to sell beeves in a known sinful place like The Flat?"

Nate stepped up on Millett's porch.

"A sinful place filled with whiskey and card games."

Nate ignored Millett's spurring. "So why don't you tell us what exactly happened to our brothers," he asked flatly and then after a short paused added, "and your number one gun hand?"

Millett grabbed the willow chair and settled it under him. He looked up at Nate and crossed his right leg over his left thigh. "Short of it is this, I paid your brothers six hundred in coin for the beeves."

"Of which none was found on his body," Foss interrupted.

Millett glanced over at Foss with dark eyes and paused briefly. "After the deal was completed, Charlie wanted a card game."

"And you let him play?" Nate snarled.

Millett uncrossed his leg and leaned forward, never relaxing his gaze at Nate. "He was a grown man. It wasn't my place to be his daddy or his big brother."

Nate's body tensed.

"Course he lost it all and then threatened me and the boys. Because I know your daddy, I cooled things off and gave Charlie thirty-dollars to get back home."

Nate frowned.

Foss looked in disbelief at Millett. "But the sheriff already said Charlie and Ben were broke."

Millett waited for both brothers to understand, then mused, "I wasn't there, but the deputy sheriff, Jim Draper, says Charlie lost it all again to Frank Coe right before the gun play."

Nate turned his head away from Millett and mumbled, "Damn you, Charlie."

Foss glanced over at Nate. "We should've known."

Nate swung his head to Foss, seething. "Shut-up, Foss," he muttered in a rough whisper.

Millett exhaled a long breath through his nostrils. "I figure you boys have a lot of things to reconcile before you see your daddy," he said.

Nate's face roiled crimson. "Don't push it, Cap," he warned.

Millett stood his ground and refused to rile at Nate's threat. "I'm serious, Nate. What went on inside the Exchange should alter your thinking on these boys you're going to pursue."

Nate's cheeks flushed white through the crimson. "I can damn well handle Pure Reston's gun play," he swore.

Millett's eyes grinned. He allowed a barely noticeable chuckle to rise in his chest. "I'm sure you can, son. But that ain't the fella you need worry about."

Nate's head shot up. Disbelief glowed on his expression. "Are you telling me, I need lose sleep about Pure's lap-dog colored boy?" he said and suddenly broke out laughing.

Millett waited patient and steady.

Foss joined in the laughter.

Millett smiled along with the pair and then said in a strong, husky voice, "That's exactly what I'm telling you."

The laughter stopped. Nate's eyes glowed black.

"Because that lap-dog colored boy, as you call him, killed Frank Coe," Millet declared.

Foss swallowed hard.

Nate rolled his eyes. His shoulder's drooped, unconcerned.

"Coe had the bulge on that boy," Millett muttered and shook his head. "Every witness there said so, and yet, Frank Coe, one of the fastest draws ever, died of a single gunshot right between the eyes."

"No matter," Nate said dismissively.

"No matter," echoed Foss.

Millett shrugged.

"Reston and his bunch have Gunn blood on their hands," Nate declared. His voice was hard and cold.

"Coe was a better at gunplay than either of you, Nate," Millett said. "You should take a minute and chew on that fact."

"Don't matter, Cap," Nate growled. "Maybe you should take a minute and understand that fact."

"Yeah," Foss said. "An eye for an eye, just like the book says."

Millett inhaled and studied each Gunn brother carefully. "Appears neither of you boys will be happy until you know," he said.

Nate forced a hard glare on Millett. "Know what, Cap?" he asked.

"Know that the colored is faster than the both of you."

"You think you can scare us, Cap?" Foss asked.

"No," Millett said. "I don't, and that fact alone will more than likely be the reason that the both of you end up just as cold as Ben and Charlie."

# JOURNAL NOTES

The ride back to Brushy Creek was at times sad reminisce and at times engaging frankness. And by the time we reached the spot where Isa was buried, Pure seemed to have shaken the feeling of doom gripping his mind. The boys helped some with that, singing hymns and recalling the good and the blockhead things that both Isa and Paint had done in their days. And this time, Pure allowed the whole outfit to dig Paint's grave. By the time, we finished, sweaty, tired, and dirty, a great deal of the grief had been flushed from us, and all of a sudden the grim job of putting Paint to rest was a welcome responsibility. We all got to have our say over both brothers and after everything was said and done, we all seemed a little less sad and a little less angry.

And the day we arrived back in McMullen County, we all breathed a sigh of relief. The ≡R ranch was a welcome sight, and the south Texas air, as usual, dripped with a heavy sweetness. Home again, Pure seemed back to his old self and the rest of us were naively enraptured with the delight and happiness of setting our boots on familiar ground. Not understanding that the end of our world was riding hell-bent, straight ahead, and resolute for each and every one of us.

# TWENTY-ONE

*October 1878*
*Gunn's Cabin, Texas*

———◆———

E.B. Gunn sat in the grayness of a chilly October morn spinning the rowel on one of Buckshot Wallace's spurs.

Deep in thought.

Waiting.

The scuff of leather against a horse's lope far off in the brasada had awakened him earlier. His attention suddenly left the spur. He pressed his back against the rough slats of a willow chair and gathered a double-barrelled shotgun from his lap. He lifted the gun chest-high and let it rest across his chest. A contemptible frown rustled his grizzled face.

*Closer now.*

Another scrape and then low voices. E.B. leaned forward and placed his left ear into the October chill, listening. His cheeks pushed heavy flesh into his eyes restricting his vision to a tight squint.

*Only two.*

He turned back, deadpanned, and set the shotgun against the front wall of the cabin. The gun inched down the wall and then rested passively. E.B. made sure the gun was stable and then twisted his shoulders into the willow, taking several seconds to find a comfortable position. His expression, stolid indifference, refused to reveal the fury brewing in his gut.

Five minutes passed before the creak of stirrups sounded from the north side of the porch followed by the tinny jangle of spurs against the south Texas earth. E.B. tilted his head toward the noise and gazed down the porch and into the yard.

"You boys must've got an early start."

The two figures stopped mid-stride.

Foss threw a hurried glance at Nate in the gradual lifting darkness and bobbed his head in disbelief.

Nate inhaled a whisper of a breath and then answered in an exhale, "What'd you do, stay up all night, E.B.?"

E.B. rocked himself forward two times and then lifted out of the willow. "Much noise as you two were making out there, I'm certain most living things in the scrub is awake by now."

Nate stepped onto the porch wearing a cowed expression. He instinctively knew E.B. wasn't happy.

"I don't hear or see them sixty beeves you was sent after."

Nate slowed his step. He sensed the showdown coming.

E.B. ran a dry tongue over his lower lip. "Where's the other, two?" he growled softly.

Nate stopped on his heels. His jaw muscle pulsed in and out. "E.B., hear me out now," he begged politely. "Charlie sold those sixty head of cattle to Cap Millett and then lost all of the money in a card game."

E.B. exploded like a wound spring. In one blink, he stood inches from Nate's face, shaking in anger. "Now why would he have gone and done a fool thing like that for?"

Nate knew better than to lie to the old man. He straightened as tall as he could stretch and in a whisper of a voice, said, "Because I sent him to see Millett."

The back of E.B.'s rough-hewn left hand struck cat-like quick and propelled Nate backward. He stumbled clumsily into Foss causing both to sprawl into a tangled heap on the rough porch decking. "Now why in the hell would you want to go and do something like that for?"

Nate rubbed his cheek in disbelief at the old man's strength and quickness. "I thought it made more sense to sell those cattle there . . . on the trail, rather then drive them all the way back here," he stammered rapidly. "He had the money E.B., six-hundred dollars, he had."

E.B. spit between Nate's legs. "Had," he said in disgust. "Had don't mean nothing to me."

Nate scrambled to his feet. A red welt showed on his left cheekbone.

"Had!" E.B. spit.

"E.B., just listen."

"Had, hell, boy, had is nothing but a prospector's dream."

Nate rubbed his cheek. "E.B.," he pleaded.

"Why didn't you watch him? You knew you couldn't let Charlie get around money or card tables," E.B. snapped. "You was the one in charge."

"E.B."

"Not Charlie!"

"I know, E.B., it's just that I thought . . . ,"

"Thought?" E.B. turned back and grabbed the shotgun. "Had. Thought," he muttered. "And by the way, Nate, just where were you all this time that your brother was losing my money?"

Nate lowered his eyes, hanged-dogged. "I took Foss to Dodge City to finish it with the Restons."

E.B. lifted his brow and cracked open the shot-gun. "And did you," he said and tapped the caps on each end of the gun's shells, "Finish it with the Restons?"

An eerie uncomfortable silence fell on the porch.

"Well, did ya?"

"I only found one of them," Nate confessed.

"Only one?"

Nate nodded. "Paint."

"That math don't add up for me, Nate," E.B. said and bit down on his lower lip.

Nate stiffened and stayed silent.

E.B. slammed the broken-down gun together with a loud snap. "And your brothers?" he asked, already knowing what had happened. "How'd it go down?"

Nate inhaled and then exhaled a long breath. "Pure Reston killed the both of them," he blurted out.

E.B. pushed both barrels of the shotgun into Nate's chest. His lips pulled back from his teeth, exposing an animal-like snarl. "Didn't I tell you what I'd do to you if you got any of my sons killed on this outing?"

"Wait a minute, E.B.," Foss shouted impulsively.

E.B. tossed an angry glance at Foss. "Shut-up, Foss."

Foss ran his tongue around his lips and then sucked in a heavy breath.

"Or you're next," E.B. growled. "And even if you do shut-up, you might be next."

Nate rolled his eyes skyward and pressed them both shut.

"But, E.B.," Foss uttered and thrust a hand into the leather wallet hanging heavily over his shoulder.

"Shut-up, boy!"

Foss fumbled a handful of coins from the wallet. "Just look at what Nate found that one Reston to be carrying."

The jingle of coin caught E.B.'s attention. "What's that?" he asked.

"Nate took this off of Paint," Foss proclaimed.

E.B. sniffed the air. His hands relaxed. The shotgun slipped to his side. "What've you got there, Foss?" he asked. His eyes sparkled.

Nate opened his eyes and exhaled in relief. "Gold coin, E.B.," he answered for Foss. "Fourteen thousand dollars worth of gold coin."

"Better than sixty straggling Reston beeves," Foss stammered.

"Let me see it all," E.B. bellowed, grabby and anxious.

Foss poured the wallet's contents into E.B.'s cupped palms. Coins overflowed from the Gunn patriarch's upturned flesh. The coins splashed onto the weathered porch and glittered in the now rising morning sun.

"Whooo, doggies," E.B. squealed.

Nate watched his father's face light up in childish delight. He breathed easy.

E.B. glanced up, locked eyes with both sons, and motioned for the wallet.

Foss eagerly handed the coin-laden wallet to his father.

E.B. exposed a yellow, tobacco-stained smile. "Hell, boys, why didn't you just tell me this to begin with?"

Nate stood stunned at the ease in which the old man forgave Charlie and Ben's killings.

E.B. stepped between Nate and Foss and plopped heavy arms around both boy's shoulders. "None of that other means a tinker's dam to me right now. Let's go inside and count all of this one more time."

Nate started forward cautiously. "What about Pure Reston, E.B.?"

E.B. looked over Nate. "What about him?"

"He killed Charlie and Ben."

E.B. lifted his forearm from around Foss's shoulder and shook the coin-laden wallet. The muffled jingle of coin against coin sounded inside the bag. "We're gonna count all of this first, Nate."

Nate smiled, uneasy.

"You understand that, boy?"

Nate looked past E.B. at Foss. His expression was confused. He was unsure of how to answer.

Foss lowered his eyes and tilted his head toward the front door.

"Them brothers of yours is dead," E.B. said, calm and deliberate.

Nate shook his head in understanding. "I know, E.B.," he said.

"Ain't nothing we can do that'll bring 'em back to this earth."

Nate swallowed hard.

E.B. shook the bag once more. "While this, on the other hand, is life, Nate."

"Sure, E.B.," Foss volunteered. "I understand."

E.B. ignored Foss and squeezed harder on Nate's neck. "Life for all of us."

Nate squirmed to pull away from E.B.'s powerful grip.

E.B. grinned at Nate's attempt to free himself and tightened his hold. "A very good life for all of us, Nate."

Nate lifted a hand and pried his way out of E.B.'s clench.

E.B. roared with laughter. His eyes sparkled. "So let's all go inside," he said. "And once the counting is done . . . once I know the honest tally for the coin inside this wallet . . . well, then I'll tell you how we're gonna end Pure Reston's lucky string once and for all."

## JOURNAL ENTRY

In late October of '78, I sent our seven hands to inspect the western boundary of the ≡R. It was on the west that we bordered the smaller Gunn ranch, and I wanted to make sure that not one ≡R branded beeve was even close to being on E.B.'s land. I told the boys to herd back any beeves grazing on the line and to keep a close watch on each other's backs. Normally I would have dispatched outriders in groups of two, with each outrider team setting up sign camps on the line. That way each would have a smaller territory to ride and inspect. We always dispatched outriders in the late fall to inspect the water and grass situation for the coming cold months. But because of the trouble brewing with the Gunns, I told the boys to stay together in one camp and make dang sure that they kept a guard working all night long. I didn't ride with the boys that morning as Pure asked me to ride into Dogtown with him. By that time the town had been renamed for that presidential candidate from New York, but to me, it would always be Dogtown. Pure was headed for the general store to tell Mr. Edwards that he couldn't pay his ranch bill due to the theft of the herd money. The Edwards Store, like most of the county back then, was as rough as a longhorn's hide.

A number of cowboys and citizens had been gunned down there and were buried in Dogtown's Boot Hill. Because of that, Pure reckoned it would be best if I rode along him, just in case any Gunns were lying in ambush. What we couldn't realize at the time was that there was indeed a bushwhacking being planned, just not for Pure and me.

# TWENTY-TWO

*October 1878*
*Outside the ≡R Outrider Camp, Texas*

———◆———

Past midnight and under a bright full moon, E.B. Gunn finished tying a half-hitch knot to his saddle horn. After a quick tug to check the knot's hold, he turned back and marched thirty-feet to the opposite end of the rope where a rag-wrapped torch, slathered in beef tallow, was tied. The crisp crackle of dried grass sounded under the heel of each boot step, which brought a devious grin to the face of the normally surly Gunn patriarch. The rare yet plentiful summer rains had produced a knee-high crop of grass in the brasada. But September had returned the county to its normal drought-like condition, and the lush native grass had quickly changed back to its natural state of brittle tinder. Picking up the prepared torch, E.B. lifted a Lucifer from his shirt pocket and struck the red-headed match against the butt of his pistol. The sulphurous demon flared immediately. E.B. pushed the match against the torch and watched in delight as a slender blue flame slowly engulfed the entire surface of the cloth.

Mesmerized by the combustion, E.B. observed the growing flame for several seconds before dropping the fire stick onto the dried grass. A slight breeze against his face fanned the flame backward and the dried foliage of the brasada soon glowed in a rapidly spreading orange hue. Satisfied with the fire's energy, E.B. hurried back to his mount and grabbing a handful of mane pulled his massive frame up into his saddle. With little time to waste, he raked his spurs against the horse's rib cage and jumped the beast into a gallop. The provocation was unnecessary as the animal's natural instinct to run from fire emerged, and the animal raced away out of hand, chased by the flame-struck torch. Unwilling to allow the horse to run strictly on its own fear, E.B. kept rolling Buckshot Wallace's spurs against the animal's ribs. The horse bounded high with each rake of the spurs, causing the trailing torch to bounce like rolling lightning through the tall kindling brush of the brasada.

Situated a hundred yards outside the Reston outrider camp on the north, south, and east, Nate, Foss, and Clark took note of E.B.'s ball of fire and just as quick spurred their horses in response to the burning signal. Within seconds, the whole of the brasada transformed into a ghoulish hell-like vision, burning in a giant ring around the ☰R cowboys.

⟫•◇•⟪

The growing thunder of a stampede encircled the fast asleep ☰R camp.

Horses whinnied and pulled violently against their stakes.

Willy Berry, enclosed in his hot roll, lifted his head at the noise. "What the—," he muttered sleepily, and then slowly recognizing the danger began to swear aloud.

The rest of the ☰R cowboys sprang to life at Willy's hollering. Curses and shouts streamed through the camp as the half-asleep cowboys tried to desperately to get out of their hot rolls and pull on their boots. Unheeding of July's orders, the men had all gone to sleep without a night guard.

"What is it?" one screamed.

The spooked horses' screams were high-pitched and reverberated eerily throughout the camp. The animals tugged and pulled at the bindings with nostrils held high into the night air.

"Where are they? yelled one cowboy as he scrambled from all fours to his feet.

"What the—!" was all Willy could muster as answer.

In seconds, each ☰R hand was on his feet and staring around the camp at the night sky's orange complexion. The deceptively calm luminescent glow quieted the cowboys and their animals momentarily. But the lull was short-lived as the deafening, yet unmistakeable, wind-fed roar of fire rose up from every direction and raced for the camp. The realization that it wasn't a stampede descending upon them but instead a growing, windstorm of flame forced a harsh reality on each man.

"It's got us circled!"

"Look," Willy barked at the others. "There, to the west. There's a small break. Leave everything! Mount up and let's get through it before it fires too."

In minutes, the cowboys had haltered their mounts and riding bareback, disappeared through the small ten foot opening on either side of the wildfire. And in all of the turmoil, not one cowboy noticed that their escape route had been raked free of grass and saturated with a large amount of river water.

# TWENTY-THREE

*October 1878*
*Outside the Hell Storm, Texas*

The four Gunns sat horseback behind the burning hell storm raging through the ≡R outrider camp. Levered Winchesters rested in each of their hands. They waited impassioned and fervid for the Reston cowboys to ride through the prepared escape chute.

E.B.'s eyes hardened. "Shoot every man of 'em," he instructed coldly. "But be damned sure that the colored goes down forever."

A deadly anticipation of the killing ahead silenced the sons and brothers. Winchesters were lifted and pressed against shoulders. Fingers rested coolly on metal triggers. Not one wanted to disappoint the father . . . some out of fear, others out of hate.

The Reston bunch appeared as if on cue. The fleeing cowboys, dark shadows bathed in the glow of a reddish outline, galloped ahead carrying with them the audible bubbling of relief. Each was unaware that their escape and thus their lives were transitory.

Nate eased forward in the saddle and with a deep inhale pulled against the slight curve of the Winchester's trigger. The gun's explosion was swallowed by the raging fire, which made the lead Reston cowboy's fall from his steed seem staged and humorous.

Clark and Foss followed quickly with shots of their own. The three brothers killed the first three riders with deadly accuracy.

E.B. shot next, and another Reston cowboy slid unceremoniously from his horse. Ejected Winchester cartridges flashed in the darkness and the metallic clink of levering arms snapped loud and cold.

The remaining cowboys pulled up hard on their mounts to avoid their fallen comrades. Amidst the confusion, all three stared into the darkness ahead and died without ever knowing who or what had unleashed such a murderous fury upon them.

———⟫·◇·⟪———

Later, with all seven cowboys laid out under the light of a rising morning sun, E.B. swung his wide-brimmed sombrero against his thigh. "Damn, he ain't here," the Gunn patriarch cursed.

Nate paced along the feet of the dead or dying men and chewed on his bottom lip. Two of the men's bodies still instinctively gasped for air at long intervals as if their brains refused to accept the end.

Clark shook his head at the grotesque death dance and laughed, "These two ain't going to let go."

E.B. glared at Clark, unamused at the comment.

Foss tilted his hat back and glanced at his father. "Where do you figure July is, E.B.?"

E.B. stroked his unkempt beard and muttered under his breath, thinking, before growling, "He must be with Pure. I reckon that oldest Reston cur is fearful for his life right now and keeping the colored nearby."

Nate watched the two Reston cowboys' final twitches and then raised his head toward E.B. "This bunch were outriders. They were out checking the grass and water situation. I imagine Pure and July rode into Tilden to see about a loan to tide them over the winter."

E.B. narrowed his brow and studied over Nate's words.

Foss lifted his chin at his brother. "Why would he need a loan?"

Nate looked down and scratched the palm of his hand. "Because, Brother Foss, we took all of his herd money. I reckon Pure's been running the ranch on borrowed coin."

E.B. poked his tongue into his bottom lip and nodded. "Your brother's right, Foss."

Nate's eyes widened at E.B.'s agreement.

"And," E.B. continued, "that means sooner or later the colored will show up here to be with his cowboys."

"So what are we going to do?" asked Clark.

134

E.B. looked down at the bodies and grinned. "You and Foss are going to wait here."

Clark's expression changed to one of confusion.

"Take these piebalds and hobble them like nothing happened here. Then haul these bodies back to camp and put them in their hot rolls like they're fast asleep."

Nate laughed under his breath.

"What?" huffed E.B.

"Like nothing happened? The whole country's burned-out and black, E.B."

"Don't get smart, boy. That fire is exactly what is going to bring that colored-boy 'a running."

Foss ignored the two and threw his hat to the ground. "Well, I ain't handling no dead bodies."

E.B. whirled and moved nose-to-nose with his mutinous son. "Oh yes you will, Foss, and when you're finished with the bodies, you and your brother are going to wait for the colored to ride in and take care of him just as we did these boys here."

Foss clenched his jaw. "And where are we going to hide, E.B.? We've just burnt the scrub to the ground for a mile or more."

E.B. turned away unconcerned and responded offhandedly, "You'll figure something out."

Nate offered Foss a knowing grin.

Foss cursed under his breath and then muttered, "And what are you and Nate going to be doing all this while?"

A depraved snarl tugged at E.B.'s lips. "Don't get smart, boy!" he growled. "But seeing how you're so keen to know, Nate and I are riding to the Reston headquarters to find Pure. And when we find him, I'm gonna send him off to be reunited with the rest of his clan."

# Twenty-Four

*October 1878*
*The ≡R Outrider Camp, Texas*

⇒•◇•⇐

J ust east of the ≡R headquarters, the heavy cloud of a wild fire became visible across the western horizon.

Pure lifted his reins at the distant maelstrom with a whispered, "Whoa."

July followed Pure's lead and glancing ahead said, "As dry as that scrub is, I reckoned it was only a matter of time before we saw one of these fires before winter."

"On almost any other occasion, I would agree with you, July, but seeing how that plume is rising from out near where our outriders are scouting, we might just have a problem on our hands."

July paused, taken aback. "Gunns?"

"Them or the devil. Both seem determined to have our souls of late."

July refocused on the smoke cloud. "But why mess with them? Why not ride full force for the two of us?"

Pure rolled his Snapping and Stretching gum forward to his front teeth. "Because I figure E.B. follows the old way of things," he said and began popping the gum between his teeth.

"The old way?" July asked.

"The Kentucky blood feud way."

"Nasty sounding when you say it like that."

Pure gave a quick shake of his head. "It is, and once it starts it takes on a life all its own."

"And that's what we're all caught up in?"

"Appears so."

"So, how does a Kentucky blood feud go down?"

Pure set a steely gaze on the horizon. "It gets personal," he said in a gravel-filled voice.

"Family personal?"

"More than that." Pure said.

"How far more?"

Pure glanced over at July and bit down hard on the Snapping and Stretching gum. "Retaliation is extended to any and all associates . . . just like they were family."

July stared into the distance and squinted. The dark plume was suddenly more worrisome. "What's the thinking of that?"

"It tends to keep any outsiders from joining the fray."

July pushed the soles of his boots deep into his stirrups and arched his back. "We best get out there then."

Pure sat silent. The Snapping and Stretching gum bounced between his front teeth.

July waited patiently for a full minute then said, "Pure?"

"I don't like the smell blowing from the west, July."

"But we ain't got much choice other than ride out there," July insisted.

"Oh, we're riding to check on our bunch," Pure said and pointed north.

July followed Pure's gesture and gazed at the darkening north horizon.

"Looks to be a storm gathering in the north," Pure muttered with a fair amount of thought.

July sniffed at the air. "This coming storm got you flustered?"

Pure flipped up his collar as the first nip of cooler air arrived. "Well, I ain't too keen on it."

"Looks to be moving fast."

"Maybe."

"Shouldn't drop much moisture."

"Hard to say with a fall storm," Pure said.

A lone matchbush rolled across the scrub in front of them.

July watched the plant with great interest. "True enough," he said.

The wind picked up and blew harder. Several tumbleweeds bounced past.

Pure reached behind his saddle and untied his oilskin. He slipped the slicker over his head and then held his gaze back north. A gray curtain of rain began to drape earthward.

July pushed his head through his oilskin. "That rain looks to be a mile or more away. Might not even reach us."

"Might not."

Rolling thunder growled across the sky as the approaching cold bumped into the warm air aloft.

July tossed his eyes skyward. "I know you well enough to know that you've been giving this some thought."

"Uh-huh."

"What's your call?"

Pure reined his piebald's head straight into the rapidly approaching front. "Just to be certain, we're going to ride in from a different direction."

A solitary raindrop dotted July's oilskin. July shivered uncontrollably. "Why?"

"Sorta feels right to me."

A swirl of dust blew up around both men.

July ducked his chin into his chest. "What sort of bushwhacking is it that's waiting for us?"

Pure squinted into the wind. His face showed a panged frown. "I don't know yet. I just know something inside me says we shouldn't gallop into that outrider camp head-on."

# Twenty-Five

*October 1878*
*North bank of the Nueces River, Texas*

⇒•◇•⇐

The norther stalled over the most southern boundary of McMullen County. Pure and July dismounted on a faint rise of scrub above the Nueces beneath an unabated downpour. Across the river, the blackened landscape of the outrider camp projected a dreary image. July had a sense that the four horsemen, themselves would soon appear to drag him to hell.

July removed a long glass from his pack and stared into the quiet camp. "Something's not right," he acknowledged and shook his head, confused. "The horses are hobbled, and the men all appear to be in their hot rolls."

Pure gazed skyward scowling. "Maybe they're staying out of the rain."

July handed Pure the glass and watched intently as the ≡R owner scanned the camp.

Pure pulled his eye away from the glass and muttered, "I think if our boys are in those hot rolls, then they're all dead."

The words caused July's chest to slump. A hiss of air rushed from his lungs. "You serious?" he asked incredulously, then added, "All seven?"

"Most likely."

"How can that be?"

Pure pushed the Snapping and Stretching gum deep into the front of his lower lip. "Dang if I know," he muttered.

July turned and gazed across the river once more. He rubbed the back of his neck and mumbled, "Can't be . . . Can it?" A long pause followed the question and then further bewilderment. "All seven?"

Pure stepped up into his saddle. "Even considering the rain, I can't

139

think of one good reason for those hot rolls to be occupied this early in the afternoon, July," he said in a low voice.

"What about the storm?"

Pure ignored the question and frowned at his ranch foreman. "And neither can you."

July grabbed his piebald's saddle horn and swung up on the horse's back. "Merciful, Lord," he whispered and looked toward Pure.

"You said it," Pure muttered.

"Now what?"

Pure flipped his reins right. "Let's ride west a little ways and cross the river."

July pushed his eyebrows together. "Why not cross here?"

Pure leaned in close to July. A hard expression gathered on his face. "Because, I imagine if we were to do that, we'd be dead before we reached mid-stream."

July straightened and glanced toward the river. Small beads of perspiration popped across the bridge of his nose. He surveyed the barren landscape across the river.

Pure started his horse west with a quick nod to the camp. "So let's ride west where we stand a better chance of crossing upright."

July turned his horse and followed.

Pure glanced back at his foreman and shrugged. "At least that way we'll have a chance to spot where our assassins are hiding."

July nodded and muttered under his breath, "Damned Kentucky blood feud."

———◇———

Thirty minutes later, both men dismounted with a tremble as the last remnant of the norther blew past. The passing rain mixed with the burnt scrub land to form a concoction of heavy black sludge that clung desperately to boots and leggings.

July took one step forward and then kicked one boot awkwardly in the air in an attempt to dislodge a bite of the dark muck. "Might be a bit hard to ambush a man in this ooze, Pure, especially with the scrub burnt to the ground."

Pure ignored his foreman's remarks and continued to flip the Snapping and Stretching gum from his bottom lip to his front teeth as his eyes intently gazed around the surrounding camp.

July recognized Pure's cogitating. Waiting patiently, he exhaled and tilted his head toward the ground. A small waterfall of water poured from the brim of his hat.

Pure walked around his piebald and carefully slid his Henry from its leather holder.

July straightened and lifted his brow. "What is it?" he asked in a whisper.

Tight lipped, Pure lifted his chin toward July's rifle.

July looked at the gun and then reached over his saddle and yanked the rifle from its scabbard.

Pure pulled his piebald's head around and rested the rifle across his saddle.

July expression became fuddled. He quickly re-positioned his horse, cocked the Henry, and then laid the rifle on the saddle seat.

"Might keep you from slipping in the mud," Pure said and pushed his shoulder into the gun.

"What are we doing?" July whispered.

Pure closed his left eye and drew a bead on the nearest hotroll. "Don't ask questions, July. Just follow my lead."

July stared incredulously at Pure and then tossed a quick glance at his boss's target. His mouth hung open, dumfounded.

The first shot hit the nearest hot roll with a dull thud. The camp remained silent and still. Pure aimed at the next hot roll and pulled the Henry's trigger.

A leaden thump sounded.

Pure opened his closed eye and glanced at July. "You gonna help or what?" he asked and then repositioned the Henry.

July took aim on one of the hot rolls and mumbled, "I don't even know what we're doing."

Both guns exploded simultaneously.

Pure's target sounded with a muffled clump.

July's shot brought forth a loud groan and then slow movement from the bedding.

"What the?"

141

Pure moved his sight in rapid succession on each of the remaining targets. "Watch out now," he shouted. "There's bound to be more!"

Suddenly, Foss Gunn jumped up from his concealment, screaming, and levering his Winchester.

Pure set the Henry's sight on the exposed man and pulled the trigger. The Henry bucked loudly.

Foss dropped back into the hot roll, dead.

A numb quiet fell over the camp.

July lifted his head from the Henry. He stared at Pure in wonder. "They didn't stand a chance."

"That's how I prefer them."

"How'd you know?

Pure swung his rifle from the piebald's back and laid the gun across his shoulder. "I could smell them both," he said in disgust.

———➤•◆•◆•◆•◆<———

The next morning, after burying the ≡R cowboys, Pure and July followed the Nueces south and west. The bodies of Foss and Clark rested face-down across the back of their ponies.

In the early afternoon, Pure stopped along the banks of the river on Gunn land and studied a sizeable oak tree.

"We'll hang them both here," he said. His voice betrayed no emotion.

July swallowed and glanced over at Pure. "They aren't going to get any deader," he offered.

Pure's face reddened at July's words. He cast a steely gaze at his foreman. "We're gonna hang them here and then set them both afire."

July's expression dropped. "We're gonna what?" he asked, incredulous.

The Snapping and Stretching gum popped loudly in Pure's mouth. "We gonna hang 'em and burn 'em," he said. His voice was strong and unwavering.

"Pure . . . we can't . . . we can't do that?"

"Why not?"

July grabbed his hat and rolled the brim downward. "Why . . ." he started, suddenly riled. "Did you ask, why not?"

Pure stared straight into July's eyes. His pupils contracted into small black dots. "That's what I said."

"Bu . . . But, why, Pure?" July stuttered.

"It's E.B. who set up our direction, not me."

"Our direction?

"The rules, July. How we conduct ourselves out here."

"Rules? What rules?"

Pure raised a hand to his mouth and removed the Snapping and Stretching gum with his finger and thumb. He glanced at the chewed chicle briefly and then tossed it into the dirt.

"I don't want any part of hanging and burning dead men, Pure."

"It's too late for that, July."

"It's not too late for me."

"You told me once that I couldn't switch my horse mid-stream."

July tightened his lips against his teeth and muttered to himself.

Pure settled the tip of his boot over the discarded gum and ground it into the ground. "I told you before; we're following the old way of doing things now."

July shook his head. His expression turned from disbelief to disgust. "Well I ain't liking it none," he said. His voice was low and strained.

"For what it's worth, neither do I."

July untied a coil of rope from his off-side latigo and stepped down from his horse. He walked briskly for the hanging tree, lariat in-hand, and mumbled under his breath, "Damned Kentucky blood feud."

## JOURNAL ENTRY

*In 1903, the San Antonio Express News interviewed me on the twenty-fifth anniversary of the feud. The interviewer told me that vendetta was an Italian word. Its origin was from Latin . . . vindicta, which means vengeance. I told that reporter that those Italian fellas seemed to have a pretty solid grip on the word.*

*And I will admit to you that since those days, I have come to realize that in many ways vengeance is sorta like a beeve stampede. Because once one starts, everyone near-by joins in. And I believe on judgement day, my participation in the hanging and setting of Foss and Clark Gunn's bodies afire after the dust-up on the Nueces will merit a lengthy explanation to my maker. Even though both of them deserved the death we gave them, I don't think either merited mutilation. But by that time, the cycle of killing, both Gunns and Restons, had proceeded to a point where the only way either family would ever have peace from the vendetta was through outside influence or by the killing of all on one side. What I didn't know until days later was that on the morning Pure and I rode into Dogtown, Pure had Mr. Edwards send for the Texas Rangers. People can think*

what they will about Pure . . . but he knew full well how deep
he was sinking into the violence and retaliation, and that the
man he started seeing every morning in the shaving mirror was
a stranger he didn't much care for. And that's why he sent for
help. The Rangers arrived a week after we killed Foss and Clark,
but by then, Dogtown had also taken sides in the feud and those
siding with the Gunns had sent word warning E.B. and Nate
about the Rangers. I can't tell you for certain how that news
affected E.B., but I can promise you he must've been none too
happy about it, because before he and Nate lit out for Mexico,
they burned the ≡R headquarters to the ground. And while the
Rangers wouldn't venture across the Rio Grande . . . it didn't
hold Pure back any. And he seemed to arrive at a peace with
himself, understanding that the only way he could end the feud
was by blood. After that day, he never talked about being tired
of killing or seeking peace with the Gunns. It seemed that the
whole reason for the feud had become lost somewhere among the
blood and the bodies.

    And what I write here now . . . is something I haven't
ever shared with another living soul. But I reckon it's time to
record what really went on when Pure and I rode across the
border in December of '78.

# PART TWO

# Assassin

(n). one who murders by surprise attack.

# TWENTY-SIX

*December 1878*
*Across the Border in Tamaulipas, Mexico*

⪼•◆•⪻

Pure twisted in his saddle and squinted back into the morning sun rising fast on the Texas side of the Rio Grande. "Now that's something," he said.

July twisted the stopper out of a water bladder and lifted the bag to his lips. "Makes a man feel kind of naked being out of his own country," he said and took a long drink.

"I was thinking more of Stonewall Jackson's last words."

July lowered the bladder. A slight shudder flashed across his shoulders. "Is that supposed to provide some comfort to me?"

Pure swiveled back around. "Well, according to our Ranger friend back there, that's how we'll most likely end up over here."

July shook his head, grimaced, and then looked skyward. "Let us cross over the river and rest in the shade of the trees," he let loose, out of tune.

"Well sung," Pure said, deadpanned.

July tossed a darting glance at Pure and hung the water bag over his saddle horn. "Yeah," he said and lowered his eyes. His jaw tightened. He focused on the Mexican soil beneath his stirrups. "'cept I don't see any shade trees right here unless you count Mexican sumac or creosote bush, and I sure don't figure you for resting any."

"Right now, I reckon we've got bigger problems than shade trees or resting."

"How's that?" July answered. His gaze still firmly fixed on the rocky ground.

"You heard what that Ranger captain told us. That we're liable to run into

149

Mexican bandits, U.S. outlaws, and Kickapoo renegades on this side of the river."

"That's what the captain said sure enough."

"Well, you might want to put a little distance between your horse and mine."

July lifted his head and stared at Pure. "What?"

"Spread out."

"Pure, what are you talking about?"

"Appears like the last of that Ranger captain's group has come to welcome us."

July squinted. He mouthed Pure's words and then glanced out across the landscape in front of them.

Seventy-five yards away, twelve mounted Kickapoo warriors stretched across the horizon.

July rolled his shoulders forward and exhaled. "So much for our sneaking quietly across the border."

"We can go back."

"Oh, so now you're ready to go back," July said sarcastically.

Those Rangers are probably only five miles or so away."

"Just turn our backs on that bunch in front of us?"

"I'm just providing another option to you."

July ignored the comment and glanced back across the river. "You see a place to fight from? Anywhere close?"

Pure shook his head slowly. "All the cover appears to be behind those Kickapoo."

July's eyes darted north. A hundred yards away the river jutted toward the border and created a high bend. "Back off to my right," he said through clenched teeth. "There appears to be a winding bend that might afford us a little cover."

Pure glanced north and nodded. "I see it."

"It might even the odds a bit."

Pure's hand's tightened on the reins. He inhaled a long deep swallow of air. "Little cover and long odds."

"Yep," July exhaled.

"That seems to be our lot lately."

July studied the warriors intently. "I guess it would be against our luck of things to actually have these fellas turn out to be friendly."

Pure rolled the Snapping and Stretching gum from back in his jaw to his front teeth.

July watched the gum's movement. He looked from Pure to the Kickapoo. "I thought so," he mumbled.

Pure narrowed his eyes. His front teeth began to pop the Snapping and Stretching gum up and down. He calculated the distance between the Kickapoo and he and July in his head.

Several minutes passed. Each group eyed the other. Waiting.

Then all of a sudden, the lead Kickapoo warrior raised a bow above his head and began to squawk. The others lifted their reins and pumped their weapons in the air.

Pure pushed the Snapping and Stretching gum into his lower lip. "July?" he said in a graveled whisper.

"Yeah?"

Pure clicked back the trigger of his Peacemaker as he slid the weapon from its holster. "That bend off to the north you were speaking of."

July eased his Colt out. "What of it?"

"I think right about now would be a good time for you and me to run like a couple of Nueces steers for it."

# Twenty-Seven

*December 1878*
*Across the Border in Tamaulipas, Mexico*

⋙◆⋘

A mid a torrent of lead and arrows, Pure spurred his piebald into a patch of lechuguilla on the high side of the river bank. July arrived three seconds later and thirty yards away. Both men jumped from their mounts, reins in hand, and rolled across the sharp points of the wax plants. Each offered up his own fit of cussing upon landing.

Pistol drawn, Pure yanked hard on the piebald's reins with his left hand, and forced his gun hand against the back of the animal's knee. "We need to get these horses down," he shouted.

July nodded and immediately worked his mount to a kneeling position.

"Down boy," Pure whispered calmly to his steed.

In a matter of seconds, both piebalds lay on their sides. Their heads faced away from their cowboys.

Pure holstered his pistol, reached across his horse's top side and with the reins still held securely, slid his Winchester from its leather scabbard. He levered the rifle with a quick motion and took deliberate aim at the fast approaching band of Kickapoo.

July half-closed his left eye and sighted in the lead marauder with a steely gaze. "Which one do you favor?" he called out.

Pure locked eyes on a warrior riding in hard from his left side. The Kickapoo, dressed in a brightly patched-shirt, nocked an arrow as he neared closer. "I'll take this one here on my left dressed in the calico shirt."

July completely closed his left eye. "How come these fellas ain't on the reservation?"

Pure pressed the tip of his index finger against the cold steel of the

152

Winchester's trigger. "I reckon they prefer the Mexican climate."

Both rifles bucked. The explosions sounded as one gun.

The two warrior targets slumped back and rolled ungracefully from their ponies, dead before their bodies hit solid ground. The remaining Kickapoo reined their ponies hard and kicked up a cloud of dust. The warriors howled in anger at their fallen comrades.

Pure quickly levered the rifle and ejected the spent cartridge. He fired quickly, missing high over his next target's head.

The Kickapoo regrouped and answered with a hail of arrows.

Pure ducked at the incoming projectiles. He pushed his head against his saddle and waited. A dull thud sounded in his ears. His horse screamed, raised its head, and then fought against the reins in an effort to gain its feet.

"Awwwh!" Pure moaned. "They've hit my horse."

The Kickapoo swung their ponies back south in an effort to put a safe distance between the Winchesters and themselves.

July clenched his jaw and jumped to his feet. He took a quick, but deadly accurate shot at the Kickapoo warrior riding drag. The well-aimed shot knocked the warrior from his pony. "That's another one!" he shouted and levered the next cartridge. "That ought to give them something to think about."

"And after they sit a spell, they'll be back quick-like."

"Only nine of them though," July said.

"Small favors," Pure muttered.

"Yeah," July exhaled.

Pure looked over at his foreman and tilted his head slightly. "Still, it's something to be thankful for."

July pulled against the reins and directed his piebald to stand. The horse rolled to a kneeling position and then rose to all fours. "There's something I can't figure, Pure."

"What's that?"

"It's almost like those Kickapoo were here waiting on us."

Pure pushed a hand against his left knee and slowly rose to a standing position. He watched his horse gasp for breath, and shook his head in disgust. "You feeling that someone alerted that bunch to our possible arrival?" he asked and slowly lifted the Peacemaker from his side.

"Can't say for sure, but here they were."

"Well that's true enough."

"Just waiting."

"Everyone has got to be somewhere during the day." Pure said. He aimed the Colt at the piebald's forehead and fired a single-shot without blinking, then said, "You best hide that mount of yours in whatever cover you can find below this bank. We sure can't afford for the both of us to be caught afoot right now."

"Strange that they'd be here, though."

"While you're looking, I'll try and dig us a wallow behind these lechuguilla."

July clicked his tongue twice and led the piebald down the scrub-filled sand slope. "You don't suppose E.B. could've had a hand in this?" he asked.

Pure pulled a thick-bladed knife from his belt and scratched at the rocky soil. "Well he had more than enough pay-off money."

"Now that is a fact," July said.

"I figure he or his boys took at least fourteen-thousand in gold from Paint's wallet."

July laughed aloud. "Ain't that something?"

"What's that?"

"Old E.B. using ≡R money to hire these Kickapoo to kill us."

"How's that something?"

"It's like we're paying for our own murders."

Pure dug harder. "That's something all right."

July stared out at the dead warriors. "You think any of those Kickapoo might be carrying gold coin in their medicine bags?"

Pure paused and glanced out at the bodies of the three dead warriors. "I reckon there's a strong possibility of that," he said.

"Maybe if we live through the next charge, we should go out there and take a look."

Pure holstered the Colt and reached down to undo the cinch from the dead piebald. "That's sounds like a good plan."

July and his mount disappeared over the slope. His booming voice echoed from the river bank below. "You know what I hope for, Pure?"

Pure tugged at the saddle. "I'm sure you're gonna tell me."

I sure hope I get the chance to share with E.B. just how I feel about his sorry ways one of these days . . . soon."

Pure freed the saddle from the dead animal and set it up on its end, cantle side down. "I hope we both live long enough to that," he muttered.

# Twenty-Eight

*December 1878*
*Across the Border in Tamaulipas, Mexico*

"**M**aybe those Kickapoo ain't coming back," July offered. Pure rolled onto his left side and stared at July, some ten yards away to the west. He shaded his eyes and looked into the slow-setting sun. "I reckon they'll return."

"How can you be so sure?"

"They're human animals and they've got dead to bury."

"Hmmm," July mumbled.

"They'll be back," Pure said. "They won't leave a warrior on the field of battle."

July rolled onto his right side and looked into Pure's eyes. "What are they waiting for then?"

"Dark, most likely."

"I thought Indians didn't like to fight at night."

"An Indian will fight whenever it gives him an advantage."

July rolled onto his back and searched the sky. "Looks like we'll be having a new moon tonight."

"I reckon that would be advantage enough."

July flipped back to his stomach and stared across the landscape in front of him. "Probably so," he said.

Pure turned and looked at the dead Kickapoo in the calico shirt. He studied the warrior with strained attention. After for several minutes, he rolled the Snapping and Stretching gum between his front teeth.

July watched Pure with growing interest.

Pure lifted his chin toward the southeast. A sliver of moon glowed white in the sky. "Going to be real dark tonight."

"On account of the new moon," July repeated.

Pure scratched the hair above his right ear. "I could sure go for a biscuit and sop right now."

"Black coffee, too."

Pure pounded the gum rapidly.

July watched, fascinated. "What's going on in that head of yours?"

"Something don't figure right here."

"By my recollection, something ain't figured right since Buckshot and the kid got killed."

"No this is different."

"Different how?"

"It's like we're being dilly-dallied along for some purpose."

"You thinking, E.B. has a hand in this dilly-dallying?"

Pure slowed the gum and paused. After a minute, he pointed toward the dead Kickapoo. "How far you think it is to that dead Indian?"

"I don't know, a hundred feet?"

"I was thinking more like ninety."

July made a face. "Why'd you ask me then?"

"I just was wondering what you thought."

"And I told you, but you already had it figured in that head of yours."

"How about the one you shot?"

"Are you going to tell me what you're thinking?"

"Yours looks to be about . . . a hundred feet."

July expelled a frustrated breath.

Pure slowed the gum once more. "You ever give much thought to your dying?"

"Not 'til you just mentioned it."

"Well don't worry about it, is all I meant."

"You must have this thing figured out."

"A fair amount of it anyway. I know we aren't dying here tonight."

"Well that's a comfort, Pure."

A shadow stretched across the ground in front of them. July looked west. "That sun's falling fast now."

"Yep."

"Well, if we ain't going to die tonight, what are we going to do?"

Pure began crawling forward under the rapidly darkening sky. In seconds the outline of his body disappeared into the landscape.

"Hey, Pure?" July called out. His voice betrayed a hint of panic. "Where are you going?"

From the darkness came Pure's subdued voice. "Shhh," he hushed, "Keep quiet and follow me low-like to the ground before you get the both of us killed."

# TWENTY-NINE

*December 1878*
*Across the Border in Tamaulipas, Mexico*

———◆———

Three shadowy, muted assassins scrambled hunched over across the intensely darkened landscape of Nuevo León. Four waited behind, to the south. And two more raced west and then back north.

Forward of all nine warriors, Pure lay death-like still, waiting. His eyes were tightly shut, and his nostrils flared with each passing breath, hoping against hope to catch an early scent of any approaching Kickapoo. He listened with strained attention to the soundless Mexican night.

*Lub . . .*

*Dub.*

*Lub. . .*

*Dub.*

His heart hammered against the wall of his chest.

*Relax.*

He held his breath and tried desperately to pace his out of control heartbeat.

*Relax!*

His heart ignored the command and continued to pound blood against his eardrums. He tightened his lips in anxious concern. A wave of trembling rolled down his spine. Fear clutched his entire body. A harsh reality settled in his mind. In the darkness, he was blind and deaf.

*Relax, Pure!*

The night creaked forward.

*Com'on Pure.*

He shivered at the voice. Isa rode across the back of his eyelids. His jaw clenched tightly. The haunting image of his younger brother heartened a sudden desire to flee. His cheekbones pushed up and locked his eye sockets shut.

*Hurry, big brother.*

"Paint," he moaned.

*You've gone and stepped off in for sure now, Pure.*

"Street?"

Then . . . riding on a slight breeze from the southwest . . . a faint smell of animal fat.

His nose naturally wrinkled in disgust.

He opened his eyes.

A great calm settled over him.

His mind focused.

The pounding in his ears quieted.

*There.*

The slight brush of moccasin on pebbles.

Every muscle in his body tensed. He was fully alert and prepared to act.

The scent grew stronger. It was the putrid smell of tallow.

*Close now.*

An imperceptible inhale. He held the breath.

*Steady.*

And then out of the darkness, a warm hand clamped firmly around his wrist. The calico shirt, he now wore, pressed into his lower arm.

A Kickapoo pulled him forward.

Then the warrior's hand relaxed against him.

Then forward again.

*Steady.*

The assassin's hand relaxed again.

Pure exhaled and locked his fingers tightly around the Kickapoo's wrist.

The warrior stopped, then struggled violently against the grip.

*Now!*

Pure pulled the scared warrior forward. The Kickapoo stumbled and nearly collapsed on top of him. The smell of dung and tallow from the man's hair were overpowering. Pure locked eyes with his enemy, and thrust his knife forward

A buffalo's breath passed.

Pure tightened his grip. Even in the darkness, he could see the yellow of the man's eyes.

The warrior's expression widened. His lips squirmed against his teeth. A whoosh of air pushed through his lips . . . a last vestige of breath in the dying warrior's lungs.

Pure clamped down harder on the man's wrist, and then waited with equal measure of respect and reverence. His thoughts held briefly on July. He prayed that his friend's ten minute head-start was time enough to do the things that needed doing. He prayed that July's knife had also found its mark tonight. And most of all, he prayed that his plan had worked.

After thirty seconds, he pulled the thick-bladed knife from the Kickapoo's sternum and instinctively wiped the blade against his pants.

Twenty seconds after that, he stripped off the calico shirt and tied the sleeves around the dead Kickapoo's neck.

And five seconds later, he was up and running, pulling the dead warrior toward his waiting tribe mates.

# THIRTY

*December 1878*
*The Kickapoo Camp, Tamaulipas, Mexico*

The Kickapoo camp fire was scarcely a fire at all.

Pure dropped the dead Kickapoo's wrist and simultaneously swung the Colt in the darkness. The Peacemaker spit fire and copper without pause. The quiet of the night was impregnated by the piercing cries of shocked and dying Kickapoo.

Six shots.

Impacted flesh and bone.

A thousand screams.

*You're Empty.*

Pure dropped one knee to the ground and methodical-like, flipped open the Colt's ejector gate. Sulfurous gun smoke, pale against the night, drifted head-high. He blinked his eyes rapidly to dispel the plume. The coppery smell assaulted his nostrils. He tried to swallow, but his mouth was a desert, parched by the hot vapors churning from the Colt's barrel. The swallow hung in his throat. Panic arose inside him. He pushed the Snapping and Stretching gum back in his jaw and began to chew nervously, desperate for moisture. The swallow slid away. He took a steadying breath and one-by-one dropped the reload cartridges into the Peacemaker. His eyes darted east to west in the darkness, waiting for an arrow or bullet to find him.

To the north, a single shot exploded in the night.

*He recognized the reverberation.*

Pure swiveled in the shot's direction and then quickly turned his attention back to the Kickapoo camp.

Another shot followed.

He exhaled through thin lips.

A deep hush settled across the Mexico landscape.

*It's done.*

Pure snapped the ejector gate shut and slowly regained his feet.

He walked among the dead, locating them with the toe of his boot, and kicking them roughly . . . just to confirm what he already knew.

*One.*

*Two.*

*Three.*

"Four . . ." he muttered aloud. It went just like he thought. He moved toward the Kickapoo stringer and untied a tall mount which displayed a U.S. cavalry brand.

The Kickapoo had sent three warriors to retrieve their fallen. Four warriors had stayed back with a sliver of a fire for the tejanos to see. The assassins wanted to make the tejano intruders feel comfortable knowing that the Kickapoo were in their camp and that no attack would come on this dark December night. Meanwhile two warriors had circled to the north. These two were sent to ambush the trespassers from across the border.

What the Kickapoo didn't know was that the tejanos had also planned for a killing night. July had propped the bodies of two dead Kickapoo back-to-back against one another and then started a sliver of a fire beside the two. A small fire that carried just enough light for a pistoleer like July to make two kills from behind a clump of prickly pear without much effort at all.

## JOURNAL ENTRY

*The morning after the run-in with the Kickapoo, Pure and I searched each dead warrior's body. And no matter how exciting and adventurous killing may sound two decades after the fact, being among men you have vanquished in battle is never arousing or daring. In my experience, death is always grisly and inglorious. And even though I did more than a man's share of killing, I never took pleasure or satisfaction in it. Never. Truth be told, I always felt like a little bit of me died with each man I killed. It chills my spine even today to talk about killing, no matter how necessary. And I came to know that the more a man killed, the easier it got to pull that trigger. The act becomes one more daily chore, like watering a horse or roping a beeve. But, it changes a man. It changed Pure. And it changed me, too. Looking back, I guess it wasn't a good change for either of us. In hindsight, I guess that's why the Creator bestowed the human animal with a conscience. Some use that conscience to correct past mistakes while others use that conscience to make excuses for past actions. And if you live long enough, sometimes that conscience is just an old man talking . . .*

*Anyway, that morning, we found gold coin in each of those Kickapoo's medicine bags. And one of the bags also held something very interesting . . . a hand-drawn map with two Xs. One X showed the location where we were ambushed, and the other X showed the town of Guerrero.*

*I know in today's world that wouldn't prove a thing, but in Pure's and my world . . . back then . . . that was proof enough. E.B. had paid those fellas to take our lives . . . and Pure reckoned they wouldn't be the only owl hoots in Mexico carrying around gold coin in exchange for our heads.*

# Thirty-One

*December 1878*
*Nuevo Laredo, Tamaulipas, Mexico*

E.B. stared at the thin copper-skinned man with his back pushed against the trunk of a squat mesquite tree. The man held a fist-sized red onion in his left hand. The onion was missing a large chunk of its flesh.

The man stared back, but on the face of it held little interest in E.B. or Nate.

E.B. noticed that the onion was straight out of the ground as it still held a fair amount of dirt on its outer shell. The man chewed contentedly on the vegetable, unfazed by either E.B.'s or Nate's presence. Five other men dressed in serapes and wide-brimmed sombreros lounged near-by.

E.B. glanced down the left side of the man's well-worn shirt.

The man followed E.B.'s gaze.

A polished Texas Ranger badge drooped from where a pocket once resided on the shirt.

E.B. raised his eyes. "You go as the law around here?"

The man lifted the index finger of his right hand to indicate he needed a minute and then continued chewing.

E.B. inhaled deeply to express his impatience.

The man grinned and then motioned the onion toward E.B., before swallowing the piece in his mouth.

E.B.'s neck flushed a deep red.

The man shrugged and took another bite. "Keeps you from airin' the caboose," he said. His smile widened and exposed a mouth full of brown teeth.

"I asked you a question," E.B. pressed again.

The man straightened and scratched his nose. "Nah, I ain't the law-doer 'round here, that's for sure."

E.B. arched his right eyebrow. "What about the badge?"

The man glanced down and lifted the sagging tin star with his thumb and index finger. "I got this off a dead fella across the border last year."

"What kinda dead fella?"

"A Ranger, I suppose. He was wearing this badge anyways."

"So where can I find the law here?"

The man leaned back against the mesquite and chuckled quietly to himself.

E.B.'s face reddened more. "Did I say something funny?"

Nate glanced around the street and tossed a quick look at each of the five men. They seemed uninterested in the conversation between E.B. and the man with the badge. *Siesta*, he thought.

The man lifted his right boot and secured it squarely on the tree. "Yeah, I guess you did, friend."

E.B. frowned and bulled forward two steps.

With cat-like quickness, the five lounging men sprang to life and drew double-pistols from under their serapes.

"Careful, friend," the man said.

E.B. stopped and took a shallow breath.

Nate raised his hands, palms out, and smiled. "Easy everybody . . . easy."

"Now, friend, why on earth are you going on such about the law?" the man asked.

E.B. exhaled with a smile. "Nothing concerning," he said. "I just like knowing where the law hides out whenever I come into an unfamiliar place."

"Old habit?"

"Suppose so."

"Sometimes old habits can git a man into trouble."

"Suppose they can," E.B. replied and shrugged.

The man raised his brow and widened his eyes. "Sometimes old habits can even git a man killed dead."

"I suppose that's true enough, friend."

The man took another bite of onion and chewed sloppily. "Curiosity can do the same thing to a fella."

E.B. smiled. "Well, I've never had a tendency toward that disposition."

The man twisted his mouth around the word. "Dispo . . . sis . . . shun. What's that?" he asked.

"Disposition, you know, inclined to being a curious sort."

The man nodded and dug a finger inside his lower lip. After a fair amount of exploring, he withdrew the finger and studied the fingertip intently. A sliver of onion skin rested on the nail. "Probably a good way to be," he said and then stuck the finger back in his mouth.

E.B. kept his smile and tolerated the man's display.

The man sucked on the end of his finger and nodded to himself. After re-chewing the onion skin, he swallowed, and wiped his finger across the front of his trousers. When he finished, he studied the cleaned finger and then looked back up at E.B. and Nate. "So you boys are looking for the law around here?"

"No, we were just wondering if there was law around here."

"Hmmm," the man said. "What's the difference?"

E.B. scratched the back of his neck in a deliberate fashion. "Maybe none," he said.

"Hmmm," the man said again.

E.B. watched the man closely.

"Are you an outlaw?" the man asked in false concern. He looked around at his companions.

E.B.'s smile widened and seemed to fill his entire face.

"'Cause we don't see many outlaws down this way."

A chorus of subdued laughter broke out among the man's friends.

E.B. narrowed his eyes. He chuckled to himself. "No, I'm just an old man come to make a fresh start in Mexico."

The man looked at his consorts and motioned with his thumb at E.B. "He's just an old man come to make a fresh start in Mexico," he laughed.

The men nodded with broad grins.

The man turned his attention back to E.B. "Those are some nice spurs strapped to your heels."

E.B. glanced down at his boots and then back to the man. "I suppose they are."

"You kill someone?" asked the man.

"Not today."

The man laughed aloud. "Someone riding after you?"

E.B. looked back toward the border. "Could be."

"Are you afraid to fight, old man come to make a fresh start in Mexico?"

E.B. ignored the question. "I was hoping to maybe find some men?"

The man rolled his eyes. "There's men down here in Mexico, that's a fact."

"Maybe six or so."

The man started a headcount on his consorts. He flashed a finger toward each and with a gush of exaggeration mouthed, *one, two, three, four, five . . .*

"Men who might slow down the men who might be following me."

The man pushed his counting finger into his own chest. "Six," he said.

E.B. forced himself to smile pleasantly at the man's game.

The man feigned seriousness. "You want to hire these, maybe six or so, men?"

E.B. nodded. "Just 'til I can make ready for the men who might be following me and my boy."

"I could go around and see if there are any men here who might do that for you."

E.B. grinned. "I'd be much obliged to you."

"Anything for a friend, friend."

E.B. glanced back at Nate.

Nate lifted his shoulders up, confused by the banter between E.B. and the man.

The man scratched the side of his head and yawned. "And the men you hire, what is it you want them to do . . . exactly . . . to these men who might be following you?"

E.B. returned his gaze to the man. "Stall them."

"Stall them?"

"Yep."

"That's it?"

"Maybe bust them up a bit"

"Stall them and bust them up a bit."

"Yep."

"How many are there . . . of these men who might be following you?"

"Two." E.B. said.

"Two?"

"Two."

The man wrinkled his forehead. "Two men?"

"Yep."

"These two men who might be following you must be some buckaroos."

"They might have killed a bunch of Kickapoo just this side of the Bravo two days ago."

The man leaned in close to E.B. "Do tell," he said.

"Not much to tell, really. These men who might be following me might have killed twelve Kickapoo, that's all."

The man looked down and then suddenly tossed the onion at E.B.

E.B. instinctively caught the vegetable with one hand, while the other hand pulled his pistol.

The man frowned briefly, nodded, and then smiled. Knowing.

E.B. rolled his hand over and dropped the onion to the ground in front of the man.

"You hire these Kickapoo who might have been killed?" the man asked.

"Might have."

The man looked at E.B.'s Colt. "You gonna put that away?"

E.B. shrugged and holstered the pistol. "You think you can find me some men?"

The man lifted a hand to his face, thinking. He tapped his index finger slowly against his cheek. "These men, who might be following you, and this job, both sound dangerous."

"Could be," said E.B. "Seems most jobs are these days."

The man inhaled. "It's the times," he said and grinned.

"Probably so."

"How do you know these men will come through Nuevo Laredo?" the man asked.

"You let me worry about that. You worry about them after they ride through Nuevo Laredo."

The man flashed a snarl. "Riding to where?"

"Guerrero."

The man tightened his lips and shook his head. "I don't know," he said with some reservation.

"The job pays fifty in gold coin."

"Fifty?"

"Yep."

"In gold coin?"

"Per man."

"Per man, you say?"

"I do."

"Hmmm."

"Half now . . . the other half when you've completed the job."

The man's expression turned to distrust. "And how will we find you afterward?"

"I'll be around."

"Mexico is a big place, friend."

E.B. exposed a wide grin. "I'll draw you a map," he said.

The man stepped forward and picked up the onion. He rubbed the vegetable against his dirty shirt and took a bite. "You must be one of those wealthy U.S. fellas."

"No, just an old man come to make a fresh start in Mexico."

The man lifted his chin and howled in laughter.

The five moved closer to the man eating the onion. Each exposed a wide smile while they holstered their pistols.

"Well?" E.B. asked.

The man chewed the onion with a wide-opened mouth. Spittle and pieces of the vegetable flew toward E.B. "Sure, but to tell you the truth old man come to make a fresh start in Mexico, the boys and me, hell, we probably would have taken the job for fifty for the lot of us."

# THIRTY-TWO

*December 1878*
*Nuevo Laredo, Tamaulipas, Mexico*

P ure and July rode into Nuevo Laredo on Christmas day. The stench of black powder, explosive residue from the previous night's celebration, drifted in the air and hung-over citizens languished in various stages of repose around the dirt square.

Pure studied the drunks with a keen eye. "E.B. sure wanted us to ride this way," he said. "Wonder why?"

"Can't say, but the map certainly made it easy," July answered. His eyes darted around the street counting the sleeping men. "Or convenient."

Pure's head swiveled from left to right. "Must have been quite a party."

"These sheep raising types always seem to imbibe," July said. "That's a fact."

"What have you got against sheep?" Pure asked. He rolled the Snapping and Stretching gum in his mouth.

July swiveled and scanned the street behind them. "They're nasty animals," he said.

A low chuckle rolled in Pure's chest. "You remember what C.A. always said about sheep?"

July frowned. His brow tightened. "Can't rightly say that I do."

Pure lifted the reins with his left hand. His right hand naturally lingered above his Colt. "Whoa," he said softly. His eyes locked on a figure sitting on a bench outside of a mud-bricked hut. The man's sombrero was pulled down low on his forehead and hid his face. A full bottle of a yellow-colored liquid rested beside him.

July followed Pure's lead and pulled back on his left rein. "Whoa, horse," he said.

Pure tilted his head to the right and tried to see the sitting man's face.

July waited patiently for several seconds and then asked, "Are you gonna tell me what C.A. said about sheep?"

Pure lifted his head and frowned. He pointed at the man in front of the hut and then glanced over at July. "What's that fella doing?"

"Where?"

"Over there."

July glanced toward the man. "From here, it looks like he's eating something."

Pure glanced back over his shoulder. He studied their trail. "Something about this square gives me the shakes."

July shook his head and muttered, "Something about being out of the U.S. gives me the shakes."

Pure turned back at the man in front of the hut. "Something ain't right with that fella."

July squinted at the man and then looked at Pure. "I think he's eating a date palm or maybe an apple."

Pure fidgeted in the saddle. His hand gripped the Peacemaker's handle. The Snapping and Stretching gum bounced between his front teeth.

July followed Pure's hand movement. The Reston boss's hand nervously clutched and then relaxed on his pistol grip. "Now you're making me nervous," he said.

"He said they were creatures come into the world just looking for a place to die."

"Huh?"

"Sheep."

July dropped his chin and stared at Pure. "What?"

Pure fixed his gaze on the bottle next to the sitting man. "It's what C.A. said about sheep."

"We back to that, now?"

"Well, you were asking."

"That was a while back, before this fella with the apple got the hair on your neck standing at attention."

"He said a sheep was a creature come into the world just looking for a place to die."

July relaxed and thought for a few seconds. "I guess that sounds just like C.A.," he said.

"It's that fella's bottle," Pure mumbled. His knuckles whitened around the Peacemaker's rubber handle.

"Huh?" July said and glanced over at the bottle resting next to the man. "It's full."

July directed his gaze on the man resting in front of the hut. "Appears so."

"That seems strange after a night of festivities."

July gazed at Pure and shook his head, grinning.

"Look at him," Pure said.

July's eyes darted back to the man.

The man's left hand disappeared under the brim of his sombrero.

July leaned over the front of his saddle and watched the man with great interest.

Pure made a face. "You'd figure the bottle would be empty . . ."

July didn't wait for Pure to finish. "Or near empty after a long fiesta."

"In my experience, men that observe holidays with a full bottle don't usually give up until the bottle's finished," Pure said.

July watched the man's head rise slightly. The man raised his hand toward his mouth once more. July caught a brief glance of what rested in the man's hand. He smiled with a quick shake of his head. "I'll be," he said.

"What's that?"

"He's eating an onion."

Pure let his eyes drift away from the bottle and over to the man. "An onion?"

"Yep."

Pure drew back his lips in disgust and squinted hard. "I reckon that's something a man doesn't get to witness everyday."

"Not especially pleasing to the eye."

"Or to the mind."

"Probably why his bottle is still full."

Pure tossed a quick glance at July and shrugged questioningly. "How's that?"

"It's an old wives tale," July explained. "Eating a raw onion like that causes your stomach to bloat, so you don't get so drunk when you're on a bender."

"Well, I sure couldn't drink mescal and eat an onion in the same set-to."

"Takes some constitution, that's for sure."

Pure turned his gaze back to the man and scratched the back of his neck. After a long minute, he shook the rein and clicked his tongue. The Kickapoo mount started forward. "Watch your back," he whispered to July.

July nodded and kept a long stare on the man sitting in front of the hut as he rode by.

The man kept his eyes hidden under the sombrero.

The peaceful silence of the street suddenly seemed sinister and foreshadowing.

"Pure?" July said in a hushed voice.

"Yeah?"

"Explain to me again what we're doing in old Mexico."

Pure looked down the road and didn't answer.

July looked back at the man with the onion. "Pure?" he called out softly.

Pure kept his eyes focused on the road ahead. "I heard you the first time."

"You figure to answer?"

"Come to get our gold coin, mostly."

"Mostly?"

"I reckon we also come to kill Gunns."

July exhaled. "Outside our own country."

"Yeah."

"Ain't that illegal?"

"I reckon Mexico law wouldn't hold favor with such planned activities."

July glanced back at the slumbering figures around the street. "Just who is the law in these border towns anyway?"

Pure straightened at the question. He didn't answer immediately. After several seconds of thought, he said, "Down here most localities have a top dog called the caudillo."

"El jefe."

"Yep."

"And who takes care of problems for the caudillo?"

Pure tossed a brief glance at July. "Probably men like those back behind us."

"Like that man eating the onion?"

"Yep."

"Like those men lounging around the street."

"Yep."

"Pure?"

"Yeah?"

July tossed another hurried look back over his shoulder. "You know what?"

"What?"

"You've got me feeling like one of those damned sheep right about now," July mumbled.

# Thirty-Three

*December 1878*
*On the Road to Ciudad Guerrero, Tamaulipas, Mexico*

⮕◆⮔

Five miles outside of Nuevo Laredo, the road to Guerrero turned west for a hundred yards. Pure reined the Kickapoo horse from the road and headed for a free-standing ridge of rock twenty-yards away. He maneuvered the horse around the wind-eroded slope.

July urged the piebald to follow.

The inside wall of the formation was lower than the outside and offered a hiding place for the men and their horses from any eyes traveling to Guerrero.

"What are we doing?" July asked.

"Making ready."

"I'm almost afraid to ask why," July said.

"There'll be men following."

"More the reason to keep breezing these ponies."

"We keep running we might not find a place to stop."

July glanced back down the road to Nuevo Laredo. He watched patiently for some sign of pursuit. "Seems quiet enough."

"They'll be coming."

"Uh-huh," July hummed.

"Won't be long."

July let the humming die in his throat. "I'm beginning to feel like nothing good ever happens to a Texas cowboy in old Mexico."

Pure's expression turned serious and reflective. "The way our luck has been drifting lately," he said. "I can't really say that I can tell the difference between Mexico and Texas anymore."

July smiled grimly. "I reckon I can still separate the two in my head."

Pure nodded and pulled his Colt. He opened the ejector gate and checked his loads. "It'll be that fella eating the onion," he said without looking up.

"And the others too?"

"Yep."

"Coming at us like the Kickapoo?"

"Probably."

July pulled his Colt and checked his loads. After he finished, he closed the gate, and then glanced back down the road. "We just going to wait here and let 'em go by?"

Pure pushed the gate closed on his Peacemaker and slipped the gun back into its holster. "Or kill them."

"What's that?"

"Or kill them."

July pushed his hat to the back of his head. "Shoot 'em in the back?"

"Well that would be one way of killing them."

July's face strained. "What about questioning 'em first?"

Pure stepped down from his mount. He began to chew the Snapping and Stretching gum rapidly between his front teeth. "You do remember that there's going to be more than a couple of these fellas riding here for us?"

July nodded. "At least six by my count back in Nuevo Laredo."

"And you figure they'll be of a mind to answer our questions?"

"When you say it like that, no."

"How else would I say it, July?"

"No need to get riled?"

Pure pounded the Snapping and Stretching between his top and lower teeth. "Who said I'm riled?"

July rolled his right leg over the saddle cantle and stepped out of the stirrup. "You know you do that whenever you have you're mind set to a thing?"

The gum flattened between Pure's teeth. "What's that?"

"The gum."

Pure stopped chewing. "What about the gum?"

"You chew it real fast between your top and bottom front teeth."

Pure leaned in close to his horse and untied his lasso from the saddle ring.

"Hmmmph," he muttered and then resumed chewing. He grasped the lasso in his right hand and started for the dirt road.

"What are you going to do?" July called out.

"See if I can snare some varmints."

"You need my help?"

"Be nice."

July followed Pure south down the road, toward Guerrero.

Fifty yards from the rock ridge, Pure stopped and held out one end of the rope. "Take this end," he said and pointed to a small mesquite across the road. "And tie it to that tree."

July dragged the lasso to the tree and tied a half-hitch knot four feet up the trunk. "You aim to snap these fellas from their horses?" he asked and pulled against his rope to check his knot.

"No, just stop them in front of it."

July glanced back to where the horses stood hidden. "That rock formation makes a pretty good ambuscade."

Pure wrapped his end of the lasso around a chest-high stand of oak scrub. "Uh-huh."

"We going to hide behind it and wait for these fellas?"

"You are. I'm going to settle in amongst those rocks behind me on this side of the road."

"Are we coming out shooting or talking?"

Pure ignored the question. "All of them will be hung-over, I reckon."

"What about the one with the full bottle?"

Pure thought for a minute and then pushed the Snapping and Stretching gum into his lower lip. "'Cepting him," he said.

"Shooting or talking? I need to be prepared."

Pure glanced up. "What's your take on E.B. hiring out for our killing?"

July smirked. "I imagine old E.B. isn't partial to even odds in his killings."

Pure lowered his chin. "We'll be needing to kill them all 'cept full-bottle."

July nodded. "So we need to kill five?"

"Five or six."

"Two against five or six?"

"I reckon the numbers will improve once we start shooting."

"I suppose."

"July?"

"Yeah?"

"Maybe this will make it easier."

"What's that?"

"We just need to kill everyone but full-bottle."

"So you said."

"That way no counting is involved."

July nodded again and rubbed the back of his hand across his mouth. "Pure?"

"Yeah?"

"All this killing . . . it ever make it hard for you to sleep at night?"

Pure straightened and locked eyes with July. "Hell, I haven't had a good night's sleep since last April."

"You figure it's gonna be that way for the rest of our lives?"

"Probably. We'll get used to it, someday, I suppose . . . I hope so anyway."

July exhaled a long exhausted breath, turned, and shuffled toward the rock formation. "Me too," he muttered.

"July?"

July stopped and turned his head back over his shoulder. "Yeah?"

"How come you waited so long to tell me?"

The ranch foreman frowned to signal his confusion to the question.

"You know . . . about the gum?"

July gave a quick shake of his head. "I don't know, today just seemed like the right time to tell you."

Pure nodded. "Well, thanks for that."

In the distance, a horse grunted.

Pure turned back north and listened. After a few seconds, he glanced over at July and nodded. "That'll be full-bottle," he said coolly and then hurried for his hiding spot.

# THIRTY-FOUR

*December 1878*
*On the Road to Ciudad Guerrero, Tamaulipas, Mexico*

J uly stroked the piebald's muzzle in a circular motion to keep the animal calm. He peered out to the road from his hidden vantage point and watched as the six riders from Nuevo Laredo pulled rein at the lasso stretched across the road. Then suddenly, from the corner of his eye, a blur of movement caught his attention. Pure had exited the hiding spot and with long, purposeful, yet hurried steps. He rushed forward toward the assassins. July's hand instinctively fell from the horse's lower lip and to his Peacemaker.

Pure's gun exploded.

Once, twice, three times.

A man straightened then arched backward. An anguished groan spewed from his mouth.

*The killing's begun.*

July sprinted from behind the rock formation, Colt raised and firing.

Chaos ensued quickly enough.

Horses reared.

Men cursed and grabbed for pistols.

The pop, pop, pop, of bushwhacking gunfire continued at full strength.

Men began to die.

One of the riders drooped forward with a heavy scream.

Another slumped sideways and rolled off his mount.

The unmistakable fragrance of gun powder filled July's nostrils. He tossed a quick glance down to his right hand. His Colt bucked vertically.

Another assassin slid to the ground.

July watched the serape flutter above the falling man and then settle

181

unceremoniously, yet peacefully around the dead figure.

Full-bottle reined his horse left with a shout of, "Heeyah!" The assassin attempted to skirt the ambush around the stretched rope barrier.

Pure raised his Peacemaker at full-bottle's maneuver with a focused and steady aim. He pulled on the trigger. Blood exploded from the horse's neck. The animal screamed and stumbled to its knees. Full-bottle pitched forward and sailed over the horse's head.

July kept his approach for the remaining figure.

The man reined his horse around and unleashed three rapid shots at July while spurring his horse back in the direction of Nuevo Laredo.

July stood straight with dogged determination. He lifted the Colt to eye level and steadied his shooting wrist with his left hand.

The horse sprinted past July at a building gallop. The man's pistol clicked empty. He reached for the second pistol.

July swiveled at the waist.

The man turned in the saddle and fired wildly.

July squeezed his left eye shut and sighted the escaping assassin with his right eye. He pulled the trigger in rapid succession.

The fleeing man fell and bounced twice on the road.

July lowered his gun and inhaled deeply.

"Shoot that horse!"

July turned and looked at Pure in confusion.

"Shoot that horse, July! Don't let him get back to Nuevo Laredo!"

July wheeled. The Colt rose automatically. The gun belched smoke and fire. The horse stumbled forward.

July inhaled and holstered the Colt. He licked his lower lip and then dragged his gun hand shirtsleeve across his forehead. He paused for several seconds and then glanced back at Pure.

"You did good," Pure said.

July nodded. "Don't feel like good," he said. "Now, we're shooting horses."

"No time for that."

July stood in the road, slack-faced. "I know," he said.

Pure motioned for July to join him. "Give me a hand here," he shouted. "It's time we got on with asking full-bottle a few questions."

# THIRTY-FIVE

*December 1878*
*On the Road to Ciudad Guerrero, Tamaulipas, Mexico*

F ull-bottle sat up. He glanced about the roadway. His expression showed disbelief and shock. He dabbed at a red welt rising on his forehead and began to ramble with lack of clear thought. "You fellas are in a heap of trouble, ambushing us like that."

Pure pushed the Snapping and Stretching gum back in his mouth. "That so?"

"The law won't go for this."

"What law?" Pure asked. He looked over at July. "Did you see any law in Nuevo Laredo?"

July stuck out his bottom lip and shook his head.

Pure looked back at full-bottle. "He didn't see any law either."

"We . . . all of us . . . are law abiding citizens here."

Pure looked back at July. "Did you see any law abiding citizens in town?"

July shook his head again.

Pure returned his gaze to full-bottle. "He didn't see any of those either."

Full-bottle exhaled a sliver of breath through a half-opened mouth. He appeared flustered. Well . . . the town will sure enough get a posse together and hunt you down and string you up for this."

Pure leaned over and backhanded the man across his left cheek.

Full-bottle's eyes widened. His left hand was immediately drawn to his cheek. He rubbed his reddening flesh in a circular fashion.

Pure leaned in close to the man and winced at the smell emanating from the man's mouth. "Law abiding citizens don't wear double-holstered pistols," he said, his voice rising with each word. "Law abiding citizens don't follow two men riding through their town!"

183

The man's expression dropped. He looked from Pure to July. "You fellas going to kill me?"

Pure glanced over at July. "Your call."

Full-bottle tensed and waited for July's answer.

"Probably so," July said.

Pure straightened and looked at full-bottle with dark eyes. "Maybe not . . . that is if you tell us what we want to know."

Full-bottle dropped his gaze to the ground between his legs.

Pure pushed the Snapping and Stretching gum forward to his front teeth and began to chomp loudly. "It's your call."

Full-bottle glanced up. A hapless look hung on his face. After several seconds, his gaze dropped back to the ground. "Whataya want to know?"

"How come you come after us the way you did?"

Full-bottle let loose with a yielding exhale and stammered, "There . . . there was two of them."

Pure leaned in close. "What'd they look like?"

"One of them wore a fancy pair of handcrafted spurs."

Pure's face flushed in realization. He squatted in front of full-bottle and bore his gaze deep into the man's eyes. "They give you their names?"

Full-bottle looked up at Pure and then glanced to July. He shook his head blankly and issued a whispered, "No."

"And I don't suppose you asked?" Pure said.

Full-bottle made a face and twisted in the dirt.

July bore a hard gaze into full-bottle. "Those Texas boys weren't as green as you figured were they mister?"

Full-bottle grabbed a handful of dirt and then flung it back into the ground between his legs.

Pure reached forward and pinched full-bottle's chin between his thumb and forefinger. He swiveled the assassin's face toward him. "What'd they pay?" he asked and dug his thumb into the man's flesh.

Full-bottle winced. He looked blankly into Pure's eyes for a handful of seconds, then answered, "Fifty in gold coin."

July whistled and looked over at Pure. "The price on our heads is going up."

"Twenty-five up front. The rest when we finished."

Pure dropped full-bottle's chin and stood up. "Finished what?"

Full-bottle's expression changed. "Only slowing you fellas down from their trail."

Pure placed both hands on his hips and bit down on his lower lip. "That's it? Just slow us down?"

"Bust you up too, if we had the opportunity."

The Snapping and Stretching gum rolled onto Pure's bottom lip. "Not kill us?" he asked. His voice betrayed his distrust.

"Nope, the man never said that," Full-bottled argued.

Pure sucked the gum back inside his mouth and began to chew. "Fifty in gold coin and you didn't have to kill us?"

"Them boys never said nothing about killing you."

Pure looked over at July. "How's that story sound to you?"

"About right. You?"

Pure chewed the Snapping and Stretching gum faster. "About right."

July grinned. "Old E.B. sure likes his game to be crippled up some before he faces them head-on."

Pure nodded in stark realization of E.B.'s plan. "There's probably another group waiting down the road."

"Reckon so."

Full-bottle glanced up. "You fellas gonna kill me?"

"Still deciding," Pure answered without a glance at the man.

"There'll be another group at the next map's X."

Pure nodded, thought for a second, then shot a hard look at full-bottle. "He leave you a map?"

Full-bottle winced and shook his head. "Yeah."

Pure extended his right hand. "Let's have it," he said.

Full-bottle reached into his shirt pocket and withdrew a scrap of dirty pasteboard. He extended the map toward Pure's outstretched hand.

Pure snatched the map and studied the charcoal drawing. After a minute, he handed the map to July. "Appears E.B. is leading us back to the Rio Grande east of Guerrero."

July looked carefully at the map. A large X was drawn on the Mexican side of the river. He nodded and then thrust the map in full-bottle's face.

"What is this place?"

Full-bottle's knees shook uncontrollably. He ignored the map and looked ay July. "You fellas gonna kill me?"

Pure's right hand brushed the handle of his Colt. "The man asked you a question."

"You can both have the gold coin."

"It belongs to us in the first place," July uttered and then rattled the map once more, violently. "What is this place?"

"*Pueblo bandito.*"

Pure stopped chewing and muttered, "Bandit town."

Full-bottle nodded once. "It's a bad place."

"What goes on there?" July asked.

"It's the place where American bandits and Mexican bandits exchange stolen cattle."

July looked away. "Sounds about right," he said.

Pure glanced at July and then back to full-bottle. "Get-up," he said.

"You gonna kill me?"

Pure walked over to full-bottle's dead horse and removed a length of piggin' string from a rawhide tie. "Only if you ask me again," he said. "Put your hands behind you."

Full-bottle obeyed reluctantly.

Pure pushed both wrists together and then expertly tied the man's hands behind his back. "How many men in this bandit town?" he asked.

Full-bottle took a second to think. "This time of year? Probably no more than a handful. It gets busier in the spring."

Pure lifted up on full-bottle's bound wrists and roughly guided him toward the rock formation.

"Hey! What are you doing?"

"Is it a real town?"

Full-bottle showed a pained expression. "Hey!"

Pure lifted the assassin's bound wrists higher. "Is it a real town?"

No . . . no, it's just a bunch of canvas tents."

Pure lowered the man's wrists. He glanced over at July. "Whataya think?"

"I guess we should ride for the river and take a look."

"No, I mean about full-bottle here."

Full-bottle's head turned sharply. He tried to glance back over his right shoulder at Pure. "You gonna kill me?" he asked. A desperate panic sounded in his question.

July stopped and pushed his eyebrows together. He looked intently at Pure. "Seems to be a pleasant enough fella."

"Pleasant enough to try and kill us."

"Well, there was that," July said.

"We can't let him go back to Nuevo Laredo."

July lifted his brow, thinking. "Or to bandit town to announce our arrival."

Full-bottle gasped. "Honest fellas, we didn't sign on to kill you. I give you my word on that."

Pure looked around the road at the dead bodies.

July glanced back toward Nuevo Laredo and the dead assassins. "We could put him to work burying his friends."

Pure rolled the Snapping and Stretching gum to the back of his jaw. "That's what I'm thinking."

"I'll do that," full-bottle panted. "Clean it up so that no one would ever know what went down here. I'll even gather up the coin off these boys and give it back to you fellas."

Pure's face hardened in disgust. "We're not taking coin off dead men."

July glared at full-bottle and shook his head. "That's bad luck," he said.

Pure reached toward his belt and lifted the thick-bladed knife from its scabbard. "And don't you take any of it either. You bury it with your friends."

"And after all that?" July asked.

Pure cut the piggin' string and glanced east. "I guess he goes with us."

Full-bottle's expression dropped. His face turned ashen.

July pursed his lips together and nodded.

"That way, he can collect the rest of the coin he's owed from E.B." Pure said.

"But . . . but, I don't even have anything to ride," Full-bottle stuttered.

July glanced around at the carnage of dead men and horses. "He's right about that, Pure. We did kill every horse."

"Well," Pure smirked. "Then it appears our friend here will just have to ride shank's mare to bandit town."

# THIRTY-SIX

*December 1878*
*Bandit Town, Mexico*

———◆———

E.B. hunched over a lechuguilla mat and cupped his hands around a tin of coffee. Across from him sat a man dressed in tattered wool trousers and a dirty undershirt. The man drank from a similar tin cup but made an irritating slurping sound with each swallow.

Nate sat slightly to the left of his father. Son and father stared at the man with equal portions of distaste and wonderment.

As if he sensed the stare, the man glanced up, glared at Nate, and smacked his lips vocally. "Ah!" he said with a fair amount of belligerence.

Nate made a face.

The man smiled and then took another loud drink.

E.B. uncupped his hands from the coffee and pulled at his beard with a rough stroke of his right hand. Good coffee," he said.

"I can't think of the time I've ever had bad coffee," the man answered, still eyeing Nate.

"Sorta like a woman," E.B. spouted.

"Sorta," the man said, and then motioned at Nate. "This your pup?"

E.B.'s eyes darted left briefly. "He's the only survivor from of a litter of six," he said flatly.

"I don't like the way he looks at me," the man said and curled his lip up. "Like he's trying to get me angered up on purpose."

Nate tightened his mouth and leaned forward. He started to rise.

E.B. pushed his right arm into Nate's chest and smiled at the man. "That ain't how it is, friend."

The man pushed the cup to his mouth and made a loud sucking noise.

When he lowered the cup, he smiled briefly at Nate and then set his gaze on E.B. "Suppose you tell me then, how it is . . . friend."

E.B. let his arm fall away from Nate's chest. "Like I said earlier—,"

The man smiled smugly. "You're looking to hire some men to git some fellas trailing you to quit trailing you."

"Not quit so much as slow down some."

"And why would I or anyone else want to help you, friend?"

"Cause there's gold coin in it for you."

The man stared at his coffee tin and shook his head slowly. A large grin spread across his face. "You're a brave man."

E.B. returned the man's grin.

"Not many would have the grit to ride into bandit town and announce they're carrying gold coin with them."

E.B. looked down at his pistol and then back into the man's eyes. "Wouldn't have said it were I not pretty good with the pistol."

The man glanced over his shoulder. "There are five others here that might be your equal with that pistol."

"Might be," E.B. muttered. "But don't overlook the boy here."

"The pup shoots like his pa does he?"

"Shoots straight enough."

The man twisted his head slightly to the right and made a face. "Still . . . considering we're six against your two."

"But it ain't really the shooting is it?"

"How's that?"

"When everything else is stripped away, it's not about the shooting, only about the killing."

"Makes sense," the man said.

E.B. lowered his hands.

"Careful," the man said and dropped his hand to his Colt.

E.B. offered a tight smile and lifted the front of his shirt up to his neck. Six circular, red-welts adorned his stomach and chest area. "See these came from shooting."

The man lifted his brow in acknowledgment.

"From a couple of blue-bellies during the war."

"Uh-huh."

"But the two of them . . . well . . . their shooting didn't actually do any killing," E.B. said and released his grip on his shirt. "You see what I'm saying, friend?"

The man nodded and kept a hard stare on E.B. After five-seconds, he lifted his chin and laughed aloud. "Mister, you're either the craziest or most dangerous soul I've ever met."

"My pa always said I was little bit of both."

The man lowered his head and exhaled a gush of breath through his nose. His expression took a sudden turn to serious. "So what's your proposition?"

"You slow down the men following us."

"You don't want these fellas killed?"

"Nobody said nothing about me not wanting these men killed."

The man wrinkled his brow. "You trying to be funny, mister?"

"No."

"Well what's this talk about hiring us to slow down some fellas you want killed but don't want us to kill them?"

"The boy and I'll kill them when the time allows that it is right to do so."

The man pushed back from the table. "Well that's all fine and dandy, friend, but what if these fellas decide they want to kill us?"

E.B. glanced around the camp. "Like you said, there's six of you."

The man's face flushed. His eyes narrowed into tiny dark slits. "And how many of these fellas?"

"Same as us."

"Two?"

"Yep."

The man took a breath and scratched his chin. "Mister, what kinda game are you running here?"

"No game."

The man leaned forward and rested his elbows on the lechuguilla mat.

E.B. shrugged. "Pays a hundred per gun."

The man stared deep into E.B.'s eyes. "For not killing?"

"That's my offer."

"These fellas, they gun hands?"

"They sure shoot like they are."

"Somehow, I figured that."

"A hundred per gun."

"So you said."

"You seem like a man who's more than capable," E.B. said.

"Six hundred for the job?"

E.B. closed one eye and appeared deep in thought. After five seconds passed, he opened his eye and said, "That's how I add it up."

The man dragged the back of his hand across his mouth. "Something don't figure right here."

"Nobody's holding a pistol to your head, friend."

The man straightened with a hard jerk. "What's that suppose to mean?" he barked.

E.B. looked down at the lechuguilla mat. The atmosphere around the table turned cold. He placed both hands on his coffee tin and spun the cup like a top before looking back at the man. "It means, friend, do you want the job, or do you figure to just waste me and my boy's time?"

"Might be easier for me and the boys to just shoot you and the pup."

"Might be."

"Then we take your gold and never have to worry about not killing these fellas trailing you."

"Sounds like a pretty fair plan."

The man leaned back and folded his arms across his chest, self-satisfied.

"The only problem I see in it, is taking the gold."

The man tilted his head slightly side-ways. "How's that?"

"Well, for starters, it belongs to those two fellas trailing us here."

The man slammed both hands down on the table, furious. "You're bringing the very men that you stole from into our hideout?"

The spinning tin cup popped into the air.

E.B. snatched the cup with cat-like quickness. "Pays a hundred per gun in them fellas' gold coin."

"A hundred per gun for slowing these two down."

"Half now, half when the job's done."

"Where you two gonna be while we slow these fellas down?"

"Close by."

"How do I know you'll pay the other half?"

E.B. didn't say anything.

"Mexico's a big place."

"So, I've heard."

"I need some assurance on where you two will be hiding . . . close by."

"Preparing."

"What?"

"We'll be preparing to kill these two, not hiding out."

"If that's what you say."

"I'll draw a map."

"What?"

"I'll draw you a map of exactly where me and my son will be."

The man scratched behind his ear and glanced down at E.B.'s boots.

"I'll put a big X on it for you."

"I'll be needing those spurs as well," the man grinned. "Call it collateral."

E.B. lifted his chin. "We'll see."

"No, the spurs come with the deal or you two fellas can fight your own battle."

E.B. pursed his lips and then clenched his jaw. "Well, I don't see any cause to negotiate a fairer price than that."

The man held out his right hand. "I'll be taking my coin and spurs now."

E.B. reached down and unstrapped his left spur. He lifted the spur from the heel of his boot and held it across the table. "Half now . . . half when the job's done."

# THIRTY-SEVEN

*December 1878*
*Near Bandit Town, Mexico*

━━━━◦◆◦━━━━

Pure and July lay in a thick stand of coyote willow situated on the upper bank of a large bend on the east side of the Rio Grande. Pure studied the movement and activity of Bandit Town with his long glass.

"How many?" July asked.

"I count six."

"E.B.?"

"No sign of him."

"Nate?"

Pure answered with a quick shake of his head.

"Whataya figure?"

Pure lowered the glass from his eye. "I 'spect there's another map in that camp."

July swallowed a half-chuckle.

Pure made a face. "What?"

"Well you have to admit that E.B. has pretty much thought out a good plan."

"How's that?"

"Well, he's running us from map to map fighting hired guns along the way."

"I suppose that's right."

"Got us using a lot of energy."

"And cartridges," Pure said.

"There's that too."

Pure pulled the Winchester even with his chest. "Maybe this plan of ours will surprise him a bit."

"Hope so."

"It will," Pure said.

July eased his rifle forward. He narrowed his eyes into a squint and lifted his chin toward Bandit Town. "I 'spect either way we're fixing to find out."

Pure braced the Winchester firm against his shoulder. "Yep."

Across the river, full-bottle stumbled straight into the bandit hideout. One of the bandits, gun drawn, rushed out to him.

July nudged Pure. "Look at that fella's right boot."

The man wore a single spur.

"Why would a man strap on a single spur?" Pure growled.

"Most likely belongs to someone we both knew."

Pure cursed under his breath.

"Yeah," July muttered.

Full-bottle and one-spur engaged in animated discussion for several minutes.

"Whataya think they're talking about?" asked July.

"I'm hoping full-bottle is telling him that the two men he was hired to kill are on the road just west of Bandit Town."

"We'll find that out in a minute or so."

Pure waited.

Another minute passed.

The remaining five bandits joined the first man.

One-spur yanked his pistol and pressed the barrel into full-bottle's chest.

A second passed.

One-spur cocked the pistol.

Full-bottle lifted his left arm and pointed across the camp and across the river.

"Uh-oh," Pure muttered.

One-spur turned and studied the far bank of the river.

July placed his finger on the Winchester's trigger and sighted in on the bandit's chest. "There goes the plan."

One-spur mouthed a string of cursing that echoed across the river.

Full-bottle turned and started to run for a stand of river cane.

One-spur turned quickly. He raised his pistol and fired once.

Full-bottle stopped mid-stride, arched his back, and then collapsed in a heap.

"Hell-fire," Pure muttered.

One-spur turned back and assumed a crouched position just as July squeezed the trigger. The bullet, aimed at the man's chest, struck the man slightly above the nose.

Bandit Town erupted into bedlam. The remaining bandits scurried for cover.

Pure fired and levered the rifle rapidly. His first shot hit one of the running bandits headed for one of the tents. The man crumbled and fell face-first in the sand.

July snapped off three quick shots. Two of the shots struck a bandit in the middle of his chest.

Return gunfire followed quickly.

"Those fellas' pistols are useless at this distance," July shouted out.

Pure sent another shot into the camp but the three remaining bandits had found cover in one of the tents.

A cloud of gunpowder drifted up through the willows.

"We best leave this spot. If those fellas have rifles in that tent, it ain't going to be hard to see where we're shooting from."

"Good idea," July said. He scooted out of the willow stand and down the backside of the bank to his horse.

Pure followed quickly.

In twenty seconds, both men were mounted.

"What now?" July asked.

Pure tightened his lips together, thinking. He rolled the Snapping and Stretching gum to his front teeth and looked across the river.

July shook his head and chambered a cartridge. "We'll let's do it then," he said.

Pure nodded and raked his spurs across the Kickapoo pony's ribs.

Five seconds later, both men topped the bank and raced across the Rio Grande, riding straight into Bandit Town.

# Thirty-Eight

*December 1878*
*Inside Bandit Town, Mexico*

Pure reined his mount to stop fifty yards in front of the tent that hid the three bandits. Calm, but working with a sense of urgency, he flipped the reins left and rolled off his mount's left side, simultaneously jerking the horse's head so that the animal's body moved parallel to the tent. Using the horse as cover, he held a firm grip on the reins, levered a round into the Winchester, and threw the rifle onto the saddle seat.

A hundred yards away, on the opposite side of the tent, July performed the same maneuver.

Confusion and disorder followed as a salvo of fire targeted the tent and its inhabitants. Near the front of the tent, a stringer of horses danced in place at the repeated explosions. Unfazed by the horses or the killing, Pure continued to sling murderous lead into the bandits' shelter.

Two minutes later, shredded in the fusillade of crossfire, the tent stood riddled with over twenty 44-40 cartridge rounds.

"Whoa!" Pure yelled.

July fired once more and then raised his Winchester off the saddle seat with a great exhale as a rush of smoke fled his rifle barrel and breezed toward the river.

Pure lowered the Winchester and began feeding fresh cartridges into the gun. "If anyone in that tent is still breathing, holler out now, before we start again!" he shouted.

A slight south wind pushed a deafening silence through the camp.

"I'm dead serious!" Pure yelled out and then levered a cartridge.

Cold silence.

Pure dropped the reins and slipped around his horse's flank. He studied the tent with strained attention, and after a deep breath, marched forward with the Winchester readied at eye level.

July hurried to meet Pure, his rifle raised and fit to fire.

Pure reached the tent opening first and flung back the flap with a wave of his Winchester's barrel. He pointed the rifle about the tent, all the while chomping the Snapping and Stretching gum between his front teeth.

"Done," he said and turned away.

July took a quick look inside the tent, inhaled once at the gore, and then settled the Winchester on his right shoulder. "Done," he repeated and backed away, unnerved.

Pure walked several yards away from the executions and faced July. "We need to find the map," he said.

July nodded but twisted his mouth in an uneasy manner.

"What?" Pure asked.

July paused three seconds before answering. "Something is beginning to feel muddled in all of this," he muttered.

"Muddled how?"

"I don't know. . . muddled strange, maybe."

Pure glanced back at the tent. He licked his lower lip and then chewed the Snapping and Stretching gum faster. "We best find that next map."

"How many men have we killed over here?"

"More than you can count on two hands."

"And why?"

"I don't follow your thinking, July."

"Why didn't E.B. and Nate just bushwhack us like they did everyone else in our crew?"

Pure turned and started for the body of one-spur. "Let's find the map, and then we'll talk about E.B. and Nate's doings."

July gave a reluctant nod and followed Pure toward the dead bandit.

Pure approached the dead man and rolled the body over with his rifle barrel. The man's tattered clothing didn't hold one pocket. He frowned and looked around the man. A sombrero rested on its crown six feet away. Pure walked over to the hat and looked inside. An exposed corner of folded cowhide rested inside the band. Pure bent down and picked up the sombrero. He removed the square piece of hide and let the hat drop to the ground. The signature X, which marked all of E.B.'s maps, immediately caught his eye. He unfolded the cow hide to its full size and studied the charcoaled lines carefully.

"Where's it pointing us to?" asked July.

Pure frowned and didn't answer. He stood speechless and began to chew the Snapping and Stretching gum faster. Angrier. Then he tossed a sudden, hard look back east toward the stand of coyote willow.

July noticed Pure's expression and stepped in close to look at the map. "What is it?" he asked.

"Hell-fire," Pure muttered.

"What?" July asked again and then glanced east.

"Get down!" Pure screamed and reached for July's shirt. He pulled hard on the buckskin material and forced July to the ground.

A warning shot whizzed overhead.

"What the—?" July hissed.

"I ain't going to kill you boys!" reverberated over the Rio Grande. The voice was familiar.

July looked up with an open mouth. His face flushed in disbelief.

"Hell-fire," Pure uttered. He spit the Snapping and Stretching gum into the sand.

Across the river, standing in front of the coyote willow stood E.B. and Nate Gunn, rifles in hand.

"Stay down, now!" E.B. shouted. "I don't wanna see either of you boy's get scratched up!"

Nate shouldered his rifle and began firing and levering the Winchester repeatedly.

Pure, his chin resting in the sand, watched in disbelief as Nate began methodically and accurately to shoot every horse in Bandit Town.

## JOURNAL ENTRY

When I look back on that time in Mexico, I . . .
sometimes get a bit wooly-minded as to that wild and exciting
undertaking . . . what I mean by that is . . . I sometimes can't
recall exact words or the order that things occurred . . . 'cepting
one . . . and that one is a memory that is as vivid today as the
day it happened on, Friday December 27, 1878. I reckon it's
fixed in my mind so well because at the time it all began, I
was laying face-down in Mexican river sand while that cold-
blooded bravo, Nate Gunn held me in his Winchester's bore. I
still get goose pimples thinking of it.

And I can see Pure's face, dark and angry, as he rose from
that Mexican ground and brushed the sand from his shirt
sleeves. He stood tall as an oak and called out to E.B., "How'd
you know?"

And E.B.'s response?

Well, he dug his thumbs into the front of his trousers, and
shouted across the Rio Grande, "You know."

Pure got even angrier then, if that was possible, and if
he hadn't spit out his gum earlier, I know he would have been
chomping on it like a boar eating an ear of corn. Instead, he

pointed his finger at E.B. and yelled back, "How'd you know?"

I reckon E.B. felt mighty cocksure about that time because he let out a loud belly laugh that echoed up and down the river. And when he finally did stop laughing, he hollered back, "Because Pure Reston, you and me . . . we ain't all that different now are we?"

And right then . . . I promise this happened . . . Pure shrunk a foot in height. And his chest sunk in and he . . . well . . . he just turned old. I 'spect it was the knowing that throughout this whole thing, perhaps . . . we had grown more like the Gunns and contrariwise.

Right after that, I gathered my feet and gave E.B. a hard stare and then locked eyes with Nate. I was mad, and I screamed out to the both of them that no matter what, I promised I was going to hunt them down and kill the two of them. I reckon that must have been a sight because E.B. started laughing again and pointed down the road behind us. "You might want hurry then, little black bull 'cause I hear tell that a local caudillo is not too contento with you boys killing so many of his hombres. I've even heard a rumor that this caudillo had two good citizens from McMullen County warn him of these murderous owl hoots. I'll bet you that jefe is riding for Bandit

Town even while we're jawing. And because I want to be a good neighbor, I'm going patrol this side of the river and make sure you outlaws don't try to escape back into the States."

And right then, both Pure and I turned and faced one another, stunned. Each of us knew that E.B. had us dead to rights. That we had become outlaw fugitives in old Mexico and it was clear to me that the two of us had done a pretty fair job of cooking our own gooses . . . and it sure felt like we were a hundred miles to water.

# THIRTY-NINE

*December 1878*
*Bandit Town, Mexico*

———⟴———

The caudillo was as brown and leathery as any Mexican that Pure had ever seen. The militia leader arrived in Bandit Town about an hour after the killings.

Pure sat in the middle of the encampment on a willow stump that he had carried from one of the bandit tents He noted that the caudillo arrived in earnest . . . heavily armed and not alone. A force of twenty-five hard-barked Mexicans rode behind him.

Pure sat with his right boot resting on top of his left thigh. He gripped the Peacemaker in his right hand but held it hidden behind his crossed-leg. By appearance, he was well fixed and comfortable.

The Mexican leader stopped his horse ten feet in front of Pure but never offered a glance in his direction. Instead he twisted left and right in the saddle and surveyed the carnage scattered throughout the camp. After several minutes, he settled back and cleared his throat, then fixed a sinister glare on Pure.

Pure didn't buckle or turn away. He just sat there quiet. Waiting. Wondering.

The caudillo exhaled roughly and then said in perfect English, "The other?"

Pure wrinkled his brow. "Pardon?"

"The other man. Where is he?"

"Couldn't really say right now."

"Killed perhaps?"

"Wasn't the last I saw of him."

The caudillo tried not to show his contempt. He tightened his lips into a straight line. After a few seconds, the Mexican leader inhaled and said, "I guess he's hiding somewhere nearby with his gun trained on my heart."

"More likely between your eyes."

A grin crossed the caudillo's face. "And is that suppose to somehow frighten me?"

Pure shrugged. "I couldn't really say."

"You have no opinion?"

Pure tossed a quick glance to his right.

The caudillo instinctively followed Pure's head movement.

"It would sure frighten me," Pure said. "But I 'spect that's a whole 'nuther matter."

The caudillo studied the surrounding brush. "Your friend must be a good shot," he said and then swung his gaze back on Pure.

"Hard to find someone better."

"Hmmm," the caudillo nodded. "I would like to meet this man."

"You'll probably get the opportunity."

"Maybe he might go to work for me?"

"Couldn't say."

The caudillo smiled. "And you?"

"No thanks," Pure smiled back. "I'm set pretty good right now.

"Really?"

"Yep."

"Because I must tell you that it doesn't appear so from where I'm sitting."

"How do you figure?"

The caudillo's eyes scanned Bandit Town once more. "Again, this is just from my view, amigo," he said and poked a finger into his own chest.

Pure shrugged. "It's your show."

"You have no horse."

"That's true."

The caudillo pointed at Pure and traced his finger from the ≡R owner's boots to his hat. "And from your appearance, you might not have any coin either."

"I can't deny that."

203

"So how is it, you are . . . as you say . . . set pretty good right now?"

Pure chuckled, "Because I'm healthy as a Mexican mule."

The caudillo and his men roared with laughter.

Pure joined in.

After more than a few seconds passed, the caudillo suddenly stopped laughing and cast an icy glare in Pure's direction.

Pure locked eyes with the man and never blinked.

The caudillo flashed a quick grin and then coughed one last chuckle. "Maybe not for long, amigo."

Pure nodded politely. "No matter what happens between you and me . . . my friend will still be out there somewhere."

"With his gun pointed between my eyes."

Pure uncrossed his leg and exposed the Colt. He raised his left hand and rested the tip of his forefinger between his eyebrows. "Right here to be precise."

"And what will you do after he shoots me?"

Pure rose from the stump and scratched the back of his head with the barrel of the Colt. "I 'spect that's when things turn sure-enough serious."

The caudillo leaned forward and crossed his hands over his saddle horn. "You know we're . . . my men and I . . . probably going to hang you," he said.

Pure lowered the Colt and slid it into his holster. "Maybe those fellas behind you will."

"What's that?"

"I'm just saying that you won't be able to participate in my hanging."

"You think you frighten me with your words?"

"No," Pure said, reluctantly. "But I'm hoping that we can scare this mob of yours a bit."

The caudillo smirked and shook his head slowly in disbelief. "You have much to learn about Mexico and its people, amigo," he whispered.

Pure walked forward until he stood even with the caudillo's horse. He admired the animal for a few seconds and then gently ran his hand down the beast's neck. "Well, I'm not real sure how much time I've got here, so why don't you give me a quick tutoring."

The caudillo glanced down at Pure. "You won't frighten my men by shooting me; you will only make them angrier. You see they hate Anglos, every last one of you."

"Except for the two back across the river that set me and my friend up?" Pure asked.

"No," the caudillo said emphatically. "They hate those two also. But, they tolerate them . . . but only because those Anglos give them gold coin."

Pure looked up. "And if we give you gold coin?"

The caudillo paused for a moment and then said, "I don't know. You and your friend have killed a lot of men in my jurisdiction."

"And we might not be finished yet."

The caudillo smiled and then chuckled, "As I said, we're probably going to hang you."

"Shame."

The caudillo shook his head. "One's life is sometimes filled with misfortune."

Pure nodded in agreement. "Shame on account of there being twelve dead."

The caudillo glanced back at his posse. "Bring up a rope," he said to no one in particular.

"You first and then eleven of your men," Pure mocked.

The caudillo swung his gaze back on Pure. "You are a very confident man, friend."

One man from the militia walked his horse forward. He swung the loop of a lariat in a wide, lazy arc.

"Well I hate bragging, but so far, we seem to have had a fair portion of luck in surviving once the shooting starts."

The caudillo regarded Pure with a hard glare. "Maybe you and your friend have yet to encounter men who are not afraid of being shot at . . . men who know how to shoot back."

"Maybe."

"Still, you must consider it, amigo."

Pure held steady and nodded at the militia. "You mean those men?"

The caudillo shrugged. "Ah, amigo, who can ever know?"

"It's a funny thing though."

The caudillo leaned back in his saddle. "What's that, amigo?"

"I was just thinking it's funny that we've been outnumbered at least three to one in every fight and yet . . ."

The caudillo leaned forward and rested both hands on his saddle horn. "Please, amigo, continue with your thought," he said.

"Yet, here we both are . . . me here, and him out there."

The caudillo's face tensed. His brow creased, and he inhaled a deep breath. He looked at the horseman moving forward and motioned at the man with his fist.

The horseman twirling the lariat stopped his horse.

Pure stood and stretched his back, more confident now. "As you keep reminding me, I'm going to die anyway. Why not try to kill some of you before I'm shut of this place," he said.

The caudillo stared toward the Rio Grande. He rubbed his right thumb along the side of his mouth.

Pure watched intently.

A lifetime passed.

Fifteen seconds later, the caudillo looked back at Pure. "Just how much gold coin are you talking about?" he asked.

# FORTY

*December 1878*
*Bandit Town, Mexico*

———⟫•◆•⟪———

"What are they doing?" E.B. said with a great deal of impatience.

Nate frowned, petulant. "I don't know, but something ain't right over there."

E.B. kicked at the sandy soil and gestured toward Pure and the *caudillo's* powwow. "Shoot Reston in the back," he snarled.

"If I do, every Mexican in that militia is going to ride across the river for us."

"I said shoot him, boy."

Nate raised the Winchester and fixed the sight on Pure's back.

"Anytime," E.B. grumbled.

Nate placed the tip of his index finger on the trigger.

"Com'on, boy."

"No, E.B., wait."

E.B. curled his lips back over his teeth. "Bedamned, boy, shoot!"

"Look," Nate said.

The Mexican leader leaned down from the saddle and placed his pistol against Pure's temple.

E.B watched the scene unfold. "'bout time," he said.

Nate lowered the rifle.

Across the river, Pure turned his head slightly north and began shouting.

Several seconds later, July rose from a clump of coyote willow.

The caudillo smiled and removed the pistol from Pure's temple. He motioned with the gun for July to drop his rifle and walk toward him.

July tossed the Winchester to the ground and with long, even strides

234

approached the Mexican leader and Pure.

E.B. slapped his thigh. "That's right, Reston, prepare yourself for the everlasting sleep."

The caudillo's militia eased their horses forward. The riders on each end of the line pulled ahead of the middle riders and soon enclosed Pure and July in a circle of horses.

"What the—?" Nate grumbled.

"Whataya think they're doing?" E.B. asked.

One of the Mexicans shouted something in Spanish.

"What did he say?" Nate mumbled.

"I don't know. I can't see or hear a thing with them horses situated like they are."

Then the same Mexican shouted louder. The man's voice carried across the camp. "*Ponerse de rodillas!*"

"Ha!" E.B. exclaimed.

"What?"

"He told Reston and the colored to get on their knees."

Nate lifted his hat and dragged a dirty shirtsleeve across his brow. "Never thought I'd see the day," he said.

Outside the circle, the caudillo holstered his pistol and dismounted. He moved heavily, through the circled horses.

E.B. squinted in disagreeable agitation. "I can't see a thing," he swore. After a second, he stretched his neck forward and then crouched trying to see through the blockade of man and horse. His maneuvering was interrupted by two quick pops from inside the circle. E.B.'s expression turned serious. He tossed a quick glance at Nate.

Nate didn't return his father's gaze.

E.B. turned back toward the caudillo and his men.

Two of the posse backed their mounts away from the circle. The Mexican leader pushed his way through the opening and strode for his mount. He thrust his pistol back into his holster with his first footfall.

E.B. looked past the caudillo. He bit down on his lower lip and then formed a tight smile.

Behind the caudillo, visible in the opening, lay the lifeless bodies of Pure

2

Reston and July Walker.

Nate let loose with a low whistle. "Just like that?"

"Just like that."

"We going to ride over there?"

"You do what pleases you. I'm heading back to McMullen County."

"Don't you want to make sure?"

"Sure? Sure of what?"

"That Reston's dead."

E.B. turned and walked for his horse. "You ride over there, Nate and you'll end up like Reston."

"Huh?"

E.B. stepped into his stirrup. "That caudillo and his men don't like us any better than Reston and the colored."

"But we paid them for the killings."

E.B. turned his horse east. "That we did."

"Well, I don't see the problem with going to see if the job was completed."

"Go west then," E.B. laughed and flipped the rein across his horse's neck. "But if you do, know that caudillo will want all the money he supposes you to be carrying."

Nate looked back across the river. The militia men milled about the dead bodies. He turned back to E.B. The old man was already fifty yards away. He inhaled and took a generous glance at the scene.

*We should make sure*, he thought.

"You coming, boy?" E.B. called out from atop his mount.

Nate turned and looked at E.B. After a minute and some thought, he nodded and hurried for his horse.

# FORTY-ONE

————⊰⊱————

O ne of the caudillo's men knelt beside Pure's body and rifled through his pockets.

Pure opened his eyes at the looter's foray. "Hey!" he said.

The man ignored Pure and glanced back at his leader.

The caudillo lifted his chin at the man.

The pillager shrugged, took to his feet, and joined his fellow despoilers, now plundering the six dead bandits scattered around the camp.

"It had to look real for your friends," the caudillo said.

July opened his eyes and assumed a sitting position. He looked at the Mexican leader and then Pure. "Are they gone?"

Pure lifted his brow in reply. "Don't know," he said and tossed a glance at the caudillo.

The Mexican leader nodded. "Your friends are riding east," he said.

Pure took a deep breath and jumped to his feet.

July followed Pure's action. "Now what?" he asked.

"I guess we owe our friend here a thank you."

The caudillo shook his head and began laughing.

Pure and July watched, confused, and then looked around the camp. The caudillo's men had all stopped their looting and were looking intently at their leader.

The caudillo wiped tears from the corners of his eyes and continued to laugh. "Did you hear that?" he choked.

The militia looked from man to man and joined in with their own laughter.

Pure cleared his throat and held a hot stare on the caudillo. "What's so funny?" he asked.

"I think you, amigo."

Pure's face flushed. "How's that?"

July looked on, concerned.

The caudillo locked eyes with Pure and then broke up laughing once more.

Pure reached into his shirt pocket and removed a stick of gum. "You care to share your joke with us?"

The strongman's militia slowly took to their feet.

July glanced around at the bunch and uttered a nervous breath.

Pure removed the outside paper from the gum and folded the stick into his mouth.

The caudillo stopped laughing. His expression turned serious. One corner of his mouth twitched slowly. He looked over Pure and whispered, "Careful, friend, I assure you this is no joke, and you don't have your guns anymore."

"I thought we had a deal."

"We do," the caudillo said.

Pure began to chew on the Snapping and Stretching gum. "Then why . . . ?"

The caudillo raised his index finger to interrupt. "I saved your life for one reason only," he said.

Pure chewed harder. His face glowed red.

"I saved your life in exchange for gold coin."

Pure lifted his chin and scratched his neck.

"Ten thousand in gold coin is our arrangement."

Pure stopped the scratching.

"Ten thousand in two weeks, amigo. That is our deal. I don't need your thanks; I only need your gold."

Pure took a breath and nodded.

"Two weeks. And just to make sure you return with the gold, we are going to hold your friend here with us."

July glanced over at Pure and shook his head.

Pure exhaled. "But I need him to help retrieve the gold," he said.

The caudillo looked at his men. "Hey," he said and then motioned toward Pure. "Bring this one his gun."

"You have my word, we'll return."

The caudillo ignored Pure and motioned toward July.

One man hurried over to Pure and handed him the Peacemaker.

Pure took the Colt and cinched the belt around his waist.

Two other men, guns drawn, moved in behind July.

The caudillo smiled. "Two weeks, friend, that's all."

Pure tied the holster to his thigh. "I'm going to need a horse," he said.

The caudillo motioned for one of his men to bring Pure a horse.

"Two weeks."

Pure began to chew the Snapping and Stretching gum between his front teeth. "I heard," he muttered.

"If you want to see your friend alive."

"I heard," Pure said, louder this time.

The caudillo smiled. "I think you can do this," he said.

Pure turned back and looked out toward the dead. "I'm gonna need that spur," he said and pointed toward one-spur's corpse.

"The spur?"

Pure nodded and held out a hand.

The caudillo tightened his brow and gestured for one of his men to fetch the item. The man shuffled lazily toward the dead man. After unbuckling the spur, the man walked at exactly the same pace toward Pure and handed him the object.

Pure took the spur, held it up at eye level, and waved it in the air. "Hammered by an old vaquero in San Antonio who went by the name Alavez," he said.

The caudillo lifted his shoulders in indifference.

Pure stepped up in the stirrup and tossed a quick glance at July. "I'll be back for you."

July smiled. "No reason you wouldn't," he said.

# Forty-Two

*December 1878*
*Bandit Town, Mexico*

———◆———

J uly and the caudillo sat on a pair of willow stumps. Both men stared east. Pure had been gone for a full day.

"You're never going see that gold."

The caudillo turned toward July. "That would be a shame for me and for you," he said.

"It's not that he won't try."

The caudillo turned his gaze back east. "I think your friend will do more than try."

July glanced over at the Mexican leader. "But the other two have a whole lot of money to fight him with."

"So you think these other two will hire some assassins?"

"History usually repeats itself," July said.

"You're sure?"

"Once they realize he's not dead, they will."

"But your friend has a history also. He has killed assassins before."

July nodded. "A string of 'em on both sides of the river."

"So maybe he will kill a few more on that side."

"Maybe."

"What else can a man expect in life but the possibility of maybe?"

"Still, if he gets killed, you're not going to see any gold."

"As I said, that would be a shame."

"Even if he kills the two and their assassins, it's most likely they would have spent most of the gold."

The caudillo shook his head once. "Then both of us will have an unhappy ending."

July lowered his head and stared between his legs at the Mexican soil. "Yep."

After two minutes or so, the caudillo slapped a dirty palm down on July's back. "How about some mescal? I have a bottle on my horse."

"Now?"

"What better time, amigo?"

July squinted, thinking. *Mescal.*

"Well?"

*Mescal.*

July raised his head.

The caudillo turned and hollered for one of his men to bring the bottle.

July turned and surveyed the bodies littering Bandit Town. On the road leading into the camp, he spied full-bottle.

One of the caudillo's men approached and handed the Mexican leader a half-full bottle of the mescal.

"This clears the mind of worries," the caudillo said.

July turned and glared at the Mexican leader. "What if I left you some ballast?"

The caudillo took a long drink from the bottle and then handed it toward July. "What's that you are saying?"

July took the bottle but did not take a drink. "Coin. What if I left you some coin as collateral?"

The caudillo grinned. "Ah, amigo, you've been holding out."

"Would you let me ride to my friend if I had some coin for you to hold until we return?"

"How much coin?"

"Three hundred, maybe . . . six-hundred in gold coin."

The caudillo's expression changed to surprise. "You have that much gold on you?"

"No, but I have a pretty good idea where it is."

"Ah, lost gold."

"Not lost."

The caudillo looked around the camp around grinning, eyes wide. "Where is this gold then?"

"I 'spect a few of your men are hiding a fair amount of it."

The caudillo straightened at July's words. His grin disappeared. "Which ones?"

July pointed toward full-bottle's body and then to the remaining six dead bandits. "Whichever ones rifled those fella's corpses."

The caudillo snatched the bottle back and took a drink. "This is a very serious thing."

July nodded. "Ask them to show you their pockets. Some of your men are hiding a fair piece of gold coin."

The caudillo raised the bottle once more. He drank the remaining brackish fluid and then stood. A frown tightened across his face. He stood, stretched his back, and then looked at July. "Come with me," he said.

## JOURNAL ENTRY

Now once that Mexican General learned that some of his men might be withholding gold from him, well, let's just say he was none too happy. He gathered all twenty-five of his militia around several piles of clothing and weapons taken from the dead. He poked through the pile of clothing with his boot and asked if anything worth keeping had been found. The seven who had searched the dead all shook their heads no. But this caudillo was a pretty cagy fella. He nodded okay to those men and then looked back at the pile of pistols, knives, and cartridges. He thanked the looters and told the seven that for their hard work they could have the first pick from the gun and knife pile. The men got excited, and all smiled and returned their many thanks for the caudillo's generosity.

The caudillo smiled and waved his right hand over the piles and told those seven to take whatever they wanted. The men immediately began pulling weapons from the pile, and when they had finished, each man held armfuls of guns and knives. But as they turned and thanked their leader once again . . . well right then, in an instant, that caudillo's face changed. I mean it took on a dangerous appearance. His smile disappeared and from deep in his throat he growled, "What about the gold coin you found?"

And those seven Mexican fellas? Well I've never in my life seen jaws drop so fast and so hard. Each one, to a man, swallowed a lump of clay. And try as they might, their faces couldn't disguise their guilt.

It's a curious thing about men. One of the things I learned during my life was that every man acts different when he senses his own death closing in around him. And those Mexican fellas, well, all of them got excited in a hurry, some denied the caudillo's claim, while a few others proclaimed they had merely forgotten about the gold during all of the excitement. And one of those fellas . . . well, he just dropped to his knees and started sobbing.

The caudillo walked up to that fella on his knees and patted his head twice like a man does his favorite dog . . . then as easy as saddling a tame pony, he put a bullet in that fella's temple.

Then, the caudillo turned and gestured for the eighteen who hadn't taken gold to pull their pistols and deal with the remaining six. And without a second's thought or a bat of an eye, those eighteen pulled their guns and shot their amigos . . .

men they had ridden with, just shot 'em dead.

The caudillo found three hundred and twenty-five in gold coin hidden on those men's bodies. I told him he would find another hundred and twenty-five on the bodies buried on the road to Guerrero.

And after that, we both drank mescal. We each took several pulls on the bottle before the caudillo looked at me and said, "Go to your friend."

I gave him my thanks and promised to return with his ten thousand in gold. He just nodded and had one of his men bring me a horse. I told him I needed two. The caudillo laughed and asked why. I told him that if I was going to catch up to Pure, I would be riding day and night and there was a better than fair chance that in doing so I was gonna kill one of the horses.

# PART THREE

# Unforgiving

(adj). not disposed to forgive or show mercy; unrelenting.

# Forty-Three

*January 1879*
*Dog Town, McMullen County, Texas*

—————◇—————

Pure tied his horse to a split rail post outside of Levi Edward's general store and, knowingly, right next to E.B. and Nate's horses. The Snapping and Stretching gum bounced lightly in his mouth. He studied the street as he slipped the Peacemaker from his holster and checked the gun's cartridges.

*Six.*

Turning back to the store, his hand naturally started the Colt toward the holster only to stop mid-action. He looked down at the pistol and decided it better to enter the store, gun in hand.

Inside, E.B. stood at the counter jawing with Mr. Edwards when the front door screeched.

Pure walked in slow and deliberate. He held the Colt chest-high. Buckshot Wallace's single spur was tucked into his gun belt. A grim and deadly look painted his expression.

E.B. turned toward the door's creak.

"Hello, E.B."

E.B.'s face went from shocked surprise to outrage. "Reston!" he muttered.

Pure's eyes darted around the small store in search of Nate.

E.B. smiled. "He ain't here."

"Who?" Pure fired back.

"My oldest," E.B. said.

Pure rolled his eyes back over his left shoulder. "Nate?"

"That's who you're looking for."

Pure turned his attention back to E.B. and raised the Colt slightly. He looked down the gun's barrel. "Well, since I'm looking for him, where is he?" he asked and then backed up into the door frame.

"No telling with that youngster."

Pure took a quick glance out into the street.

"Probably off in some kind of trouble somewhere."

Pure nodded. "Sounds about right."

E.B. gestured at Pure. "Thought you was dead."

"What do you think now?"

"That maybe, I should give the boy his due."

Pure turned his gaze back to E.B. "How's that?"

"He told me that you weren't dead."

"I'd say that makes him smarter than his old man."

"You're mighty brave when you've got the drop on a man," E.B. fired back.

"Not every man can be as honorable as Gunns, E.B."

"That sounds like smart talk."

"Probably," Pure said.

"Just what the hell do you want, Reston?" E.B. said. His voice betrayed his testiness. "Coming in here and holding me at gunpoint."

"You don't know?"

E.B. turned and looked at the store owner. "You're a witness to this, Levi." Edwards nodded and winked at Pure.

Pure looked past E.B. to the storeowner. "Levi, have you seen Nate?"

The storeowner made a slight nod of his head toward Pure and said, "No."

Pure glanced back through the door again and then moved forward toward E.B.

"What now, Reston?" E.B. asked. "You gonna shoot me?"

Pure moved with inches of E.B. and thrust the Colt into the elder Gunn's chest. "Naw, I just feel less skittish standing over here beside you, E.B."

E.B.'s upper lip curled into a snarl. "I never took you for the nervous type," he said.

Pure grasped Buckshot's spur with his left hand and removed it from his gun belt. He lifted the spur and dangled it in front of E.B.'s face. "Put it on," he said.

E.B. glanced at the spur and flushed red. Tiny specks of spittle emerged from the corners of his mouth. "You've gone loco, Reston," he swore. "Crazy loco."

Pure pressed the spur into E.B.'s cheek. His mouth twisted unnaturally. He rolled the Snapping and Stretching gum between his front teeth. "Put it on, I said!"

E.B. tensed and then grabbed the spur. In defying anger, he bent down and strapped the spur to his right boot.

"Where's the other one?"

E.B. straightened and stood nose-to-nose with Pure. "Don't know what you're talking about."

Pure turned his attention to Levi Edwards. "He killed Buckshot Wallace and the kid."

The storeowner lowered his chin. "Hold on, Pure."

"I'm telling you he did, Levi."

"He couldn't have."

Pure frowned, stunned. "He's been wearing his spurs, Levi," he said through clenched teeth. "He left the one strapped to his boot right now in Mexico not four days ago."

"Pure, on the day I first heard about Buckshot," Levi paused. "E.B. got into a fight with one of Frank McElroy's cowboys over in the saloon."

Pure inhaled. "Word about Buckshot couldn't have got here for a day or so, Levi."

The store owner looked up. He stared into Pure's eyes. "E.B. had been here drinking for almost the whole week."

E.B.'s eyes glistened. "Seems you've been found out for what you are, Reston."

"Shut-up," Pure uttered.

E.B. turned his head toward Edwards and smiled smugly. "And it 'pears you're strong-arming days are done as well."

"Shut-up!" Pure screamed.

"There's witnesses now," E.B. shouted.

Pure trembled in rage. He pushed the gun further into E.B.'s chest.

"Don't do it, Pure." Levi Edwards said.

"He killed my brothers and my cowboys."

"That a 'nuther one of your stories, Reston."

A long slow screech sounded from the doorway.

Pure froze at the sound.

E.B. grinned.

Levi Edwards made a face.

E.B. glanced over Pure's shoulder. A broad grin flashed across his mouth.

Pure cursed to himself. A familiar voice crawled up his spine.

"Best put down that Colt, Reston, or stand there and be killed," said Nate Gunn.

# Forty-Four

*January 1879*
*Dog Town, McMullen County, Texas*

———⋙◆⋘———

E.B. reached out and eased the Peacemaker from Pure's grip.

"Careful, E.B., I'm a witness to all of this," Levi Edwards said.

Nate cast an evil smirk at the storeowner. "Watch your tongue, shop keep," he said.

E.B. scanned Pure from head to toe. "Well, look what we've got here, Nate. It's the big-bug from the ≡R outfit."

Edwards leaned forward and placed his left hand on a shot gun under the counter. "I'm warning you, E.B.," he threatened.

E.B. brushed Edwards off with a wave of his hand. "Put that double-barrel away, Levi. Me and Nate are just gonna take big-bug, Reston here next door for a drink."

Nate smiled at Edwards and raised his brow. "You heard E.B., we're just gonna try and talk some sense into this fella."

"Yeah," said E.B. "We're done feuding with the Restons."

Edwards looked up at Pure and waited.

Pure raised his chin at the storeowner. "It's ok, Levi. This pair relies on the dark of night or others to do their killings."

Edwards removed his hand from the gun under the counter. "If that's how you want it, Pure."

Pure cocked his head to the left and glanced out of the corner of his eye toward Nate. "That's how it'll be for now."

# FORTY-FIVE

*January 1879*
*Dog Town, McMullen County, Texas*

———⊰◈⊱———

Five minutes later, Pure sat at one of three tables in Dogtown's only saloon. Two glasses filled with half-a-finger of rot-gut rested in the middle of the table. E.B. took the chair opposite from Pure.

Nate sat down three feet away and behind Pure. A Colt pistol rested across his lap.

E.B. reached across the table and picked up one of the glasses of whiskey. "Reston, I 'spect it's time we end this thing," he said.

Pure studied E.B. carefully. After a few seconds, he leaned forward and pushed the second glass toward the man. "Why now?"

E.B. made a face, thinking, and then slanted his head to the right. "I dunno," he said and lifted the whiskey glass to his lips. After a long drink, he said, "It just seems like the right time. I figure there's been too much killing between us."

Pure took a long pause. His eyes narrowed on the elder Gunn. "I've got eleven dead," he said.

E.B. licked his lips and softly set the glass back on the table. "Only two family though."

Pure's neck muscles tensed. "Not to me," he said. "All eleven count."

E.B. shifted in his seat and glanced down at the table. "Yeah, we'll I've got five sons, all family, all dead."

The air in the saloon changed.

Pure lifted one of the empty glasses and stared at the cloud of whiskey grease that blocked the container's transparency. "Four sons and a bastard, E.B.," he said.

226

Nate let out a muffled breath. He leaned forward and jammed his pistol into Pure's spine. "Say one more word about Street that way, and I swear I'll put one in your back."

E.B. raised a hand and patted the air. "Easy, Nate, he's just trying to rile us." Pure leaned back in his chair.

E.B. picked up the remaining glass and motioned it toward the barkeep. Looking back to Pure, he broke out into a belly laugh. "Well in strict interpretation, I'd say you were correct, Reston."

Nate clenched his jaw. "E.B., what are you saying?"

E.B. pushed against the table and jumped to his feet. "I'm saying Street was the bastard son of C.A. Reston! And you know it to be true!" he growled, then lowered his voice and stared down his nose at Pure. "And you know it too, Mister high-and-mighty Pure Reston."

Pure sat unmoved.

E.B. slapped at the table top. "Look at him, Nate. He's a pretty smug bug right now."

Nate scooted his chair forward until it rested inches away from Pure. He leaned in close to Pure's ear and hissed angrily, "How about my, ma, Reston? Where do you figure she rests in all of your number counting?"

Pure inhaled and tightened his lips against one another.

E.B. composed himself and sat back in his chair. He glanced at Pure and smiled. "The boy has a point, Reston. That's why this thing needs to end now."

Pure exhaled. "From my side it sounds like you two are just all-of-a-sudden 'fraid of dying."

E.B. chuckled. "I don't follow your logic, Reston. I mean you're the one sitting unarmed and Nate's pistol shoved square into your back."

Pure cleared his throat with little force. "You better go ahead and kill me then, E.B., because I'm not listening to you anymore."

"Don't force my hand, Reston."

Pure looked around the saloon. His eyes drifted on the approaching bar keep. "I'm not too worried about dying, E.B."

"Why's that?" Nate whispered in Pure's ear.

Pure lifted his eyes and turned his head toward Nate. "Because I realize it now . . . I should have seen it earlier . . . the both of you just have too much to lose," he said.

"What kinda nonsense is that, Reston?" E.B. grumbled.

The bar keeps placed a glass of whiskey on the table and lifted his brow at Pure.

Pure looked at the man and shook his head slightly. "Everything's fine here," he said.

Nate tossed a hard gaze at the bar keep. "You heard him. Everything's ok. Move along."

Pure glanced back at E.B. "What I mean is you've got gold coin now. My gold coin. Fourteen thousand of it."

E.B. sat back and waved a finger in Pure's direction. "I always knew you were a smart one, Reston."

"I figure that's more money than you've ever had in your pitiful life, E.B."

"Maybeso," E.B. grinned, angry. "Maybeso."

"So, I going to stand up and walk right out that door."

Nate raked Pure's back with the Colt. "You forgetting something, buckaroo?"

Pure gripped both arms of his seat and slid the chair back into Nate. He rose to his feet with measured dignity. "You know what I'm looking forward to the most, Nate? The day I kill you."

Nate tossed Pure's chair aside and sprang to his feet. "Why you son-of-a-dog!" he screamed. "I'll shoot you down right now and enjoy the show of it!"

"I don't think you will, Nate."

E.B. roared to his feet. "Are you crazy, Reston?"

Pure turned and started for the door. "Some think so."

Nate looked at E.B. anxious and bewildered. He raised the Colt. The hammer clicked back.

E.B. placed his right hand atop the pistol and forced it down. "What makes you so sure we won't shoot?" he shouted out.

"Because of that gold coin, E.B."

"What?"

"It's what gives men like you a reason to live. Truth be told, it's giving you fourteen thousand reasons to live."

"Reston! Don't you turn your back on me!"

"All that gold has got you fearing the possibility of hanging. That gold has got you all balled up."

"You're loco crazy, Reston."

"Am I? Look at you, you can't even shoot an unarmed man anymore."

"Don't push your luck, cowboy."

"All because of some gold coin."

"You miserable—," Nate spewed.

Pure chuckled at the pair. "Because if you did, then you and Nate wouldn't be able to spend any of that coin of mine."

"You just can't let it go, can you, Reston? You've got to have your blood killings."

Pure walked for the door. "Killings?" he whistled. "You've tried a half dozen times with more than a dozen assassins to kill me, E.B."

"I'm offering a truce. I'm willing to put this thing behind us."

"Ain't that just the way," Pure said.

"I'm warning you, Reston," E.B. muttered, then in a much weaker tone said, "I'm warning you."

"Sorta funny though," Pure said. "Because right now, I'm the one with nothing to lose."

"Reston . . . Why do this, this way?"

Pure looked back over his shoulder. His eyes contracted. E.B. and Nate stood there amazed in disbelief. "Why? Because of something you'll never understand, E.B., probably something you can't understand. It's the code . . . a man's code."

E.B. trembled with rage. His hands balled into fists.

Nate shoved the Colt back into his holster. He glared furious at Pure.

Pure turned his head back and walked deliberately toward the street. "Watch yourself, boys. I've got less than a week to kill the both of you and get that gold back to Mexico, back to that caudillo you hired," he called out and then disappeared out the door.

# FORTY-SIX

*January 1879*
*Outside of Dog Town, McMullen County, Texas*

⇒◦◦⇐

Twenty yards off the main trail and a mile out of Dogtown, Pure sat atop his horse. The Snapping and Stretching gum was pushed deep into the back corner of his jaw. Every few seconds he lifted the gum with his tongue, rolled it around his mouth, and then poked it back into his jaw. Contemplating.

Deep in thought, he took no notice of the clop of a horse and rider approaching from his back.

July slowed at the sight of the ≡R owner and walked his mount right up beside Pure's horse. "And hello to you," he said.

Pure didn't look over. Instead, he lifted a bladder from his saddle horn and held it out to his friend. "Might help cut the dust," he said.

July grinned and took the water. "You letting any rider come up behind you these days?"

"I knew it was you."

"How so?"

"Because trouble's starting."

July swirled a mouthful of water in his mouth and then spit out the liquid. "Starting?" he laughed and raised the bladder back to his lips. "When did the last of it end?" he said and took a drink.

Pure stared down the road. "E.B. and Nate will be coming down this road soon."

July cleared his throat and bit down on his bottom lip, contemplating. After three seconds he asked, "You haven't mixed with them yet?"

"We spoke."

July handed the bladder back to Pure. "Just spoke?"

"Yep."

"No gun play or harsh words or nothing?"

Pure chuckled inside. "It was downright civil."

"What was the cause of it?"

"It seems the two of them are having some difficulty regarding the subject of their sudden wealth."

July slumped in his saddle. "I don't follow."

Pure glanced over at his ranch foreman. "It appears that there is a certain level of wealth that makes a man more cautious about his possible demise."

July thought for a minute or so and then mumbled, "Hmmmph."

"Yeah."

"It's amazing how fast men aspire to respectability when they get enough gold coin in their possession."

"Even more amazing when the coin is stolen," Pure added.

July leaned back and broke into a rousing fit of laughter.

Pure grinned at July's uncontrollable attack and choked back his own laughter. "So, anyhow those two were all fired up to strike a deal with me."

"They wanted to make a deal with the son of C.A. Reston?"

"Yep."

"What was the offer?" July asked, still choked.

"End all of this right now."

July calmed himself. "Your sitting here tells me how that played out."

Pure turned his head toward July and shrugged. "That's a deal couldn't be made by me."

July nodded. "Well there's Isa."

"And Paint."

"And my seven cowboys."

"And Buckshot and the kid."

"Seems like a lifetime ago."

"Yep."

Both men stared down the trail, remembering. The land turned unnaturally quiet.

After minutes passed, July pushed his lips together and said, "Hey, what

231

was the kid's given name anyway?"

Caught unaware, Pure stopped rolling his gum. His brow wrinkled. Five seconds went by. He glanced at July. "Billy . . . something."

July frowned, trying to recall. "Yeah, Billy. But what about his last name?"

Pure started chewing the Snapping and Stretching gum in a deliberate, slow fashion. No answer came forthwith.

July scratched the back of his neck. "Seems like something I should remember."

Pure considered July's words. "Seems like."

July shook his head. "It'll come to me."

"Most likely in the dead of a good night's sleep."

July grinned. "Ain't that the always the way?"

"Seems so."

"Anyway, that's eleven good reasons not to end this thing I reckon," July said.

Pure rolled the Snapping and Stretching gum to his front teeth. "Can I tell you something?" he said.

"We're friends, aren't we?"

"That's why I feel like I need to tell you this."

"Won't matter?" July said.

"What's that?"

"No matter what you tell me, I'm still going to stay here with you."

Pure allowed the slightest of a glint of what might have been a smile to crease his lips. "Deep inside, I don't figure to be doing this for the eleven," he said.

"I know that."

Pure's expression flushed curiosity. "You do?'

"Yeah."

"How could you know?"

"I know you."

Pure chomped down on the gum. "Yeah. I suppose that's right," he allowed.

"Never been my way to judge."

"Not a bad way to be," Pure said.

"I suppose."

Pure turned. "How long have you known?" he said.

"Since the dust-up in The Flat."

Pure nodded. "Because of my shooting of Ben?"

July interrupted quickly. "Nothing more needs saying."

Pure lowered his chin. "Suppose not," he said.

A moment passed.

Then another.

Suddenly, July rose up in his saddle. His eyes sparkled. "Green," he said.

Pure frowned. "What's that?"

"The kid, I believe his last name was Green."

Pure took a deep breath. "Sounds about right," he said.

In the distance, the distinctive clop of unshod hooves on grass and sand sounded.

Pure turned an ear toward the sound. He listened intently for ten seconds and then pulled the stem-winder from his pocket. "Seven minutes past," he said.

July nodded. "What's the hour?"

"Three o'clock."

July nodded again. "So as to these Gunns, what's the plan?"

Pure closed the Elgin and slipped the watch back in his pocket. He fixed his gaze square on July and then slid the Winchester from its sheath. "Try not to get killed, I suppose."

## JOURNAL ENTRY

*At six minutes past three o'clock on the afternoon of January fifth in the year 1879, Pure and I sat horseback in the middle of a scrub trail one mile outside of Dogtown. It's strange how a man can remember in detail a day that happened almost fifty years prior. But that day, that day is as keen in my mind as a fine whetted blade.*

*We waited on the far side of a sharp bend, killing time, plotting . . . and waiting . . . for the arrival of E.B. and Nate Gunn. Sixty seconds later, at seven minutes past three, E.B. and Nate Gunn rode headlong into us and what followed was certainly not the outcome expected by any of the parties involved.*

*And on that day, in that time of no organized law in McMullen County, Pure and I became the law . . . became our own law. I guess maybe we had been for some time. But we weren't alone, for most men in those days, during those times, became their own law.*

*And sometimes that law was, if not just, at least good . . . and at other times it was just sure enough bad. I reckon it's an* easy enough thing to do . . . look back . . . and make a judgment fifty years forward.

But five decades later with the difficulty far removed, an outsider can expend little effort and absolutely no blood in pronouncing that we should have behaved better on that fateful day. But for all the hell that was to occur at eight minutes past three o'clock on January fifth . . . I can tell you with great certainty that we comported ourselves as men must in lawless times when dealing with that defiant outlawry.

# FORTY-SEVEN

*January 1879*
*One Mile Outside of Dogtown, McMullen County, Texas*

E.B. Gunn stared straight down the barrel of Pure's Winchester. "It don't have to be this way, Reston," he said.

"You ain't the law," Nate hissed.

"That's true enough," said Pure.

"But close enough," July remarked. The bore of his Winchester was level with Nate's heart. "Now hold on to those reins good and tight with both hands, boys."

E.B. shot a quick glance at his holstered Colt and then looked back at Pure. "You aim to shoot us down in the middle of this trail? Like dogs?"

"That seems to be the best we could come up with on short notice," Pure said.

E.B. grimaced. "We've both suffered dead through this thing."

"Some more than others," Pure said.

"Weren't Gunns who started this?"

"Then it won't be Gunns who end it," Pure said.

"Be reasonable, Reston. You know one cartridge won't stop me from yanking my pistol and getting off a shot or two at you."

"Didn't plan on stopping at one cartridge, E.B."

"Why don't we split the gold coin straight down the middle?"

Nate shot a hard look at E.B. and mouthed *what?*

Pure's expression glazed dark. "Split my own gold coin with me?"

"Better'n men dying here today."

"Some might disagree."

July kept a hard gaze on Nate.

"So whataya want, Reston? All of the coin?"

"Just what's mine."

"What about what you took from me?"

"I guess we can discuss that after."

"After? After what?" E.B. asked frantic.

"After I get back what's mine and justice."

"And what of our justice?"

Pure rolled the Snapping and Stretching gum to his front teeth. He bit down hard on the chicle and said, "That's something you might want to fight for . . . same as us."

E.B. frowned. "You're a hard-barked son-of-a-dog, Reston," he said.

Nate fidgeted in the saddle. "Justice," he spat. Bright red flushed across his throat. "You're the one who killed Street!" he screamed out. "It was you that night, Pure Reston. We all saw your piebald, Mr. high-and-mighty!"

Pure glowered at Nate. "*La muerte de vaca, Nate?*"

Nate's fidgeting stopped. His face flushed with the truth.

"It was you, wasn't it?" Pure said. His voice was rich and thick. "It was you who started all of this."

Nate swallowed hard. "Like E.B. said before, you're loco, Reston."

"You're the one who wrapped them boys in Reston hides!"

"You can't prove any of that, Reston!"

Pure raised his brow. "Buckshot gave you the spurs, didn't he?"

"Don't know what you're talking about."

"He did," Pure said. He was suddenly aware of exactly what happened in Cañón Cerrado. "What you couldn't know, Nate was that Buckshot knew whoever we found with his spurs would be his killer."

"I didn't have Wallace's spurs, Reston? Looks like you got it all wrong again."

A dark grin tugged at Pure's lips. "But old, E.B. took those spurs from you, didn't he, Nate?"

"I ain't afraid of you, Reston," Nate said, with little conviction.

"I know it was you, Nate."

"I told you before, you got it all wrong," Nate protested.

"You want to know how I know? Because Levi Edwards told me so this morning. Levi told me that your pa was soused that whole week . . . in Dogtown."

Nate grinned and dropped hold of his reins. "I'll see you in hell, Reston," he swore. His hand flashed for his Colt.

Pure swivelled the Winchester away from E.B. and fired once into Nate's stomach.

A low, guttural moan oozed from Nate's mouth. He grabbed his belly with his left hand and then slumped forward across his horse's neck. Although his face was buried in the horse's mane, he still tried to yank the pistol, but the gun never left the holster.

A shocked E.B. turned toward the gun fire and screamed, "Damn you, Reston!" His face turned an enraged purple. In the blink of an eye, he dropped off the left side of his horse, and almost simultaneously, shots blazed from his pistol. On the ground, he tugged at the reins in an attempt to turn the horse's head into him and create a shield between himself and his assassins.

Pure wheeled and sighted the Winchester on E.B., "Damned, Gunns!" he cursed. Suddenly, a dull pressure drilled through his right shoulder. The shock of burning fire hit immediately and spread throughout his chest.

E.B. shouted, "How's that, Reston?" His first shot had caught Pure in the shoulder socket. E.B. kept up a relentless barrage of gun fire. His second bullet passed through Pure's right lung. The third whizzed overhead. "You're gonna die right here."

July swung his Winchester away from Nate and onto E.B.'s horse. He pushed his boots against his stirrups and rose in the saddle looking for a clear shot at E.B. over the horse's neck. Blocked, he cursed the elder Gunn, moved his aim down, and shot E.B.'s horse twice through the ribs.

The horse screamed and fell forward on its front legs, away from E.B.

E.B. pulled against the reins, but the horse's weight yanked him forward into the dying beast.

July's horse danced on its back legs. He took a wobbly shot at E.B., hitting him in the left thigh. "Be still, damn you!" he yelled at his horse and then levered another round.

E.B. fumbled to his feet and fired a quick charge into the ≡R foreman's exposed left side.

July recoiled from the bullet, inhaled, and then squeezed the Winchester's trigger. His shot veered right of E.B.

Pure's horse screamed and reared on its back legs. His right arm nearly useless, Pure slid from the saddle and crumpled to the ground. Unable to gain his feet, he placed the butt of his rifle into the ground and pushed himself to his knees. An agonized expression colored his face. Struggling against the pain, he let out an excruciating scream and fought against blacking out.

E.B. screeched at July. Spit flew from his mouth. He raised the Colt and extended his arm. "Gotcha," he laughed, crazed.

Pure cursed loudly and swung the Winchester from the ground. With deliberate indifference to his afflicted state, he pushed the rifle into his broken shoulder. The pain twisted his face. He cussed louder. And without conscious aim, he pulled the trigger. The explosive kick forced a louder string of curses to fly from his mouth. The crack of bone against bone resonated in his ears.

E.B. collapsed forward, mouth open, face down, and instantly dead. His Colt was forever encased between his palm and fingers.

Pure immediately looked in July's direction. "You ok?" he groaned.

July rolled off his horse and landed on his back. His expression locked in a painful grimace. He placed the palm of his right hand across the gun wound. "I've been better. You?"

"Yeah."

Ahead, Nate, still prone over his saddle horn, groaned. He reached forward and gathered up his rein and then pulled the horse's head around so he could see Pure. "This ain't finished, Reston," he soughed. "I'll be back, ya hear?"

Pure reached across his body with his left hand. He tried to pull his Colt, but the movement paralyzed him in pain.

Nate tried to rake a spur across his horse's ribs, but he couldn't raise the heel of his boot. The horse, its head hung low, walked forward past Pure and continued west, headed for home.

Pure gasped for breath. His eyes followed Nate as the horse shuffled by.

"I'll never stop, Reston," Nate whispered. "Never."

Pure tried to turn and keep a line of sight on the oldest Gunn but instead collapsed on his side. A mixture of dried grass and dirt flew into his eyes.

The matter blinded him. He blinked rapidly and tried to clear his vision, but Nate became lost in a murky haze.

"I'm coming back to kill you and anyone who rides with you." Nate moaned. He coughed up a mouthful of blood with his tortured promise. "If you marry, I'll come back and kill your wife."

Pure panted for air. He ignored Nate and looked across the trail at July. "Can you get up?" he said.

Nate continued his threats in a raspy, rattling voice. "If you have kids, I'll come back and kill every last one of them."

Pure lay back. "July, can you get up?" he asked again.

July strained to lift his head. He glanced down at the red liquid oozing out of his body and then fell back. His wide-opened eyes stared into the bright afternoon sky. "Not right now," he said. "I think I might need to rest here for a bit."

Pure's face contorted in acute pain. He closed his eyes and gasped in rapid puffs. "Yeah," he said roughly. "Me too."

## JOURNAL ENTRY

*We lay there until sunset. That evening, a couple of cowpunchers headed home from an afternoon of high spirits in Dogtown stumbled across us. Those boys hauled us into town, and Doc Morton had a go at us. We both survived, but how is still a mystery to most folks in the county. Pure's right shoulder was broken at the shoulder joint and his right lung had collapsed. Me? I was shot right in the top half of my right kidney. I bled a fair amount, but as you can plainly see, I can still get around pretty good. It took six months for me to get to where I could ride a horse again, but Pure's recovery took longer . . . almost two years, and even then he never had the use of his right arm again.*

*E.B., of course, was quite dead. The day after the shoot-out, Levi Edwards recovered Pure's cattle money rolled up in E.B.'s hot roll and Buckshot's spurs. As Pure had figured, there was just under fourteen thousand in coin. After settling his bill with Levi, Pure had just enough coin left over to pay the caudillo in full. Pure sent word by messenger to the caudillo before our two-week deadline had passed. In his message, Pure explained why we couldn't show in person and invited the*

*Mexican leader to come visit us at the ≡R headquarters.*

*And Nate . . . well . . . we were just left to wonder about*

*Nate for a long time after that day . . .*

# PART FOUR

# Ending

(n). the last part; finish; death.

# FORTY-EIGHT

*April 1879*
*The ≡R Headquarters, McMullen County, Texas*

———◆———

The caudillo sat on a cowhide chair in the large great room of the Reston bunk house. The Mexican leader stared into the rock fireplace on the north wall of the building and then over at Pure. A stream of sweat glistened from his neck.

"Can't seem to get the chill out of my bones since the shoot-out," Pure said. A wool blanket covered his extremities.

The caudillo nodded and then lifted the end of a wide piece of cloth hanging from his neck and swiped at the sweat. "I'm sure it will go away in time," he said and then allowed his gaze to drift down at his lap. A leather wallet hung over his right knee.

July looked at the caudillo and grinned. "I told you we'd get you your gold."

"So you did, amigo," the caudillo said. "And me, I never doubted that you would."

Pure cleared his throat and looked over at the caudillo.

The caudillo turned back to Pure and smiled.

"There's a favor we need," Pure said and then lifted his chin toward July.

"For you amigos, I would be happy to help."

July lifted a small leather pouch from his chair. He tossed the bag toward the caudillo.

The Mexican leader caught the pouch in mid-air and raised his brow.

"More gold," July said.

The caudillo glanced over at Pure.

"Five hundred in coin."

245

"And what is it that you need?"

"We want you to find Nate Gunn," said Pure.

"Ahhh," the caudillo nodded. "The one who rode away."

Pure nodded and glanced at his right arm. The extremity hung limp and useless from his shoulder. "Busted up as we are—,"

The caudillo motioned at Pure with a sweep of his hand. He untied the string on the wallet and opened the satchel. "I understand," he said and stuffed the leather bag inside. "And if I find him?"

July glanced over at Pure.

Pure twisted his back against his chair. After settling in a comfortable position, he looked at July and then the caudillo. "Do what you figure to be the right thing," he said.

"And if I don't find him?"

Pure stared up at the ceiling.

The caudillo waited patiently.

After a long pause, Pure lowered his head and said, "What was it a fella once told me in Mexico?"

The caudillo rocked back and forth in his chair. A wide gin split his lips.

Pure set his gaze on the Mexican leader. "Oh yeah, that fella told me, I think you can do this," he said.

"Ok, amigo, I will try my best."

July rocked forward in his chair. "But, just in case you don't find Nate."

The caudillo swung his gaze over to July.

"Then make sure you let us know."

"I understand," the caudillo said and rose from the chair.

"Good fortune," Pure said.

The caudillo shrugged and lifted the wallet to his shoulder. "Very good fortune," he said. "I will try my best to find this man, this I promise."

"Not much more any man could do," Pure said.

"Or promise," July said.

The caudillo bowed and then looked once more at July. He paused for several seconds.

"What's on your mind," July said.

The caudillo held his thumb and forefinger almost together. "I have a small curiosity," he said, puzzled.

Pure looked at July.

July swung his gaze over to Pure, shrugged, and then looked at the caudillo. "Please," he said.

"You took two horses that day in Bandit Town."

"Yes."

"You said you needed the two because if you were to going to catch your friend, you were going to ride day and night."

"I remember."

"That in doing so you would probably ride one of the horses to its death."

July nodded.

My curiosity is this, did you do this thing?"

July allowed a knowing smile to settle across his mouth. "Yes, I did," he said.

The caudillo nodded and moved for the door. "Now that, amigo is a story worth telling," he said.

# JOURNAL ENTRY

*Neither of us ever saw the caudillo again; although once a year until 1881, a messenger would arrive on the ≡R with a message from the Mexican leader. And every message was always the same . . . as far as he could promise us, Nate Gunn was not in Mexico. In 1881, we heard rumors that the caudillo had been hanged by his militia. I suppose it was true.*

*And Nate Gunn? Well he was never heard from again. Not by us anyhow. Some said he had ridden north and was hanged in Nebraska in 1883 for stealing cattle. Still others told stories of his living in Mexico and running a great cattle ranch down there. Who can really say if he lived through Pure's bullet that day in 1879? But dead or alive, he continued to plague the ≡R.*

*Although, later, after the shoot-out, Pure had a few opportunities to settle down, marry, and raise a family, he spurned every chance. He said he couldn't risk his family to Nate's revenge. It was his code. He always felt that Nate was alive and gunning for him. And I reckon he was miserable for the rest of his life just by that way of thinking.*

*In October 1886, two months past his thirty-fourth*

*birthday, Pure wanted to take a ride through the scrub. He hadn't ridden much at all since the Gunn shoot-out and preferred to travel back and forth to Dogtown by carriage in those years. And his health . . . well, truth be told, Pure never regained his vitality after we ambushed the Gunns that day in January. He walked all hunched over and looked decades older than he really was. His right arm and hand, once as quick to the holster as any shootist in McMullen County, now hung like deadweight from his shoulder.*

*Still, I saddled his favorite piebald that morning, and we rode through the brasada like we once did in the wild days of our cowpunching youth. Late in the day, we rode upon Cañón Cerrado. Looking back, I reckon that's where Pure was headed all along. He rode into the canyon, the place where the misery started and found where we buried Buckshot and the kid . . . or at least where he recalled them both to be laid. He got off his horse in front of the graves and untied the hot roll from behind his saddle. He spread his sleeping gear on the canyon floor and tucked away inside were those spurs. That was some day, I tell you. A day, that in this old man's last years, still wells up tears inside me like a spring thunderstorm.*

# Forty-Nine

*September 1886*
*Cañón Cerrado, McMullen County, Texas*

———◇———

Pure hung Buckshot Wallace's spurs from a cactus pad near the old cowboy's grave.

"I figured it was time to return these," he said.

July smiled. "I'll bet they're tired of hearing that story of his in the great beyond," he chuckled.

Pure nodded and stared steadily into the cactus.

"What are you thinking on so hard?" July asked.

"Back to that morning."

"Which morning is that, Pure? The good Lord has certainly afforded you and me more than most men."

Deep lines wrinkled around Pure's eyes making him appear much older than his years. "That morning in April."

July stood in respectful silence.

"I believe it was April."

July nodded, tight-lipped.

"Wasn't it April?"

July gentled his hand on Pure's shoulder. "I believe it was April."

Pure stretched his neck above his shirt collar and pressed his lips together. "That was some morning."

"Yes, yes it was. Some morning for sure," July said.

"I thought the world was ours that morning."

"The cards sure seemed stacked that way."

"How'd it all get away from us so quick, July?"

"I don't know, Pure, it just did that's all."

Pure cleared his throat and wheezed out a breath. "I wish I knew," he said.

July patted his friend's back. "I reckon that sometimes life is nothing more than an old moss back hiding out in the scrub."

Pure coughed hard. A small moan followed. "Like a rangy old longhorn, July?"

July's voice bristled with excitement. "Yeah," he said. "You know the feeling you get when you reckon you've put out the perfect loop?"

Pure's eyes glistened. He nodded and smiled.

"But you ain't figured how much that old steer is willing to fight back."

Pure straightened. "He's a fighter," he said. "That's true enough."

"He's fighting for his way of life."

"He can see the shadow of that lariat in the air," Pure muttered.

"That's when those horns get to thrashing the air."

Pure laughed. "And those backs legs get to kicking toward the sun."

"He's fixin' to run."

"But which way?" Pure muttered.

"Made many a brush-popper waste a loop trying to know."

"More than a few of 'em was mine," Pure chuckled in the recall.

"That's instinct," July whispered. "Five hundred years of breeding behavior."

"Hard to beat," Pure said.

July turned and nodded at Pure. "But you had to try," he said.

Pure paused. His eyes watered a bit. "And so did that old moss back."

July inhaled deeply and tipped his hat back. "Of course he did," he proclaimed. "The both of you could only do what was bred for you to do."

"To do contrariwise would be against the code," Pure uttered in full realization.

July dropped his hand from Pure's shoulder. "In our time, we could only be what the time demanded we be," he whispered.

Pure turned his shoulders and looked away from July. He studied the canyon at some length. "Wasn't really any other way," he stated.

"Not for us. Not back then."

"Let's not speak anymore of this, July."

"Probably for the best."

"What's done is done."

July wiped the corner of his mouth. "And no amount of talk or regret will ever change that."

Pure nodded and glanced up at the afternoon sun under a shaded hand. "Might hot out today," he said.

"Well it's October."

"October, you say?"

"Yep."

"October?" Pure asked in a shaky voice.

"It's October, Pure." July said.

"What day?"

July lifted his eyes. "Hmmm. The sixteenth, I believe."

"Hmmm," Pure muttered. "Sure feels hot for so late in October."

"I reckon that's so."

Pure lowered his gaze. "July?"

Yep?"

"I'm gonna pull my bedding over in the shade of the canyon wall and rest a bit."

July nodded. "You want me to drag it over there for you?"

Pure turned and surveyed the wall. He paused for a moment calculating the distance in his head. "Probably best," he said.

———◆———

An hour later, July was startled awake by Pure's snoring. He rubbed his tongue over his bottom lip and then glanced over at Pure. The ≡R boss slept soundly. July took a deep breath and glanced toward the west wall of the canyon. Lengthening shadows told the lateness of the day. *Best get going*, he thought. "Pure," he exhaled and gently shook his friend's left arm. "We best get saddled and head on back home."

Pure opened his eyes and rolled his neck to the left. "What?" he said.

"It's getting late. We best ride out of here if we want to make it back to headquarters before dark."

Pure yawned. "Yeah," he said and sat up showing a sullen scowl.

"What is it?" July said.

"Could you get a stick of my gum from out of my front pocket?"

July nodded.

"My arms useless these days, you know."

July unbuttoned Pure's front chest pocket. He removed a single stick of Adams No. 1, unwrapped the stick, and then placed it in front of Pure's mouth.

Pure leaned forward and grasped the gum with his teeth. After a minute of chewing, he rolled the gum into the back of his mouth. His expression showed satisfaction. "Thanks. My mouth was getting powerfully dry."

July nodded. "We best be going. You ready?" he asked.

"I 'spect so."

Then a long pause.

"July?"

"Yeah?"

"Where are all the boys?"

July frowned. "The boys, Pure?"

"Yeah, Paint and Isa and the rest?"

Pure glanced around the canyon, confused.

July bent over and placed his hands on his knees. He studied Pure's face intently and exhaled loudly. "Why they're all gone, Pure," he said.

Pure sat quiet for several seconds. Thinking. "Gone?"

July nodded.

Pure inhaled a deep breath and then asked, "Gone? Gone where?"

July dragged his palm across his mouth and spoke into his hand "To the feud."

Pure made a face. "All of them?"

July nodded and lowered his hand from his mouth. "Every man one of them," he said.

Pure nodded and lay back on his bedding. "Boy we had some times out here didn't we?"

"Not many have had better," July said.

"And we were always a hundred miles to water weren't we?"

"Sure seemed so," July said.

Pure rolled the gum toward his front teeth and chewed on the chicle softly. After some time, he looked up at July and said, "I think I'm going to lay here awhile."

"But, Pure . . . it's getting late."

"You go ahead. I'll be ok."

"But—,"

Pure reached up and pulled his hat down over his eyes. "Go on now," he whispered.

July's lips trembled slightly. "Pure," he muttered.

"Go on, now."

"But . . . I . . . I just can't up and leave without you," July said.

Pure grabbed the brim of his hat and tilted it up. "I'll be fine, really I will. I just need a little rest that's all."

July looked deep into Pure's eyes. He grimaced at the sight.

Pure smiled weakly. "Go on. You go on back and fix us up some grub."

July nodded solemnly. "Ok, Pure," he said. "I'll have some biscuits and bacon waiting for you."

Pure stared blankly into the sky.

July bent over and waved his hand in front of Pure's eyes.

Pure continued to gaze ahead, unblinking. "I'll be fine, July . . . out here with all the boys."

July fixed a long gaze on Pure's figure, and then said, "I'll guess I'll be leaving now."

Pure crossed his hands over his chest. "Probably for the best," he said.

July turned and walked toward his horse. He dragged his shirtsleeve across both eyes as he walked. *Yep,* he whispered to himself, *Probably for the best.*

## JOURNAL ENTRY

*That October afternoon in 1886 was the last time Pure and I ever spoke to one another. 'Course we really didn't need to speak then . . . as a lifetime of talk had come before that moment. And think what you will about Pure or any of us ≡R buckaroos, there is one fact that can never be disputed . . . right or wrong; we stayed true to one another and the code, no matter the hardship, no matter the consequence. And I figure that's about as close to purity as a man could ever achieve in this world.*

# THE HISTORY BEHIND
## *A Hundred Miles to Water*

In early November of 1493, a fleet of seventeen Spanish ships carrying over one thousand men, including Christopher Columbus, landed on an island that Columbus named, Dominica. Also on-board the ships were domesticated pigs, horses, and of course, cattle.

Twenty-six years later, Hernán Cortés began his conquest of New Spain, (Mexico) with six hundred soldiers and fifteen horsemen. The horses were descendents of the original herd brought to Dominica in 1493. In 1521, Gregorio de Villalobos transported the first cattle, also descendents of the first herd, from Dominica to New Spain.

New world cattle soon became a form of currency for the Spanish. Owning a great herd provided men with disposable and liquid wealth. Cortés stocked his great estate in New Spain with significant numbers of the animal. His estate was named *Cuernavaca*.

As the Spanish began their campaigns to conquer their new world, they took with them horses and cattle. In 1540, one conquistador, Francisco Vázquez de Coronado set off in search of the famed Seven Cities of Cibola. He departed with thousands of sheep, goats, hogs, and, by most estimates, five-hundred head of cattle. Coronado's 'five-hundred' were the first cattle to set 'hoof' in what is now the United States.

Over time, escaped, dispersed by Indian raids, abandoned, or left behind purposely, these strays or wild cattle propagated prolifically. Left to their own survival, Spanish cattle developed the traits necessary to survive and reproduce efficiently and providently in the new world environment. These traits included robustness, vitality, fertility, and most importantly browse-efficiency. By 1835, wild cattle, sometimes referred to as mustang cattle, and later, Texas cattle, could be found from the Red River to the Rio Grande. Some records of the same year put the total number of cattle and horses running wild inside this area as three million head. These Texas cattle, what we today call longhorns, were, in the words of Captain Richard Ware, "… wilder than deer."

Another chronicler, Colonel Richard Irving Dodge offered the following comment on wild Texas cattle. "…animals miscalled tame, fifty times more dangerous to footmen than the fiercest buffalo."

After the Civil War, men returned home to Texas to find untended fields and millions of wild Texas cattle. A few far-thinking men looked at the vast cattle herds and saw a profitable future ahead. These far-thinking men began to round-up, brand, and then drive these wild Texas cattle toward railheads that serviced burgeoning northern markets, markets "hungry" for beef. We know these men by names such as *cowboy, rannie, buckaroo,* or *cowpuncher,* but they are all descendents, not by blood, but instead by the common love of their occupation from the Mexican vaquero.

The cattle drive era was short in duration but provided millions in gold to those few entrepreneurs who saw the potential of a rangy, long-legged animal that was shaped by Mother Nature for self-preservation. The Texas longhorn could live on a diet of browse that would kill other breeds. It was an animal that could go tremendous distances without a drink, swim the broadest rivers, and run, when needed, like a mustang pony. In short, the longhorn of that period was the right animal to accomplish what those far-thinking men had in mind. The longhorn, *Cuerno Largo,* was without peer.

In *A Hundred Miles to Water,* the two feuding families, the Restons and the Gunns are actually a mixture of one of the most notorious ranching families in the history of the state of Texas, the Olives.

In 1843, James Olive, moved his family from Mississippi to Williamson County, Texas. James had four sons, Thomas, Ira, Bob, and Isom. Isom, or Print, as he was called, fought on the side of the Confederacy during the Civil War. After the war, Print returned home to Williamson County and with his three brothers soon turned the family holdings into one of the largest cattle operations in Central Texas.

But the Olives, like the open range of the times, were never far removed from lawlessness and violent aggression in protecting their operation. One event in particular, the killing of two rustlers by a torture method practiced by the Spanish, "the death of skins" led to the Olives' reputation as lawless thugs. The Olives bound the rustlers alive inside wet Olive-branded cowhides and left them on the prairie. The green cowhides shrank in the Texas sun, suffocating both men. The Olives were hauled into to court over the murders but acquitted on both accounts.

In his book, *We Pointed Them North*, E.C. Abbott, (Teddy Blue), describes hiring on with the Olives in Austin, Texas, in 1879. Abbott writes, "The Olives were noted as a tough outfit – a gun outfit . . . violent and overbearing men." Abbott rode up the trail with the Olives in the spring of 1879. He notes that they drove 7,000 horses and an unknown greater amount of cattle to western Nebraska. It was on this drive that Abbott became familiar with the notorious black cowboy and Olive wrangler, Jim Kelly.

Kelly's parents worked for James Olive. Kelly grew up on the ranch and was well known for his ability to "break" horses. Kelly moved to West Texas in the 1850s but returned to Williamson County after the Civil War where he reunited with a young Print Olive.

Kelly was proficient with any manufacture of gun and soon gained a reputation as a gunslinger. He also became the chief enforcer for Print Olive's cattle operation. To most along the trail, he was known as the Ebony Gun. One incident involving Kelly was described in Harry Chrisman's *Ladder of Rivers*. Chrisman writes of saloon owner Bill Green refusing to sell Kelly a bottle of bourbon. After a string of racial slurs was passed his way, Kelly gripped his pistol and told Green, "I come here to buy a bottle of whiskey, not to be made a fool by a bartender . . . pass me a quart of that bourbon and I'll be peacefully on my way." Green gave in and was later told by a Texas cowboy present during the altercation, "That's Nigger Jim, Print Olive's bad nigger. Pay you to treat him right or leave him alone."

In 1872, after selling his herd in Ellsworth, Kansas, Print became involved in a well-reported gun fight. Print's foe in the shoot-out was card-cheat, James

Kennedy. Kennedy had accused Print of cheating at cards on the previous day and, finding Print at the tables once again, shot Print through the hand, groin, and thigh. Jim Kelly was sitting outside the saloon when the commotion began. Seeing Print's attacker ready to fire the killing shot, Kelly drew his pistol and shot Kennedy in the thigh. Kelly stayed in Ellsworth with Print until his boss and friend was able to travel back to Williamson County.

In 1878, Print determined that with the disappearing free range and his continued troubles with the law in Texas, it was time to move his operation north. He settled on the Loup River in Central Nebraska strategically situated near the railhead at Plum Creek. By 1879, Print and his brothers owned one of the largest cattle operations in the state, holding thirty thousand head of cattle and several thousand horses. To combat the rustling problems that had dogged him in Texas, Print helped organize the Custer County Livestock Association. He became the organization's first president, and in turn, Jim Kelly became the association's chief gunman.

Once again, as in Texas, tensions soon arose between Print's cattlemen and the ever-growing population of farmers or "sodbusters" as they came to be called. Whenever a dispute arose, whether it was over water rights or furrow boundaries, Kelly was sent in to settle the disagreement . . . with force.

One such disagreement occurred in 1878 between the Olives and two local farmers, Luther Mitchell and Ami W. Ketchum. Print asserted that the two "sodbusters" were stealing and butchering Olive cattle. Sheriff Dave Anderson of Buffalo County, Nebraska deputized a posse led by Bob Olive to arrest Mitchell and Ketchum. In trying to serve the arrest warrant on the sodbusters, Bob was shot and later died.

The remaining members of the posse arrested both Mitchell and Ketchum and started them for Plum Creek in a wagon. However, seven vigilantes seized control of the prisoners before they could reach Plum Creek. The vigilantes were led by Print Olive and Jim Kelly. Mitchell and Ketchum were hanged from an elm tree. Later the men's bodies were set on fire. The blame for the fire, mistakenly, was placed on Print. After the incident, a new nickname was attached to Print, that of, "man burner."

Print was convicted in the murders of Mitchell and Ketchum and sentenced to life in prison, but the conviction was overturned on a technicality less than two years later. Jim Kelly had his charges dismissed. Some speculate that Kelly was let go because the jury was intimidated by area ranchers.

Little is known of Kelly's life after 1880, other than he spent his last years in Ansley, Nebraska. Kelly died in 1912 and is buried in the Ansley town cemetery.

Print separated from his brothers in 1882 and set up his own operation north of Dodge City, Kansas. In 1884, after a partner stole all the assets from a business operation, Print found himself broke and owing creditors ten thousand dollars. In 1885 and 1886, the Great Plains was struck by a series of winter storms in what many called the worst winter ever. Print lost over forty percent of his cattle to the storms. He not only owed money, but money was owed to him.

Ruined financially, Print moved to Trail City, Colorado. In Trail City, Print started a stable business to service the growing cattle trade there. In late 1886, he decided to move back to Kansas and set about collecting his debts. One of his clients was Texas cowboy Joe Sparrow, who had once ridden up the trail with an Olive herd. The collection demand resulted in Print drawing his pistol and threatening to shoot the Texas cowboy. Sparrow is reported to have told Print that he didn't even have money to get a meal. The next day, Print encountered Sparrow once more. Sparrow drew on the unarmed Olive and shot him twice and then finished him off with a shot to the head.

Sparrow was tried and found guilty in Las Animas, Colorado. The decision was overturned due to a "breach of rule." The jury deadlocked in the second trial. The third trial was moved to Pueblo, Colorado. The jury there found the Texas cowboy not-guilty.

Isom Print Olive was buried in Dodge City, Kansas.

Joe Sparrow died in Tampico, Mexico, in 1924.

<hr>

Thomas Adams (1818-1905) was the first person in the United States to manufacture chewing gum that had chicle as the base ingredient. Large quantities of chicle, which comes from the sapodilla tree in Central America, had been given Adams by friends of General Antonio López de Santa Anna. The former Mexican dictator was in exile at the time and spent time at Adams' house on Staten Island. Santa Anna persuaded Adams that the inexpensive chicle could be compounded with the more expensive rubber to make an economical alternative for carriage tires.

Adams tried for a year but was unsuccessful at every attempt to accomplish the ex-dictator's "get-rich" scheme. One day, after yet another rubber failure, Adams is reported to have popped a piece of chicle into his mouth. He remembered that Santa Anna enjoyed chewing chicle gum. Adams realized that the softer chicle gum was superior to the paraffin wax gum that was popular at the time in the United States.

Shortly after that, Adams and his oldest son, Thomas Jr., made up "penny sticks" of the gum and distributed them to a local drugstore. The chicle gum was an instant hit. Adams sold his chicle gum with the slogan "Adams' New York Gum No. 1—Snapping and Stretching."

In 1888, Adams' Tutti-Frutti flavored gum was the first gum to be sold in a vending machine. By 1899, Adams Sons and Company had become the largest and most profitable chewing gum company in the United States. In that same year, Adams and five other chewing gum companies joined forces as the American Chicle Company. Thomas Jr. was named chairman of the board of directors for the new company.

Thomas Adams Sr. died in 1905.

In 1944, Thomas Adams Jr.'s son, Horatio, related the following recollection at a manager's banquet for the American Chicle Company. "...after about a year's work of blending chicle with rubber, the experiments were regarded as a failure; consequently Mr. Thomas Adams intended to throw the remaining lot into the East River. But it happened that before this was done, Thomas Adams went into a drugstore at the corner. While he was there, a little girl came into the shop and asked for a chewing gum for one penny. It was known to Mr. Thomas Adams that chicle, which he had tried unsuccessfully to vulcanize as a rubber substitute, had been used as a chewing gum by the natives of Mexico for many years. So the idea struck him that perhaps they could use the chicle he wanted to throw away for the production of chewing gum and so salvage the lot in the storage. After the child had left the store, Mr. Thomas Adams

asked the druggist what kind of chewing gum the little girl had bought. He
was told that it was made of paraffin wax and called White Mountain. When
he asked the man if he would be willing to try an entirely different kind of
gum, the druggist agreed. When Mr. Thomas Adams arrived home that night,
he spoke to his son, Tom Jr., my father, about his idea. Junior was very much
impressed, and suggested that they make up a few boxes of chicle chewing
gum and give it a name and a label. He offered to take it out on one of his
trips (he was a salesman in wholesale tailors' trimmings and traveled as far west
as the Mississippi). They decided on the name of Adams New York No. 1. It
was made of pure chicle gum without any flavor. It was made in little penny
sticks and wrapped in various colored tissue papers. The retail value of the box,
I believe, was one dollar. On the cover of the box was a picture of City Hall,
New York, in color."

Kentucky is well recognized as the home to some of the bloodiest feuds in
the United States. One of the better-known feuds, the Hatfields and McCoys,
began when Floyd Hatfield penned a number of wild hogs he captured in the
forest. Sometime later, Randolph McCoy passed the pen and claimed the hogs
as his. Other well known feuds in the state were the Tolliver-Martin-Logan
vendetta, the French-Eversole war, the Howard-Turner feud, and Bloody
Breathitt, which included the Little-Strong and the Hargis-Marcum feuds.

Clay County, Kentucky, is located in the foothills of the Cumberland
Mountains. In late 1775, the county's first settler, James Collins, tracked
game to a large salt lick located on Goose Creek, a tributary of the south fork
of the Kentucky River. The value of salt in frontier America soon became
apparent as settlers who followed Collins into the area began to sink salt
wells up and down "Goose Creek."

One of the longest running feuds in Clay County began in 1844 when
Abner Baker, a man thought to have suffered from mental illness, shot his
friend, Daniel Bates in the back. Baker and his wife, Susan (White) Baker
lived in the Bates home. It is thought that Abner believed his wife and Bates
were engaged in an affair.

Before he died, Bates dictated his last will and testament, in which he instructed his son to take revenge on his killer. A local magistrate, T.T. Garrard, joined sides when he refused to turn over the unstable Baker to the sheriff or the Bates.

Enraged, both the Whites and the Bates joined forces and persuaded the Commonwealth to indict Baker for murder. A jury found Baker guilty. He was hanged in 1845. Baker's hanging caused lines to be drawn among the families with the Bates and Whites on one side and the Bakers and Garrards on the other.

The feud lasted fifty-plus years and by some estimates took over one hundred lives.

---

McMullen County, Texas was formed from parcels of land in Atascosa, Bexar, and Live Oak counties in 1858. The county was named for Irish empresario, John McMullen. McMullen and James McGloin settled the area with two hundred Catholic immigrants in 1828, but none of these original grantees ever settled the land assigned them. After Texas independence, the land remained unoccupied except for native peoples.

After the county's establishment in 1858, thirty settlers built a crude settlement at the junction of Leoncita Creek and the Frio River. The settlement was named Rio Frio, and later, Dogtown. One legend is that the town was so named because the ranchers used dogs to help work wild cattle and that "more dogs than men" lived in the county. Still another popular explanation is that a group of drunken cowboys went on a shooting spree and left a pack of dead dogs in the town's thoroughfare.

Levi J. Edwards built a general store in 1862 and soon after expanded his interests with a saloon. After the Civil War, returning men found an economic opportunity along the Frio River where large herds of wild mustangs and cattle roamed. After 1867, these same men discovered the growing consumer demand for beef in the Northern states. These new markets meant that wild cattle, not mustangs, would bring wealth to those who engaged in "cow hunts" and built up herds to drive north to Kansas cities such as Dodge City and Abilene.

In 1871, the town's name was changed to Colfax, but residents still referred to it as Dogtown.

The county was officially organized in 1877, and Colfax (Dogtown) was named the county seat. That same year, the town's name was once again changed, this time to Tilden. The new name came from the defeated Democratic presidential candidate, and then New York governor, Samuel J. (Whispering Sammy) Tilden, who came to Dogtown in 1876. Candidate Tilden was defeated by Rutherford B. Hayes.

⇒•◇•⇐

The brush country of south Texas, also referred to as the brasada, is home to numerous and varied species of plant life, each equipped with its own armament of thorns and barbs. The brasada of 1878 was thick with prickly-pear, cats-claw, Spanish dagger, black chaparral, twisted acacia, all-thorn, wild currant, and mesquite.

The brasada required that a brush cowboy's equipment be suited to working in these dense and dogged thickets. Every brush hand's armor included toe-fenders on his stirrups, leather leggins that covered his legs all the way to his waist, (no respectable brush cowboy ever referred to his leggins as chaps), gloves that extended past his wrists, and a wide-brimmed hat that could be tied around his chin.

J. Frank Dobie wrote in *A Vaquero in the Brush Country,* that, "In running in the brush a man rides not so much on the back of the horse as under and alongside. He just hangs on, dodging limbs as if he were dodging bullets, back, forward, over, under, half of the time trusting his horse to course right on this or that side of a bush or tree. If he shuts his eyes to dodge, he is lost. Whether he shuts them or not, he will, if he runs true to form, get his head rammed or raked. Patches of the brush hand's bandana hanging on thorns and stobs sometimes mark his trail. The bandana of red is his emblem."

The brasada was also home to Texas and Mexican bandits and desperadoes. In the parlance of the time, they were known as owl hoots, bad men who rustled, robbed, and murdered at their own will. Texas and Mexican bandits used the brasada as an exchange point. The Texas rustlers often had Mexican cattle to dispose of that carried no known state brand and contrariwise.

———◆———

The word, *caudillo,* as used in Mexico, came to mean a political-military leader. *Caudillo,* translated into English as "leader," or "chief," but as in most peasant societies, the word came to express a dictator or potentate. The Merrimam-Webster dictionary defines *caudillo* as "a Spanish or Latin-America military dictator."

One of the best known *caudillos* in Mexican history was José Doroteo Arango Arámbula, also known as Pancho Villa. Villa was a provisional governor of the Mexican state of Chihuahua from 1913-1914.

Villa led a 1916 raid on Columbus, New Mexico, which resulted in a year-long expedition by General John J. Pershing to find the "bandit." Pershing's pursuit proved unsuccessful.

Pancho Villa was assassinated in 1920 by seven gunmen outside of Hidalgo del Parral, Chihuahua, Mexico.

Other historically famous Mexican *caudillos* were Antonio López de Santa Anna Pérez de Lebrón, Agustín Cosme Damián de Iturbide y Aramburu, José de la Cruz Porfirio Díaz Mori, and Álvaro Obregón Salido.

Iturbide marched troops into Mexico City on September 27, 1821. The following day, Mexico was declared an independent empire. Iturbide is known as Mexico's first *caudillo.*

———◆———

Pure Reston's "code" in *A Hundred Miles to Water* is a mixture of principle and honor that can be found in literature dating from medieval times. The "code" is a descendent of the chivalry practiced by the Knights of the Round Table which still stands as a standard for good behavior.

During the cattle drive period in American history, the "code" was a necessary and guiding rule for cowboys. These were men who more often than not worked in isolated and dangerous conditions. The "code" guaranteed help and protection to any cowboy riding for a brand who was of a need. Unfortunately, during the rise of the cowboy and those early cattle towns, the "code" also protected bad behavior. A cowboy's first obligation was to his fellow cowboy, no matter that cowboy's disposition to his own desires and no matter the rules of conventional society.

In 2005, authors, James P. Owen and David R. Stoecklein wrote, *Cowboy Ethics: What Wall Street Can Learn from the Code of the West*. Some of the "code" rules to live by listed in the book are: (1) Be tough, but fair. (2) Ride for the brand. And (3) Do what has to be done.

Today, many ranches in the West still practice the "code". Code cowboys of the twenty-first century still work cattle as their predecessors did in the nineteenth century, from rounding up cattle on horseback, to the use of lariats and branding irons in the field.